K CALLAN

How to sell Yourself as an ACTOR

Sixth Edition
revised and updated

© 1990, 1992, 1996, 1999, 2003, 2008 K Callan
ISBN 1-878355-21-X
ISSN Library of Congress Catalog Card Number 91-65952
First Printing 2008

Other books by K Callan

An Actor's Workbook
The Los Angeles Agent Book
The New York Agent Book
The Life of the Party
The Script is Finished, Now What Do I Do?
Directing Your Directing Career

Illustrations: Katie Maratta
Photography: Timothy Fielding
Editor: Dan Curran

⚜ Table of Contents ⚜

Invest energy in your private life. Study or work in a foreign country. The professional and personal rewards of travel. Stardom looks great from a distance. Assume responsibility for keeping yourself whole.

The purpose of unions. Your place in a union. When to join. How to do it. What it costs. Financial Core. Be part of the solution.

Owning your own business is a 24/7 job.

⚔ 1 ⚔

You, Me, Brad, Sally
& George

At first glance, it may be a stretch for you (and even me) to think of our names in the same sentence as Brad Pitt, Sally Field, and George Clooney, but as you learn more about the business and their early careers, you'll see that their journeys, though maybe not as long as ours, were all filled with challenges.

Brad was from Oklahoma and attended the Missouri School of Journalism. He came to Los Angeles in 1987 and "broke through" in 1994 after years of study with Roy London and parts (large and small) in film and televison.

George came to Hollywood in 1982 with $300 in his pocket from picking tobacco. He sold insurance, drew cartoons caricatures on the mall, and sold lemonade from a stand. In 1984 he began to work, but it's been a long journey. Take a look at his fascinating bio online at *www.tiscali.co.uk/entertainment/film/biographies/george_clooney_biog/2.*

Sally's mom was an actress and her dad was a stunt man. A star in her teens in both *Gidget* and *The Flying Nun,* she recently won another Emmy for ABC's successful series *Brothers and Sisters*, but she has been through her years of unemployment, just like every actor.

✦ *"It's never been easy, it's always been a struggle," she says of a career that ranges from the 1960s sitcoms "Gidget" and "The Flying Nun" to Oscar-winning performances in "Norma Rae" (1979) and "Places in the Heart" (1984).*
Dana Kennedy, *The New York Times*[1]

I struggled for three years in New York before I broke through in *Joe* (1970), a film that put me in the system. It didn't make me a star, but I was much further in the door than before and never really poor again in the way you are at the beginning. It's a good thing I saved my money though as twice in my career, I've gone without job or audition for eighteen consecutive months.

Knowing that a working and even star actor still has many of the same insecurities and fears (financial and psychological) as someone who doesn't yet have that first job is both depressing and comforting. It's tough to hear that your problems are not all going to be magically solved if you could just get that job or agent, but knowing the truth now could save heartache later.

Sometimes I accidently find mentors in the newspapers. This quote from Oprah Winfrey gave me a new perspective on my career even at this late stage of my life:

✦ *She has worked hard for what she has, she says, but she attributes much of her success to a talent for clarity. "I ask people what it is they want," she says, "and you would be amazed at how few of them know. They say they want to be happy. So I ask them what that happiness would look like, feel like. And they don't know. Now, I believe that the universe responds to energy, and particularly to clarity. If you focus on what you want, things clear up. If you don't, you get stuck in this muddled, fuzzy place.*

Oprah Winfrey, interviewed by Mary McNamara, *Los Angeles Times*[2]

So, if you want to be an actor, answering Oprah's question is essential. What would that look like? What would that feel like? It takes a lot of quiet, focused thinking to come up with the answers.

I only came to understand my deeper motivation for becoming an actor over time. I was pretty invisible and lonely as a kid. School plays gave me the chance to join a family and have some attention, so my real motivation was a need to be liked and interact with people.

My database of information about an actor's lifestyle was composed mostly of old MGM movies where Betty Grable was showered with roses, attention, and friends. Betty and her crowd seemed to be living a much more exciting life than any grown-ups I ever saw.

In Dallas, no handsome men were bringing bouquets of long stemmed red roses to anybody I knew. I had the idea that being an actress was something like *The Dolly Sisters, Tin Pan Alley, The Daughter of Rosie O'Grady*, or any one of a number of old 20th Century Fox movies depicting life backstage.

After twenty years in the business, I must tell you that life as an actress has not been like a Betty Grable or Esther Williams musical. Men have brought me long-stemmed red roses, but it had little to do with my being an actress.

Well, maybe a little.

I have been liked, chosen, and when working, have had people to hang with. But for me anyway, there has been much more rejection and not working than being chosen and working.

Also I never saw Betty or Esther running around town picking up scripts, needing to create an appropriate emotional climate for themselves to work in, or auditioning for a room full of executives who had already seen ten other actresses who looked just like them. I never saw them changing hairdos and clothes at red lights, rushing from one appointment to another, trying to find parking or get to an audition on time in Manhattan without resorting to taxis, or dealing with surly secretaries, while trying to stay centered and concentrated on audition material.

I'm not knocking this. I'm tickled to have an audition to go to. I just didn't have the faintest notion that acting involved these things.

I never saw Betty or Esther take an acting class or work with the flu or worry about a sick child. But then, they never had children in those stories either. Just roses. They never passed through age categories that put them out of work for years. It seemed they changed from young and adorable to middle-aged and responsible and were then magically grandparent material in a cinematically authentic manner, without a hitch.

Of course, in real life, neither of those ladies had a life-long career; Betty phased out when she got a little older and Marilyn came in, and Esther quit the business when she married.

There is nothing I'm going to be able to say that will either dissuade you from your life's dream or really convey what the actor's lifestyle is about, so I won't even try.

Wherever you live, find some showbiz related place to work. An ad agency, the radio station, the television station, industrial film company. If no job is available, volunteer to work free one or two days a week. Be a go-fer. Do whatever needs doing. Get inside some showbiz related door so you can begin to demystify the system. It's only when you get past the velvet rope that you're going to get even the faintest idea of what the lifestyle is about.

This Is Your Life

Life decisions like who to marry and what profession to strive for ultimately boil down to lifestyle choices. How do you want to spend your time?

Unless you are working on the classics in repertory theatre, the amount of time you actually get to work on good material in a fulfilling role is minimal.

The actor's chief job is pursuing work. Stardom is just unemployment at a higher rate of pay.

You will need to harness all your creative resources to create your own work, agent yourself, pay the rent, keep your spirits up, and search for work. Any freelance life requires those skills on a daily basis. There are those of us who thrive on the problem solving and uncertainty, and there are some who do not.

If you need a more structured life, re-evaluate your choice of career now because an actor's life is one long freefall. The Screen Actors Guild (SAG) statistics say that the average lifespan of an acting career is only five years and, even then, the time spent actually acting is minimal.

See how you feel as you begin to acquire insights into what you'll need to do (over and over again) if you want to live the life of an actor. You may love it, but don't be afraid to rethink your choices.

You'll get the most out of this book if you read it all the way through, get the concept, and then go back and read it again as you begin to formulate your plan of attack.

Wrap Up

✓ all actors take the same path
✓ an actor's life is unstructured
✓ broaden your horizons
✓ SAG statistics say average length of career is five years
✓ primary job of actors is looking for work
✓ enjoy problem solving

⚐ 2 ⚑
Focusing Yourself

Many actors prefer to see their profession as art rather than business. Sometimes it is, but mostly, at a professional level, acting is about being able to make money at something most of us would do for free, if someone else would only pay our rent and buy our food.

Since few have that luxury, teaching yourself to be businesslike is merely an extension of your acting education. Some people think actors lack the ability to be businesslike. I believe many actors just never think about it.

If the actor were playing the part of a creative business person, his brain would be teeming with business ideas. It's just a head set. If you can master the ability to break down a character, pinpoint acting obstacles and objectives, then you can learn to research the marketplace, focus yourself, call on people, schedule your days, pay your bills, and generally conduct yourself like a responsible adult.

The competition is fierce, the pitfalls deep, and the rewards fleeting, so you must call upon all your resources to prevail. The one thing you really can control is your ability to organize all your resources and focus your energy on the nuts and bolts aspect of your life.

Michael J. Fox says in his biography *Lucky Man* that his inability to deal with the business side of his career almost torpedoed him as a young actor.

Sixty years ago, film studios signed actors to long indentured contracts within what was called the studio system. Young actors of a certain look were chosen, schooled, groomed, and developed by featuring them in ever-larger roles until the actors graduated into starring parts.

The only vestiges of that system exist within the television networks where actors are signed to development deals while the network seeks to have a vehicle built for the rising star. But, as far as I know, there is no training involved. There is no opportunity for the actor to sharpen his skills. That has to be done on one's own.

The rising stars these days are most often stand-up performers who have already spent entrepreneurial years on their own, creating a character and/or material that showcased them to the networks in a commercial way. Sometimes a fortunate actor whose part (large or small) in a current successful movie has garnered attention will also be the object of the networks' ardor.

You'll notice that I am not describing anyone here who was just walking down the street and fell into a network contract.

Going into Business

A smart business person planning to invest time, energy, and his life savings in a new business commits himself to relentless research. He interviews people in the field, checks the library and/or the Internet for information, and conducts a market survey to see if there is a need for his product.

He identifies potential customers, checks to see how much money they have to spend, investigates what they are already buying, and seeks to become a specialist in his field. He knows he will have to produce a product that is superior, unique, and/or impacts the marketplace in some new way in order to access the system. An actor is no different than any other business person. He needs a Mission Statement and he needs to produce a service and/or a product. Part of producing the product is to analyze it. On paper you should answer these questions:

- Who am I?
- Why do I want to act?
- Where do I want to act?
- What do I have that no one else has?
- How will I go about entering the marketplace?
- Am I ready?

Who Am I?

Although "Who Am I?" seems a pretty innocuous question, the answer I'm searching for has more to do with your psychological make-up than a physical description — although that's also important.

Are you emotionally balanced? Excitable? Passive? Are you a self-starter? Do you have enough drive for the task ahead? How well do you get along with people? How are you at meeting people?

Although one's physical beauty is paramount in the diverse components of your showbiz persona, your capacity to roll with the punches, change directions, be entrepreneurial, and think clearly and quickly are the qualities that will ultimately reward you with the ability to make a living as an artist.

And then the physical and racial realities. Are you in good shape? Fat? Thin? Ugly? Tall? Short? Gorgeous? Average? White? Black? Chicano? Asian? Indian? Male? Female? Old? Young? Beautiful? Homely?

Your visible personhood, age, race, sex, and beauty (or lack of it) significantly influence how you will be received in any marketplace as proved by an actor who rose to the next level when he took his career into his own hands. French Stewart starred in 139 episodes of *Third Rock from the Sun* after he changed his perspective and his appearance:

✦ *Finally, after appearing in more than fifty plays in the Los Angeles area, Stewart started to look at his career as a business in addition to being an art and at himself as a product. "After several years of struggling, I felt I should have been doing better. I mean, I was working a lot, but I don't think I was necessarily working smart."*

It was a sobering moment for the actor. "I had to figure out, 'How was I going to market myself? What can I do best?'" The answer came to him quickly: 'Be weird.' The first thing he did was shave his head.

"I got myself this blue jacket that looks like a utility jacket," he says. "I even have real scars on my head, so when I shaved it, I really looked weird. The combination of those two things knocked the retardation look right over the wall."

It was that change in persona that got him noticed. He started getting bit parts on shows like "Seinfeld" and "The Larry Sanders Show." "Shaving my head sort of got my foot in the door," he says.

Kathleen O'Steen, *Emmy*[3]

Terry and Bonnie Turner, the husband and wife producing team casting *Third Rock*, said that although French did stand out because of his odd look, it was his ability to deliver that set him apart from other odd-looking guys and clinched the deal.

Yes, but first he had to get their attention! He looked at the business, looked at himself, conceived a character, adjusted himself to fit that character and once he had people's attention, had the acting chops to deliver.

The same creativity that led him to head-shaving, inhabits his work. If you check him out on imdb.com, you'll see that he worked a lot before *Third Rock* and even more afterward. With hair.

Why Do You Want to Act?

Many successful actors routinely confess in the press that they decided to act in college as a way of meeting girls. It's true, actors get more than their share of adulation from the opposite sex, but basically, that's true of all successful men and women regardless of their profession. Everyone wants to be around winners.

It's romantic to consider winning your Oscar, driving your Rolls, eating at swell restaurants, kissing beautiful co-stars, and signing autographs, but unfortunately, that's the climax of your story. Before the kissing and the autographs, you may be walking around New York City or Los Angeles every day dropping off pictures to people who won't open the door and have signs posted saying specifically, "Actors, do not ring our bell".

It's painful to be thought of as a necessary evil. It's heartbreaking to be forty years old and not have a decent place to live. Being perennially unemployed damages the soul.

If you see yourself able to be happy and fulfilled in any other endeavor, do it. There is not enough money in the world to compensate for the actor's life. It has to be done for love or you will drop out along the way, bitter and cranky over the many wasted years.

Where Do You Want to Act?

Before you buy that ticket to New York or Los Angeles, mine the opportunities in your own backyard. You'll grow as an actor and as a person. You won't be quite as green when you assault the larger marketplaces. You'll have to use the same business skillset you'll need when you reach the center of things.

The more you do at home, the better equipped you are when you finally do move away from home to start a totally new life with no support group.

What Do You Have That No One Else Has?

What makes you so special? Why should someone hire you? If you can't find a reason, other than your deep *need*, then you probably won't work until you find yourself. If you were selling shoes, why would I want to buy yours if they were the same price, color, quality, and style as those already on the market? Familiarity is everything; I've already found the shoes that are right for me. Why should I try yours?

You must find a way to separate yourself from the pack like French Stewart did. What is it about you that would make a director choose you over the thousands of others who are your competition?

Are you prettier? Wittier? Uglier? Fatter? Thinner? Is your point-of-view more informed? Do you even own who you are? Do you know your strengths? Your weaknesses? If you don't own them, you can't fix them.

What do you want to communicate? You may not know the answer to this question right now, but it must be on your mind constantly in order for you to formulate the answer. You need to discover what you communicate by just walking through the door.

"Your life is what you bring to any story. This is a life craft. It's 'How do you feel? Who are you? What do you have to say?'"
Sean Penn interviewed by Shawn Hubler, *Los Angeles Times*[4]

How to Enter the Marketplace? When?

When you can sit down and write a Mission Statement specifically detailing what you want, what it would look like, feel like, who you want to work with, what you want to do, how you see your journey unfolding, what you see as first steps and second steps and on and on, then you are ready to begin.

If you can't/won't write a Mission Statement for your small business, you are starting further down on the food chain than you need to and perhaps you aren't yet 100% committed to your goal.

Are you ready to start right now? Are you waiting until you are out of school? Until your kids are grown? Until you save enough money to quit your current job?

If you are going to be an actor, there are steps in your preparation that you can take as soon as the decision is clear in your mind. You may not be ready to make the leap of quitting your day job or even being in a play, but you can begin to train yourself, discipline your thinking, modify your expectations, and create your new life.

This book is designed to help you look realistically at the profession and the kind of energy, creative thought process, and follow-through necessary to market yourself successfully and withstand the rigors of the actor's life.

Begin as soon as you finish this book. You can speed your journey along as well as receive the slings and arrows of a difficult life with perspective. It will still hurt to get rejected, but if you understand the rules of the marketplace, you may in time be able to take it less personally.

Wrap Up

✓ learn business skills
✓ analyze and focus your product
✓ establish a time frame for your goals
✓ write your Mission Statement
✓ identify the uniqueness of your product
✓ understand the rules of the game
✓ create your life

⊰ 3 ⊱

What Are Your Chances?

One's feelings about choosing acting as a profession/lifestyle often correspond to the early stages of being in love. Lovers frequently only see the glamorous surface. They are either unwilling or unable to take a closer look. It's difficult for the smitten to listen to the bystander dispassionately view and detail the pitfalls ahead.

As in marriage, you're not just choosing the love object, but the attendant lifestyle. Before you waste time pursuing this elusive career, consider whether or not you are suited to it.

Are you and the acting profession right for each other? Forgetting specialness and talent until later, do your sex, age, ethnic, physical, and emotional packages match your choice of career?

Physicality Is Destiny

Whether you like it or not, it is true that your face is your fortune. If you are Naomi Watts, Halle Berry, or Brad Pitt, your face can/will open many doors; if you are not perceived as a beauty, reviewers won't necessarily focus on your acting:

✦ *"New York Magazine" theatre critic John Simon never even got around to reviewing Kathy Bates' acting ability in his review of her work in the off-Broadway production of "Frankie and Johnnie in the Clair de Lune" writing instead that "it was unfortunate her leading man should play opposite an actress who, even for a midnight snacker, is enormously overweight."*
Nikki Finke, *Los Angeles Times*[5]

If you'll note, John Simon (always a severe critic of less than physically perfect women) was mainly cranky because Bates was playing a romantic lead, something out of reach for those folk deemed character actors.

Sans a theatrical or screen love life, Bates enjoys an enviable career playing leads and winning an Academy Award for her work in *Misery*.

Bates is now also a successful director (*Six Feet Under, Oz, NYPD Blue, Dash and Lilly*).

There are a lot of beauties in Hollywood and only one Kathy Bates. It's harder to carve out your niche when you don't physically fit the Hollywood beauty standard personified by Halle, Angelina, and Julia, but once in, they can't get just another pretty face to replace you.

Even people who you or I might pronounce pretty don't measure up to Hollywood standards.

✦ *"I was never pretty enough, I was never sexy enough," says [Sally] Field in the den of her cozy, modest Brentwood home, where her two Oscars and one Emmy sit inconspicuously on a shelf next to her youngest son's sports trophies. "Casting directors would say it to my face. I've spent a whole lot of my time being devastated. The business can be profoundly painful."*

Dana Kennedy, MSNBC[6]

In every walk of life beauty wins. Beauty is nourishing, whether it's a beautiful day, a walk on the beach, or smelling a lovely flower. And those perceived as beautiful are just going to have an easier time of it — while their beauty lasts. But if you're not one of the young beauties, don't despair, someone has to play the un-beautiful one.

✦ *Hollywood values can be distracting and aren't always the most meaningful. The turning point for me was "My Blue Heaven" (1990). I had a tough time with the director, Herbert Ross, which shook my sense of self. Trying to get grounded, I approached a channeler and then went into psychotherapy. After a lot of hard work, I came to terms with the fact that I'm never going to be the perfect young ingenue - - and have to work with who I am. I set out to find a husband and, in 1995, married a lawyer, someone not in the business. When I told him I'm an actress, he asked if I did community theatre. Now I have a sense of balance. I'm the leading lady in my own life.*

Joan Cusack, interviewed by Elaine Dutka, *Los Angeles Times*[7]

No matter what you look like, you can have a career if you really believe in yourself, pursue your dream in a focused way, and trade on the appeal of your atypical looks, but don't fool yourself, the business is about beauty.

And Men

Since films, plays, and television reflect the world surrounding us, it is no surprise that there is more opportunity for any man to work than any woman.

Every year, a majority of films (usually action films) feature twenty-five to thirty men in a cast with possibly two women, frequently both of whom are blonde, beautiful, eighteen, and naked. When Halle Berry won the Academy Award, though not blonde, she was naked, young, and extremely beautiful.

✦ *Role distribution by gender continues the well-established patterns of prior years, whereby males garnered the lion's share of roles. With regard to age, previous casting trends prevail, with a majority of roles going to actors under the age of forty. The nexus of gender and age creates an enormous impact on female performers over the age of forty as their employment rates fall substantially compared to male counterparts over the age of forty. For example, men over forty account for 40% of all roles for men, whereas women over the age of forty make up only 26 % of all roles for women.*

Screen Actor Guild Casting Data, Los Angeles[8]

Women in the Marketplace

Dr. Martha Lauzen, a communications professor at San Diego State U., has regularly studied TV roles by age and gender and found remarkably little variance over the last decade, with women over forty accounting for only about 12% of all primetime roles and men accounting for nearly 80% of characters in their fifties. So despite examples such as Candace Bergen or Lena Olin's sultry, ass-kicking mom on "Alias," Lauzen said, "If the past is any predictor of the future, I wouldn't expect much change this season."

Brian Lowry, *Variety*[9]

Bette Midler is another talent who doesn't fit the mold and therefore has always had to generate her own work. Some of the films she and partner Bonnie Bruckheimer's production company, All Girl Productions, have put together are *Beaches, Ruthless People, Outrageous Fortune,* and *Big Business.*

After *The Rose* (which did good business and brought Midler a 1979 Academy Award nomination) not a single job came her way until 1986 when she starred in *Down and Out in Beverly Hills* and *Ruthless People.*

✦ *"Being a female production team is a real tribute to both of them," observes Robert Cort, who is working with them on Iris Dart's "Show Business Kills." "This town is a boys' club, so they start at the back of the endzone instead of on the 20-yard line."*

Midler and Bruckheimer refuse to cry victim, however. "Disney treated us as bad as [it does] everybody else," quips Bruckheimer. But in Hollywood, as in the rest of life, gender inevitably factors in. As the first women to penetrate that studio's production ranks, they were grateful for a deal that gave them office space but no capital.

Elaine Dutka, *Los Angeles Times*[10]

Ladies Million $ Club

Meryl Streep took heat for complaining that women are not paid as much as men for the same jobs, and though women are still not on a par with men, their salaries are expanding.

Two young actors have big quotes. Emma Watson was paid $4 million for the latest *Harry Potter* movie and Dakota Fanning makes $3 million per movie.

While the number of actresses who have cracked the $10 million mark still lags behind their male counterparts who are now working on the $20+ million mark, some women's salaries have become a force to contend with.

Reese Witherspoon $15-$20 Million	Sandra Bullock $15-$20 Million
Angelina Jolie $15-$20 Million	Julia Roberts $15-$20 Million
Cameron Diaz $15+ Million	Drew Barrymore $10-$12 Million
Nicole Kidman $15-$20 Million	Jodie Foster $10-$12 Million
Renee Zellweger $15-$20 Million	Halle Berry $10 Million

Although one could make a case for financial inequality since the men's salaries can be much higher, the fact is, in today's marketplace, it's action movies and men who put butts in the theatre seats.

✦ *"Like it or not," she [Nikki Rocco, president of distribution at Universal Pictures] says, it is the males who go out to the movies on a Friday night, when all too often young females stay in with their friends -- as Rocco says she did when she was younger. Because of that, she says, "we are targeting mostly males and hoping females come along. But the films that open the biggest are, without a doubt, films that are driven by the male audience."*

Stephen Galloway, The Hollywood Reporter[11]

Other than bits here and there about specific actors (Tom Hanks and Will Smith both get $25 million per picture), there is no recent data on male star salaries. The male list below all have made $20 million or more per picture though with corporate America taking over, those paydays may be a thing of the past.

$20 Million + Club

Nicholas Cage	Robert De Niro	Brad Pitt
Jim Carrey	Vin Diesel	Adam Sandler
George Clooney	Will Ferrell	Ben Stiller
Tom Cruise	Harrison Ford	John Travolta
Matt Damon	Mel Gibson	Chris Tucker
Leonardo DiCaprio	Mike Myers	Denzel Washington
Johnny Depp	Eddie Murphy	Bruce Willis

Though De Niro and Tucker are $20 million plus members, their membership in the Club is courtesy of high visibility sequels.

Many Million $ Clubbers also write, direct, and produce, so some numbers reflect payment for chores over and above acting. Those who make the money are action/adventure stars or comedians.

Women are still considered ornamental or less, so the big bucks usually go to the beauties. Character men and women can make good money in television, but Stephen and Billy Baldwin never made as much money as Alec. Dennis Quaid will always make more money than brother Randy.

Although statistics and many actresses over forty say otherwise, Barbara Niven says she's working even more now that she is in her fifties.

✦ *Caucasian actor Barbara Niven, a national SAG board member and chair of the guild's women's committee, said she hasn't seen that trend among women in her fifties age group. She said she is working more now than ever. "I think my parts get more delicious now. When you're younger, you rely maybe more on your looks or maybe on being the pretty girl. That's the time when you need to get in and really learn your craft, so you're prepared to develop your career as you develop your life," she said, adding that she has shot 18 movies in the last three years and has a recurring role on the new ABC midseason drama "Eli Stone." "You can hear all the negativity and buy into it and give up," Niven said. "I think what you just have to do is work it like a business and work harder than anyone else."*

Lauren Horwitch, *Backstage*[12]

Niven may be getting more delicious parts now, but that's not the norm.

Manager Joan Hyler (whose clients include Diane Lane and Sharon Lawrence) says the kinds of parts available are real problems:

✦ *Hyler added that the dearth of meaty characters for women is even more pronounced in feature films. According to her, "An entire generation of women is being eliminated by this emphasis on the teen market."*

Lauzen's research has found a sharp decline in the number of roles for women over forty in prime time from 26% during the 1995-1996 season to 12% during the '97-98 campaign.

"Women sort of fall off the face of the Earth when they reach forty years old," Lauzen observed.

Brian Lowry, *Los Angeles Times*[13]

✦ *"Try to find a woman in a contemporary movie in the last few years who didn't have a job that wasn't girlie," says producer and former United Artists president Lindsay Doran.*

"If you were a Martian and you looked at American movies, you would think 80% of the women in America write for magazines -- they write for magazines, they are food critics, they are artists, some of them are musicians. But try to find a woman in a business suit at the center of a movie." When one does, like Tilda Swinton's diabolical corporate lawyer in "Michael Clayton," Doran says, they are either villains or their movies "struggle to find an audience."

Why women should be relegated to minor or cliched roles is puzzling, given that women are reaching new levels within society at large. As Sony Pictures Entertainment co-chairman Amy Pascal points out, "We could soon have a woman president. And wouldn't that be awesome?"

Stephen Galloway, *The Hollywood Reporter*[14]

Ultimately Age Determines the Career

Even if you are a member of the preferred food group, age exacts its toll. When Robert De Niro complains about age and availability of parts, you know things are bad:

✦ *Now, at fifty, after thirty-nine pictures, he is aware that age can be an obstacle. "The whole thing," he says, "is for younger people who are sexy and youthful."*
Robert De Niro interviewed by Elizabeth Kaye
The New York Times Magazine[15]

A hot young scriptwriter friend of mine was advised by studio heads to change the gender of his film's lead because "it's much harder to raise money for a film if the protagonist is a woman."
Another script of his called for his leading man to be in his forties. The age of the hero was not arbitrarily chosen, but plot driven. Yet studio powers insisted he rewrite the film and shave ten years off his hero's age.
You're twenty or thirty and you think it could never happen to you. It can. It will. Don't panic. Plan.

Jodie Foster actually planned for her career to be over by age forty, but things didn't turn out that way.

✦ *"I honestly believed my career would be over at forty, and I did some movies back-to-back thinking, "This is it!" Then I realized that it's going to last as long as it lasts, and when it no longer makes me happy, I'll do something else. I was never the beautiful girlfriend, the ingenue or the one you wanted to put on the covers of magazines. It's not who I am, it's not who I ever wanted to be, and I'm not very good at it. And that put me in a different career, so now I don't have to worry so much about getting older. I'm not getting Botox, and hopefully when I'm seventy, I'll be the one getting parts because I still look it."*
Staff Report, *The Hollywood Reporter*[16]

Age/Process Time

Years ago I read an illuminating interview with one of Los Angeles' most powerful casting directors, Lynn Stalmaster. Lynn had a great eye and started many actors on the road to stardom. Richard Dreyfuss auditioned for several projects before he connected.
Instead of giving up on Dreyfuss and scratching him from his audition lists, Lynn just said, "Richard isn't ready yet," and continued calling him in to read until he finally scored the part in *American Graffiti*

that birthed his career.

This story clarifies the ubiquitous *process*. Conceptualize an actor, writer, or director as a cake that's baking in the oven. All the ingredients are there; they just need to be cooked properly. Richard just wasn't *done* yet.

I can't emphasize enough how important it is to have a feeling for the importance of time and process over a career, any career and actually, almost any endeavor.

I read an article about a woman who was remodeling her house and the job took much longer than she had envisioned. Her remarks could be applied to any part of life: "It was a slow process, but realistic. I needed the time to process all the decisions. Now I'm glad the project didn't go faster, because I got exactly what I wanted and I didn't always know at the moment."

The prospect of getting exactly what you want is daunting. Unfolding your story slowly over time gives the most opportunity to begin to perceive the possibilities. There may actually be more to life than leading parts. You think?

Age/Demographics

Surely you've heard ad nauseam how the preferred audience age for television is 18-49. Some people call it ageism and threaten legal action, but what is perceived as ageism is simply a realistic product adjustment related to the economics of the marketplace.

I spoke with Barbara Brogliatti when she was still Senior Vice-President of World-Wide Television Publicity for Warner Bros. about why those of us over fifty are perceived as a less desirable audience by advertisers and studio heads than those in the coveted 18-49 year old demographic.

✦ *The major assumption is that by the time people are fifty to sixty years old, they have already established their favorite brands: they've established their favorite toothpaste, their favorite soap; they're either Pepsi drinkers or Coke drinkers. If their income has risen, they might choose a different car, but companies selling more expensive cars don't do the bulk of their advertising on television. They advertise mostly in magazines which reach a narrower audience.*

Cable is narrow casting. A limited amount of people will target fifty+, so that's for cable. Broadcasting is supposed to be broad. In order to have those big budgets, you have to aim for a large number of people. You need mass appeal. Cable is not

unlike magazines. One of the largest magazines in the world is "AARP: Modern Maturity," but they still have many fewer subscribers than "TV Guide," which has the largest circulation. "Modern Maturity" makes a good living even though they have 50% or fewer of the population.
Barbara Brogliatti

Since it's human nature to be interested in people like yourself, that means all those people (18-49) who supposedly have not yet made up their minds between Coke and Pepsi will be more receptive to making choices while they are watching stories and listening to music that deals with their fellow undecideds.

Those of us already in the know will have to make do with the knowledge that although we are not the coveted group, at least we know who we are and what we want.

Well, that's television. Brogliatti didn't say anything about films. Perhaps the film companies care about those unfortunates over forty-nine.

✦ *Major movie money is made by the repeat business of kids and teens. At Warner Bros., they have established (both in television and features) a policy of trying to appeal to all demographics, even the less popular ones.*

You'll see in the films that come from Warner Bros., not only "Batman," but in stories that are family-centered ("The Little Princess") or films that are controversial or may not make a lot of money. The less profitable projects have "Batman" to subsidize them.

In order to do all the dramas that we do, we have to have the comedies to pay for it. This company has established itself in diversity. They have made a decision, "Okay, so our profit margin, instead of being ten, our profit margin will be one."

A lot of companies don't have that luxury. More studios keep their menus less diverse and go for the home run. We are a studio that likes to go for singles, doubles and triples, both in television and film.
Barbara Brogliatti

I'm talking a lot about aging because I think it is important for every age group to understand why younger actors will work and earn more than those who are older. If you are in the preferred age group today, your days are numbered, so prepare for a career that can span your whole lifetime by diversifying now.

We aren't all going to be put to death on our 50th birthdays; there will be jobs for some. There are jobs in theatre, on the networks, and on cable, but the employment possibilities for most of us will never equal our prime earning years from twenty to forty, just as in most any business.

Movies like *In the Bedroom, Innocence,* and *Sexy Beast* do, however, reflect some basic changes happening in the minds of viewers that are just going to grow as the core population continues to age. For the moment at least, those of us over fifty get to have sex:

✦ *John C. Cavanaugh, a provost at the University of North Carolina at Wilmington and author of "Adult Development and Aging," agrees. "There has been a fundamental shift in attitude toward midlife and aging," he said. "We no longer think of midlife as downhill, or of sex as something specific to younger people. We are becoming more aware that both interest in sex and sexual activity continue well into late life."*
Ruth La Ferla, *The New York Times*[17]

Whew! That's a relief.

Is It Possible to Make a Living Acting?

Well, yes, but it is difficult. According to the Screen Actors Guild's records, only 6% of the almost 120,000 actors who are already in the union make what SAG speaks of as a 'middle class' earnings of $30,000 to $70,000 a year and only 2% make over $100,000 annually.

✦ *Internal SAG documents show that 23% of guild members did not work during 1996-2000 and that 36% have worked less than five days in those five years. The confidential statistics show that only three branches (Hollywood, Minneapolis, and New York) saw over 40% of members log at least thirty days work during the 1996-2000 period.*
Dave McNary, *Variety*[18]

Almost 60% of the members of SAG worked only *five days* total in a recent four year period. Out of every 100 actors, only six made between $30,000 and $70,000 and 80% of SAG members made less than $10,000 a year. Almost one third made no money at all.

✦ *...a whopping 70 percent earn $7,500 or less through the Guild each year. But this is the range that represents a realistic goal for those just breaking in and the 18% who fall in the $7,500-$30,000 range. And this is the segment that pays a*

good portion of the Guild's income-scaled dues, feeds its health and pension plans, and gives it clout.
Valerie Kuklenski, *Daily News*[19]

The news gets worse. Even working actors who had persevered within the system for years are asking themselves and their families if it isn't finally time to throw in the towel.

✦ *They have had The Conversation before in their nine-year marriage, but [Michael] O'Neill did not expect to be having it now. He expected to be having his best year ever, and he had reason.*

Last year, in addition to loads of TV work, including five episodes of "The West Wing" as Secret Service agent Ron Butterfield, O'Neill had small roles in "Secondhand Lions" and "Seabiscuit." As jockey Red Pollard's poetry-loving father, O'Neill became a man worn down to such literal and emotional rags by the Depression that he gives his adolescent son into the care of strangers. It was the sort of performance that could change a career, lead to bigger film roles, or a regular spot on a TV series.

Only it hasn't.

Making it in Hollywood has always been a bit like Peter Pan's recipe for flight: All it takes is faith and trust; oh yes, and a little pixie dust. For twenty years, O'Neill has had the faith and trust; he's done the work and accepted that most actors never become big-deal movie stars. He was happy just to be an actor, to support himself and his family by acting. But lately, cost cutting, offshore production, the explosion of reality television shows and a shift in pay scales have made life harder for the journeyman actor to make a decent living.

"It saddens me," O'Neill says. "Because I'm not ready yet. I am an actor, that's who I am, who I've been most of my life. But the industry I'm in now is completely different than the one I got into.

"It's not that there's no work. There's never been any work. But the work you get now does not recognize the value of your experience; it certainly does not compensate you for your experience. All the rules have changed."
Mary McNamara, *Los Angeles Times*[20]

When I interviewed independent film producer/entrepreneur Scott Herman, he made a compelling statement:

✦ *Acting is similar to professional sports in that the top 2% make 98% of the money. Last year an actor whose earnings in SAGs 50th percentile, his/her income would be $0 (doughnut). If you looked at someone in the 50th percentile of a*

business such as IBM, he/she is making a comfortable living.
Scott Herman/Producer

SAG Member Earnings

27.5 % earned no money at all
39.5% earned $1 to $3,000
2.8% earned $100,000 +
1.4% earned $200,000 +

Still sure you want to do this?

Minorities and Women

Making a living as an actor is difficult at best, but breaking down the numbers of who gets the work by age, gender, and ethnicity can be sobering for anyone except the favored food group, young white men.

According to the most recent statistics, the major Hollywood guilds (actors, writers, directors, and producers) are 80% to 90% white.

The 2007 *Hollywood Reporter's Women in Entertainment* annual Power 100 list featured only seven African Americans (one was Oprah) and two Asians. Only two major talent agencies have woman partners: UTA has five and Endeavor has four. There are no minority women partners.

✦ *"Until minorities are in a position of power and until the people doing the buying have a vested interest, you are not going to see many drastic changes," said Park, who is Korean American. "Directors and showrunners hire their friends; this is a town of relationships. You hire who you know. The key is getting people of color to a level where they can hire their friends."*
Lorenza Muñoz, *Los Angeles Times*[21]

When Denzel Washington and Halle Berry won their Academy Awards, Berry emotionally extolled that "the gates are now open for Black actors." In fact, Forest Whitaker and Jennifer Hudson won the next year, but packaging and selling minorities didn't get any easier.

✦ *"None of this is going to change the fact that you cannot package or sell [a movie] to the world market today with a black woman," said James Ulmer ("James Ulmer's Hollywood Hot List") which tracks actors' global marketability. "I don't see [the Oscar win] as changing an industry where white male actors drive the train of the international marketplace."*

Behind the camera, minorities are just as under-represented. Hollywood may be seen by outsiders to be a politically progressive enclave, but "the industry's hiring practices and the opportunities available for nonwhites have not progressed much in thirty years," said Todd Boyd, professor of Critical Studies at USC's School of Cinema-Television.
Ibid[22]

Perhaps Will Smith will change things.

✦ *At a time when the world is growing more multicultural by the minute, movie studios cling to the notion that black performers cannot sell as many overseas movie tickets as their white counterparts. But Smith is shattering that perception: He's become Hollywood's biggest post-racial movie star. "It doesn't matter what the genre and it doesn't matter what date the movie opens -- people just want to see him," says Amy Pascal, whose Sony Pictures released Smith's hits "Hitch," "Men in Black" and "Bad Boys."*
John Horn and Chris Lee, *Los Angeles Times*[23]

Will Smith, Forest Whitaker, Don Cheadle, Chiwetel Ejiofor, Samuel L. Jackson, Denzel Washington, Morgan Freeman, Danny Glover, and Wesley Snipes are all part of a growing fraternity of African American film actors with clout. However, on television, other than *Oprah* (who crosses every barrier), the only minority voices are *House of Payne* from Tyler Perry, *Everybody Hates Chris* from Chris Rock, and *Cane*. The phenom known as Whoopi is now holding forth on *The View*.

✦ *Whoopi Goldberg is the only woman whose name on a project will flip open bankers' wallets posthaste, to the tune of $20 million for two Buena Vista films. Among the high-scoring women, though, Goldberg continues to be most remarkable in the international marketplace.*

"She's fascinating because she breaks through three major barriers internationally," notes sales veteran Kathy Morgan of Kathy Morgan International. "She's a female superstar in a man's world, when women stars tend to be these very sexy Sharon Stone types. She's an African-American actor who is strongly accepted outside the U.S., which is rare.

And she's comedic, when the old saying goes that comedians don't travel overseas. She's a very unusual superstar."
James Ulmer, *Variety*[24]

✦ ...*as a group, African Americans have far more opportunities in prime time than other minorities. Latinos, for example, comprise 12.5% of the nation's population but account for only 2% of characters on all prime-time network shows.*

By contrast, African Americans and whites jointly comprise 82% of the population yet account for 92% of all prime-time characters.

Greg Braxton, *Los Angeles Times*[25]

We are a vast melting pot of a nation, yet the 2001-2002 television season saw Latinos starring only in *Resurrection Boulevard* (cable), *American Family* (PBS), and *George Lopez* (network). Not since 1994, when Margaret Cho's *All American Girl* was on television, has there been any kind of programming acknowledging Asian audiences.

✦ *A 1999 vow by the major TV networks to include more minorities in prime-time series has largely gone unfulfilled, according to an analysis by Children Now, a research and advocacy group.*

"Fall Colors 2001-02," the group's third-annual study of prime-time programming, examined the first two episodes of each evening series airing last fall on ABC, CBS, Fox, NBC, UPN and WB. Its findings, released Wednesday, said the networks are "telling the same old tale," in which younger white males predominate, ethnic actors are relegated to supporting roles, and female characters are often stereotypes. Shows in the sitcom-dominated 8 p.m. hour, when young viewers do most of their prime-time viewing, tend to be the most segregated on prime-time TV, "Children Now" reported. Only 7% of comedies had ethnically-diverse starring casts, compared with 14% a year earlier, it said.

Elaine Dutka, *Los Angeles Times*[26]

It's hard to develop without a place to learn and grow.

✦ *"We have yet to develop a more prominent talent pool," says film and TV star Esai Morales, who was instrumental in creating the National Hispanic Foundation for the Arts, which not only strives to improve the quality of Latino images in the industry, but aid potential talent in finishing their studies through grants so they might better integrate into the industry. "But with the advent of stars like Jennifer Lopez and Benicio Del Toro, who won an Oscar, and filmmakers like Robert Rodriguez, who hit a home run with 'Spy Kids,' people are becoming aware."*

"Latinos are an emerging middle class," says Arenas Entertainment's Santiago

Pozo. "In the coming years, we're going to develop more writers, more directors, more actors." "Nothing ever happens overnight and stays that way," says Morales. *"The population likes to see repeat performers, people who strike gold again and again. I don't see it as a color issue, but a gold issue. We've got to deliver in that sense, as individuals and as a community."*
 Steve Chagollan and Paul Karon, *Variety*[27]

✦ *Latino/Hispanic roles fell slightly as a percentage of total roles in all categories from 2005 to 2006, with the exception of theatrical features. In theatrical feature presentations, their number of lead roles grew from 31 to 52, while their number of supporting roles grew from 302 to 364.*
 Lauren Horwitch, *Backstage*[28]

One reason Latinos are not further along is they are not as organized as African Americans. Another is economics:

✦ *Money drives decisions in Hollywood, and advertisers won't back Latino programs on the major U.S. networks because they can reach most of the nation's twenty-six million Latinos for less than half the price by advertising on Spanish-language TV.*
 Dolores Kunda, Vice-President and account director for the Leo Burnett USA Hispanic Unit in Chicago (whose clients include Kellogg, McDonalds, and United Airlines) says, "Many big advertisers sell to moms, and the moms are watching Spanish-language TV. If you try to market the younger Generation X Hispanic, the question is 'How fine do you want to split up your media dollars?' A lot of advertisers are already getting that consumer through the Spanish-language market."
 A recent study by A. C. Nielson seems to confirm that notion: more than 40% of U.S. Latinos speak Spanish at home meaning that the English-language Latino audience really consists of no more than about fifteen million potential viewers. "It would get me into big trouble to say this," says the leader of one Latino group, "but once you subtract the Latinos who are Spanish-dominant, the theory of a fractionalized market is correct. I don't blame the studios or the networks."
 Jill Stewart, *Buzz Magazine*[29]

Morgan Freeman feels that color may well not be the problem:

✦ *"Contrary to popular belief," he says, "Hollywood is not necessarily race conscious. It's money conscious."*
 David Ehrenstein, *Los Angeles Times*[30]

And he is right. Show me someone of any color or sex who has produced or starred in a box office record breaker and I'll show you someone who is going to work, at least during the next twelve months. So everyone not in the preferred food group might as well give up?

✦ *On the "Hancock" set, [Will] Smith said, "If I say, 'I'm black, so I can never be the biggest movie star in the world, a black person could never be the biggest movie star in the world,' I wouldn't try to be the biggest movie star in the world. I'd be creating a barrier for myself. It rarely crosses my mind -- purposely."*
John Horn and Chris Lee, *Los Angeles Times*[31]

Research Your Employment Opportunities

Where are the jobs for you? Spend every evening for a month in front of the television set with a paper and pencil. Assuming you were trained and in the right place at the right time, are there parts for you? On commercials? On nighttime television? On daytime television? As you look closely, you'll begin to get an idea of how or whether you can fit into the marketplace in a way that will enable you to make a living.

Look closely at yourself physically and the impact this has on your earning power. Extremely tall men who have any natural grace and athletic ability are recruited to be basketball players. If you are a gifted athlete who yearns to be a basketball star, but are only five feet tall, all the heart and determination in the world isn't going to make you into Kobe.

This applies to actors as well. Look at yourself. Will you physically fit into a casting niche in the business? Consider yourself in relation to the people who are working. Are you the right age? Do you need to be older to logically sell who you are? If you do, don't starve while you age; there are alternatives.

I was conducting a seminar in New York when an offbeat, not traditionally attractive, thirtyish man came up and spoke to me. He had a job in local television in Connecticut and had been considering making the move to the big marketplace in New York City. Until the seminar, he had not really analyzed the fact that he is a character man who has not yet grown into himself and that he will be more physically employable in fifteen years. Since he's already employed in the business, he decided to continue growing into himself where he is and postpone the move to New York until his visual age catches up to his presence.

I read an interview with Geraldine Page when she was nominated for an Academy Award for *The Pope of Greenwich Village*. She had spent the previous several years totally unemployable. She said: "I don't know who it is that has finally decided it's okay for me to work again."

In fact, she had just been through a growth period where she was changing from one type to another, visually.

Cinematic Age

Even though sixty is supposedly the new fifty, that's not true on film. We have ingrained ideas of what age looks like. If you're sixty looking forty-five, you're not going to read "grandmother" walking in the door. The sad news is that your sensational looks are probably not going to play forty-five either. Unless you're playing a woman who's "had work done", you're not going to fit in either category.

What They See Is What They Want

In my early career, I made money in commercials. There were several reasons why, not the least of which was my Midwestern American face, a gift from my parents for which I can take no credit.

As successful as I was in New York in commercials, when I moved to Los Angeles, that particular success did not translate. In Los Angeles, they prefer prettier people. I was perfect as a real person in New York. In Los Angeles, reality is not the strong suit.

Because I was on the crest of an age category change, I did fewer commercials in Los Angeles. No longer the mother of young kids, I was moving into Mother of the Bride territory. Not only are there not that many parts for MOBs, there were other MOBs more securely in that age range who were cinematically better able to fill that role. Interestingly, this image problem did not interfere with my film and television career during that period.

Go figure.

Actors pass through many age ranges during their careers. Some will be lucrative, others dismal. Because of age and overexposure, everything can stop without warning. One day you are doing great, finally heaving a sigh of relief: "Oh, boy, it's going to work out. I'm not going to have to worry for a while."

And then it's over for six months, or a year, or a year and a half. I don't know a single actor who has been in the business for any length of time who has not had this experience. I've been told that no young, excited actor is going to believe this will ever happen to him, and I do agree that I might not have believed it either. But no one ever told me about age ranges and changes.

When I faced this challenge for the first time, it was painful. You think that it's all over, that you'll never work again, and that it's never happened to anyone but you. It would have helped a bit if I had been able to say, "I never believed it would happen, but at least I know it's part of the process and not just me. Now, I believe."

Emotional Strength

Do you have the temperament to withstand the stress of constant unemployment and daily rejection? New York agent Jerry Hogan told me he began his career as an actor, but stopped when he realized his nature couldn't handle constant rejection. The wear and tear on his ego was too much.

Of course, I contend that actors do not really go into acting because they are necessarily in their right minds. My theory is we are all drawn to this business because we come from a background of real or imagined rejection. We are, therefore, familiar with the feeling and have ways of coping with it. If we are lucky, we get healthier along the way.

Sometimes we stay in the business because we are making more money than we could make any place else. And sometimes we leave.

Wrap Up

✓ physicality is destiny
✓ beauty wins
✓ white men make the money
✓ everyone works considerably less after age forty, particularly women
✓ minorities are still not getting their share of the work
✓ research the marketplace for jobs for your type
✓ real age is not synonymous with cinematic age
✓ emotional strength is vital

≥ 4 ≤

Why Do You Want to Be an Actor?

Youth is over in about 15 minutes so it's important not to squander what our society prizes as the most energetic, attractive part of life by chasing a rainbow whose pot of gold may not be what you want.

Just because acting seems to appeal to others doesn't mean it would appeal to you. I sometimes think the unavailability of the jobs is the thing that appeals to actors the most. Maybe if everybody chose me all the time, I wouldn't even be interested. So far, that hasn't been a problem.

What is it about acting that appeals to you? Are you truly interested in the process of creating a character? Does being a psychological sleuth attract you? Do you have a need to communicate? Are you an exhibitionist? Are your feelings about being an actor based on any realistic appraisal of what an actor's life is all about?

Before You Study Acting, Study the Lifestyle

In order to make an intelligent decision about acting as a way to spend your life, do the research. It's a shame that biographies are only written about successful actors. It would be more instructive to talk to actors who never made a dime in the business. Because the public is usually exposed only to star actors' lives, most folks' idea of the actor's life is pretty much what we see in the movies except for Bravo's short-lived reality series *The It Factor*. It's too bad the show is over. No film or television show ever portrayed the struggling actor's life so realistically. I know reality television is usually not that real, but this was. No one can perceive what the life is about unless he has lived it.

I have a friend who is a television editor. He has worked in the business all his life. Even so, he had never had an actor for a friend before we met. He was dumbfounded to find out all actors did not make the salaries reported in the newspapers. Nobody really wants to read that although an actor's minimum pay for a day on film is $757, he may not work more than two days per year, if that.

Acting is a profession. Any profession requires a big commitment. Years of study. Years of struggle. If your family is very wealthy, that may not be such a sacrifice, but the real challenge is not just doing without money, it's doing without validation.

When your life is spent with people saying "No, thank you" all the time, it takes effort to stay positive. Not only that, it depletes your energy. Psychologists tell us that we get our picture of ourselves from our work. In that case, if you are not working, it's difficult to get a valid sense of self.

The reality is that every actor spends more time unemployed than employed. His real job is looking for work and it's grueling. For a long time, he may not be able to have a life other than pursuing work and when he finally does get work, he will work and pursue his next job at the same time.

Choice of career is not just the choice of one's nine-to-five endeavor, but the choice of lifestyle. Within the instability of the actor's life, it is difficult to plan for children, vacations, illness, and other life necessities, luxuries, or surprises.

When you are unemployed, it's difficult not to be depressed; when you are working, there's little time for a mate and family.

So when you're available, you're depressed and when you're happy, you're unavailable. That can make an actor an undesirable mate.

If, however, you are able to get out of yourself, you'll realize that your mate and your kids will be there for you when management won't. You'll be able to enjoy what some might call the downside of your lifestyle.

Periods of not working can be seen as a luxury, giving you time to be there when your kids get home from school, to help them with their homework and watch them play baseball or attend their recital. You'll be able to be a reliable friend and partner to your mate.

Then when you do get a job, your family will be able to enjoy your good fortune, confident that you will not go to work and forget to come home. They will know family life is the first priority.

Communication

So far, we haven't even dealt with the word communication. Most actors might not cite the need to communicate as their initial reason for getting into acting. Whether or not it is your goal, there is no way you can play a role and not communicate your take on the character. It's easy to acknowledge the influence that writers can have on the public, but we tend to think of actors as merely delivering the writer's message, without realizing that the persona of the actor determines the message.

Roseanne was a stand-up comedienne who wrote her own material when she created the character that has made her famous. That creation came out of what she felt about being a working class wife and mother. If she had written this material and someone else had played it, let's say Sally Field (who also plays working class women), wouldn't Sally, just by being Sally, have made the material completely different?

And if the producer had chosen Sally for the role of Roseanne, he would have been choosing Sally's trademark vulnerability instead of Roseanne's edge. Casting directors and producers can alter the material dramatically by their choice of actor.

You communicate by the way you carry yourself, the clothes you wear, your tone of voice, and the time you take before you speak. If you wear an Armani suit, people will not only get the idea that you have money, but that style and trend are important to you. If you never comb your hair nor take a bath, you're definitely giving an antisocial message.

It's not just our clothes, of course, but also our mannerisms, tone of voice, and body language that communicate who we are.

I remember a conversation I had years ago with a friend of my daughter's. As a student at UCLA, she was appalled that another student had spit on her as she was sitting on campus. I agreed with her that no one had the right to spit on her just because her normal attire was green hair, clown white makeup, and strange clothes, but I did ask her to consider the message she was sending by her choice of clothing.

If you were lost and penniless on the subway platform, who would you ask for help? I'd be talking to the person who looked most like me. Someone with resonance.

Check the message your packaging is sending and make sure you are expressing your true voice. One of the problems with being trendy is that the meaning is generally: "I don't really have a message here, so I'm latching onto someone else's."

Communicating at Auditions

If you create a character and attend an audition in that guise, you are making a statement about how you see that character played. It may or may not be the idea the director has, but you will have at least impressed him as someone who has a point of view and is not afraid to take responsibility for it.

Whether you are the good one, the bad one, the weird one, the banker, or the killer, the more identifiable you are as a something, the easier it will be for casting people to plug you into the system. The bad news, of course, is that you will feel typecast. We should all be so lucky. Worry about that after you are employed.

Billy Bob Thornton's quirky character in *Slingblade* is not the only person he can play, but if you've seen other performances by this talented actor/writer, you will probably agree that you could not get another actor to play weird vulnerability more successfully. Gwyneth Paltrow's lovely sensibility was finally showcased perfectly in *Shakespeare in Love*. The vulnerable upper-class young woman seeking adventure is her most winning role. John Malkovich's most effective characters are people I wouldn't like to meet on a dark street.

Sally Kirkland is extremely career-oriented and won an Academy Award nomination in *Anna* for playing an actress who will do anything to get a job.

The biggest break I ever had as an actress was my first film. In *Joe*, I played the wife of a working class man; a woman who was raised to say yes and keep her man happy. I had been in training for years as a Catholic wife and mother. I don't think I was that great an actress necessarily, it's just that my persona turned out to be perfect for the part. It was one of those rare synergistic miracles.

Meryl Streep is a good example of someone who has played a wide variety of parts. She's the queen of characterization using different accents and wigs, body behavior, and varied social class. The one thing that is common in her work is her intelligence. You have never seen her play someone who is dumb.

When I see Sigourney Weaver, I think strong; Drew Barrymore is adorable no matter what she plays; Meg Ryan can do lots of other things, but I'm disappointed when she's not 'Meg Ryan'; and who could be more devilishly dangerous than Jack Nicholson? If you catch any of these performers' early work on television, you will see the essence even then; time, experience, and no doubt, self knowledge have honed that essence to its most commercial aspects.

Separating Yourself from the Pack

Elizabeth Dillon at HB Studios in New York was one of the best teachers for beginning actors in the business. Her ability to be clear about acting choices set her apart from all other teachers I have experienced. Dillon said drama is heightened reality. Not just a sigh, but the most profound sigh. Not just a tear, but the most poignant tear. Not just a laugh, but a contagious laugh.

New York agent Michael Kingman, a whirlwind personality on his own, spoke of his ideal client: an actor with contagious emotions.

Look in the dictionary. It says that dramatic is "vivid, startling, highly effective, striking." Are you? It takes a lot of energy to be fascinating and it doesn't happen by accident. It takes energy to focus your essence that much.

You better not be just pretty. You better be beautiful. Pretty is a dime a dozen in the marketplace. You can even be ugly and have a career, but you better be really ugly. Phyllis Diller is an attractive woman, yet her career and material relied on her ability to make us think of her as horse-faced.

Whether you are extremely fat or extremely thin, you'd better have or create a look for yourself that is unique and then develop a persona to match it.

Confidence, Determination & Drive

Talent, looks, and youth are all good, but nothing succeeds like confidence, determination, and drive. The ability to feel within yourself that you can do anything (even if you can't) will take you far. You have to set fear aside and go for it. Will Smith is a stunning example of just doing it.

Will's father, a military man, built his own refrigeration business. One summer he remodeled his ice house, tore down its old brick wall, and told Will and his brother that they were to build a new one:

✦ *I couldn't believe it. He wanted us to build a wall 50 feet long and 14 feet high. I remember standing there and thinking, "There's no way I will live to see this completed. He wants us to build the Great Wall of Philly!"*

I remember hoping my father would get committed, because if he were in an insane asylum, then we wouldn't have to finish the thing. But finally we did. And

I remember my father standing there looking at us, and all he said was, 'Now don't ever tell me there's anything you can't do.'

He'd been waiting six months just to deliver that line. And I got it: there's nothing insurmountable if you just keep laying the bricks, you know? You go one brick at a time and eventually there will be a wall. You can't avoid it. So I don't worry much about walls. I just concentrate on the bricks, and the walls take care of themselves.

Will Smith, interviewed by Joe Rhodes, *Premiere*[32]

Will was a successful rapper mugging in music videos when Quincy Jones managed to sell a network on the idea of the young musician starring in his own sitcom. A week before shooting, Will began to get nervous:

✦ *This is ridiculous. Is anyone ever going to ask me whether or not I can act? So, I'm sitting at home, flipping though channels, and there are all these shows, sitcoms, movies, soap operas and all these actors, thousands and thousands of actors. And that's when it hits me, I said to myself, "it's not mathematically possible that all these people are better than me. Nature doesn't allow that. At worst, I have to be better than half of them, right?" And this weird comfort washed over me. I knew I'd be okay.*

Ibid.[33]

Will Smith is a multi-talented superstar with success in music, television, and film, but he says his greatest asset is his drive:

✦ *I see people all the time who are better rappers than me, better actors than me, better-looking and stronger than me. But my ace in the hole is my dangerously obsessive drive, you know? I'm a terminator. I absolutely, positively will not stop until I win.*

Ibid.[34]

Being who you really are sounds easy, but most actors have spent a lifetime trying to become what they thought would please others or, at the other extreme, behaving badly just for effect. The process of owning one's real feelings comes in fits and starts.

Do you prefer red or blue? Corduroy or velvet? Rice Krispies or yogurt? How do you feel about gay people? Politics? Violence? What's your favorite music? Do you like candy? Do you eat meat? Are you formal? Casual? Flamboyant? Private? Do you even take the time to listen and find out the answers? Perhaps one of the answers is not to do so much: to listen more, to yourself as well as others.

Are the big stars all awake and we are asleep? I have no idea. What I do know is that your sense of self is all you have to sell. You will play many parts, but it's your defined presence that makes the statement interesting or not.

I'm spending a lot of time talking about philosophy. That's appropriate since life is a mind-set. If you can conceptualize your goals accurately and specifically, you can plan a time table and select a role model. The more precise your mind-set, the more efficient your efforts and the more fruitful your results.

Wrap Up

You need to know the answers to these questions:

✓ Why do you want to act?
✓ Do you really want the lifestyle?
✓ What do you want to say?
✓ What makes you special?
✓ Do you have the drive and determination?

✄ 5 ✄
There's No Place Like Home

If you want to be an actor in order to play Macbeth or Lady Macbeth, perhaps you can do that in your own hometown. Local theater productions can be very rewarding. You might play bigger parts with more regularity than you ever would as a professional actor. Perhaps you need to take a fresh look at your hometown to discover what might be showbiz related jobs.

Looking for Work at Home

Most people looking for work as an actor would never think to look in the Help Wanted section of their newspapers, but when there is a nationwide or local casting search there is usually a press release to newspapers across the country and ads in the classified section. Google (*www.google.com*) is a great place to start for everything. I typed in "casting Dallas Tx" and came up with several leads. If you work your way through the menus, Craig's List (*www.craigslist.com*) has an employment section for almost everyplace. Need a job in Turkey?

Actors Access is a free service for actors allowing them to post two pictures, resumes, contact information and (for a price) video links. In addition to this service, the actor has access to casting information and electronic self-submission via The Breakdown Service. These jobs are typically non-union, or very small parts, or a "when all else fails" plea that a casting director might release for general viewing. These Breakdowns cover the entire country and could be that much more valuable for actors outside the large entertainment centers. There is a $2 charge for each submission on Actors Access and each download of sides from Showfax. A $68 annual membership fee gives you unlimited submissions and sides.

These two resources cover the entire United States as well as Vancouver and Toronto. Check them out online at *www.actorsaccess.com* and *showfax.com*. I'd try the service for a while, paying each time until you determine if this is something that works for you. You should find at least one job if you use these tools intelligently.

The Yellow Pages of most cities list Entertainers and Entertainment Agencies. When I checked, there were many musical or variety agents for singers, comedians, magicians, etc. Some listed speakers and most listed those services having to do with conventions and fairs. Phoenix listed something called Ladies Choice (your guess is as good as mine). The Bag Lady in Tacoma also piqued my curiosity.

When I lived in Dallas, long ago, one of the lucrative jobs for local actors was the annual Automobile Show at the Texas State Fair. If you were pretty/handsome enough, you might be employed to stand by the car all day in evening attire looking like an expensive accessory. If you were p/h and could also talk, you might be the spokesperson while another p/h illustrated features of the car.

If you are in New York or Los Angeles, it is easy to figure out that the major areas of employment are theatre, film, television, and commercials. Yet even there, the life of an actor is not all Macbeth and Excedrin commercials. As a matter of fact, most of it isn't.

In the primary entertainment centers, actors are spokespersons for conventions and do voice-overs for radio and television commercials. They supply American dialogue for foreign films or appear in front of Madison Square Garden wearing sandwich boards and handing out buttons. They work industrial shows or do weird commercials on *Saturday Night Live*, *The Tonight Show*, and *The Late Show with David Letterman*. They spend a lot of money sending out pictures and resumes, They spend hours waiting in line for open calls for parts that have probably already been cast. Not only that, most of them feel grateful for any opportunity to get up in public to perform, to add to their resume and mostly to make money in anything related to the business.

Even if there are no opportunities to act in the theatre, there are many other ways to make money as an actor: Perhaps you can be the film critic on local radio or television or create an innovative cooking show with public access as your entree into television. These days with hosts and reality shows, the sky's the limit.

Create your own show on the Internet. Commit yourself to posting a one or two minute segment for *www.youtube.com* every week. Your stuff may suck at the beginning, but you'll improve. We all do.

I frequently consider where I would be today if twenty years ago, instead of producing books, I had started making film. When I wrote that first book, I had no plans to write a second. Fate stepped in and I've now written twenty-nine books when you consider all the different editions. I had no idea how primitive the first book was at the time. I look back now and smile. The learning curve entailed not only people and business skills, but computer literacy on many levels.

Think what you could do today if you started producing films. You would probably know at least as much as I did about writing books, which was zero, but at the end of twenty years you might be Woody Allen or Judd Apatow. One step at a time, regardless of who you turn out to be.

Finding Local Agents

You can do anything if you have nerve. One summer after the regular season was over at Dallas' world famous Margo Jones Theatre, where I was lucky enough to apprentice, I wondered, "What is it like to go into an agent's office in Dallas, Texas?"

This was in the fifties and Dallas was not the entertainment center it has become. I looked in the phone book and found that, indeed, Dallas did have an agency. It was called The Molly O'Day Agency. I showed up without an appointment and announced that I was a singer. Coached by Betty Grable movies, I was expecting to be shown the door. The conversation went something like this:

Molly: Do you have an accompanist?
Me: No.
Molly: Well then, do you have any music?
Me: No.
Molly: Wait here.

Miss O'Day went down the hall and reappeared with an accordion player. I had sung twice in the variety show in college and knew my key for a couple of songs. After a couple of choruses of *I'm Looking Over a Four Leaf Clover* and *It Had to be You*, the accordion player left and I was offered a job singing in the officer's club of a nearby Air Force base. My natural chutzpah got me that far, but my Catholic school training prevailed when I stood in front of my audience and I was unable to look at them. My Air Force singing career was pretty short.

For a convention, I was dressed as a woman from space who did a voiceless skit. The audience had to pick up earphones to hear what we were mouthing, but they could never figure how our mouths matched what was coming out of the earphones. They didn't know we had little earphones under the space caps. This job entailed being able to move well, learn dialogue, and lip sync.

I had a lucrative recurring job with Polaroid requiring that I pose with and take pictures of all the guests at a particular trade show. They trained me to set up the lights for the camera, take test pictures, and deal with all the equipment and the guests.

I also taught acting at my high school alma mater, started a children's theatre, and wrote my own material. I worked out an arrangement to use the community center room at the bank for free in return for providing holiday-themed entertainment on special occasions. I wrote and produced short plays and the shopping center provided space, prizes, or handouts and publicity for the event.

My students had the chance to perform for more than their parents and friends. The event was successful for both merchants and students, and I was making my first money in show business. It was not an extravagant amount of money, but when you start any business, you have to be prepared for meager earnings the first few years.

If you live in a small town, you might have to travel to your next largest town to find work. When I moved to Norman, Oklahoma, the first thing I did was check out advertising agencies in the phone book in nearby Oklahoma City.

I asked if they produced television commercials and the procedure to become involved. Since I had done commercials in Dallas, those credits added to my credibility. My husband was a grad student at the University nearby, so I called their motion picture department and subsequently worked on educational films. Money for me and film for my future.

Every working actor has a pocketful of similar stories. Successful actors call and ask where the jobs are. You need to have the imagination and determination to call everybody.

If you are computer savvy, you can probably find a local agent in your city by tapping into the Internet. Power up a search engine and type in "talent agents" + your city and see what you find. I wanted to see all the SAG franchised agents in my hometown of Dallas. I was also able to access casting director numbers as well as agents and actors in London. The possibilities are endless.

The Big Apple and the Big Orange

If you are sitting in Des Moines, Iowa or Avon, Montana, you may feel New York/Los Angeles considerations don't apply to you. You're not trying to get a job on *Law & Order* or star in Ang Lee's next movie, so what does that have to do with you?

Everything. What happens in the larger marketplace is reflected locally. Commercials cast in Oklahoma City reflect commercials cast in Manhattan. NY/LA commercials follow trends set by current films. Plays performed in Dayton, Ohio were on Broadway or in Los Angeles last year, so your educational process should include an overview of what's happening in the major production centers.

Australian actress Toni Collette (*Little Miss Sunshine*) was proactive from the get go.

✦ *Raised in Melbourne, where she still lives, she studied art, drama and dance in college before settling on acting. "The first year I came out of college," she says, "I wrote three plays that were performed in various fringe festivals and alternative spaces. I was working for my friends, and my friends were working for me."*
Manohla Dargis, *The New York Times*[35]

Staying Home

Even if you intend to enter the national marketplace eventually, the best thing you can do is spend a number of years in your own city exploiting and developing all of your talents.

Many of the Los Angeles job opportunities that I mention have some counterpart in your hometown. Working with creative people anyplace will move you along your path, whether it is at a university, a museum, or your local radio or television station. Get involved any way you can.

When I worked at the Cherry County Playhouse in Traverse City, Michigan, our cast visited a restaurant that had three shows nightly featuring singing, dancing, and skits. This work was grueling, demanding, and didn't pay a lot, but the young entertainers who were fortunate enough to get these summer jobs were, in essence, being paid to go to graduate school. These students all found their opportunities through notices at their local colleges.

Worthy, Livable Goals

I'll probably say this about a million times before I finish this book, but acting really is but a small piece of the pie. You will have a greater chance of success and a more rewarding career if you can have the vision to embrace all areas of the business.

While I was researching *Directing Your Directing Career*, I happily discovered Roger Corman's book *How I Made a Hundred Movies in Hollywood and Never Lost a Dime*. That book made me want to be starting my career all over again.

Roger gave so many young people opportunities. Tyler Perry is doing those same things today.

✦ *In its opening weekend "Diary of a Mad Black Woman" was number one at the box office, bringing in $22 million, besting superstar Will Smith's hit "Hitch" and doubling the take of the $100 million film "Constantine." "Diary" went on to gross $50 million in theaters; the DVD sold 2.4 million copies its first week.*

And that is how Tyler Perry, who wrote "Diary," played three of its characters and put up $2.5 million of his own money to finance it, made his official debut in Hollywood. Perry, 36, had been one of showbiz's best-kept secrets.

He had spent a decade writing and staging plays across the nation, selling more than $100 million in tickets, $30 million in videos of his shows and an estimated $20 million in merchandise. His e-mail list of devoted fans exceeds 400,000, and the 300 live shows he produces each year are attended by an average of 35,000 people a week.

"When I started, a whole level of people weren't going to the theater," Perry says. "We started raising awareness and getting the DVDs out there. People could see that if they spent their hard-earned money to go to my shows, they were going to have a good time."

Brett Pulley, *Forbes.com*[36]

And that quote doesn't begin to tell the story. Tyler lived out of the back of his car to make enough money to buy his own theatre when no one would produce his plays. He bought his own theatre and put up his plays and lost everything. He did that twice again before he hit.

It's always hard to break into a closed system, whether it is show business or IBM, but if you allow yourself to go through any door that is open, instead of waiting for the special one you have your heart set on, your chances for success are greatly enhanced.

You're likely to find work sooner, and may even find a niche that would have never occurred to you. Not only that, acting is looked upon as the lowest rung of the creative ladder by the rest of the creative community.

✦ *At one point, I came to realize that it's the ordinary things that are extraordinary. Everything doesn't have to be grand. That's the message of "School of Rock." It's what's inside that counts. Besides, playing character roles takes away the pressure of carrying a film and permits for a life outside. Lining up meaningful work of any kind is like winning the lottery because there are a million talented people out there.*

Joan Cusack, interviewed by Elaine Dutka, *Los Angeles Times*[37]

At dinner after his high school graduation comedian/actor/writer Dave Chappelle, the child of academics, announced that he was going to be the first person in his family not to go to college. Trying to dissuade him, his father made a point that anyone considering a career in show business should weigh carefully.

✦ *"Acting is a lonely life. Everybody wants to make it. You might not make it."* I *[Dave] said "Well, that depends on what making it is. You're a teacher. If I could make a teacher's salary doing comedy, I think that's better than being a teacher."*

My father started laughing, "If you keep that attitude I think you should go ahead, but name your price in the beginning. If it ever gets more expensive than the price you name — get out of it." Hence *Africa.*

Dave Chappelle, interviewed by James Lipton, *Inside the Actor's Studio* [38]

Become Your City's Robert Rodriguez

Robert Rodriguez wrote, directed, produced, edited, composed the music, and did a million other things on both *Spy Kids* and *Spy Kids II* and more recently *Sin City*. These are all the things he had been doing since he started making movies in his hometown of San Antonio when he was a kid and before he became famous and ultimately rich from selling his body to science in order to finance his breakout movie *El Mariachi*. I'm a big Rodriguez fan and can't recommend his book *Rebel without a Crew* and his webpage *www.exposure.co.uk/makers/minute.html* highly enough.

In a small marketplace (Robert still shoots in Texas), it is easier to become the writer, director, and/or producer of whatever is going on. The steps it takes to bring a creative idea to fruition are the same in your hometown as they are in New York or Los Angeles.

When I lived in Dallas as a young woman, it was easier to make money as a director than as an actor, so I directed. I also wrote and produced. At that point my mind was totally open; I was pretty clear about the fact that I didn't know a lot, so I asked anyone I could corner for advice and help. I just wanted to be engaged in theatre, film, or television.

I remember my first day of acting class in college; the venerable Myrtle Hardy telling us that we should take any opportunity to get up in front of people. What a gift she gave me. Until that time, I had thought people would think my getting up to perform would be pushy or conceited (it was high school, after all). Now I had been told that as part of my training I should take every chance to perform. I can still remember the sense of freedom I felt.

People probably did think I was stupid, pushy, crazy, or worse. It didn't matter, for I was on a mission. From where I am sitting now, I can only wish that my aspirations had been higher. Although I was willing to do whatever it took, my mind was clearly set on acting, not acting as a means to direct, produce, or write. Today, I realize that actors with truly great careers do not just act.

✦ *For all her well-known setbacks in the 1930s, including her disastrous 1933 Broadway appearance in "The Lake" (which inspired Dorothy Parker's famous putdown that she "ran the gamut of emotions from A to B"), Katharine Hepburn never had trouble making her own opportunities. She had the wherewithal to tie up the film rights to "The Philadelphia Story," the Broadway vehicle that she knew she could ride to a Hollywood comeback.*
Frank Rich, *The New York Times Book Review*[39]

So open your brain. Write. Direct. Produce. Let your goal be success in showbiz wherever that takes you. Some of the best directors I have ever worked with were once actors and they would never trade the power and vision they command as directors for the mere visibility of being an actor. Many writers and producers from acting backgrounds feel the same way.

Advantages of Staying Home

If your hometown isn't New York, Los Angeles, or Chicago, your job options won't be as numerous, but you will have mom's home cooking, cheaper rent, a familiar environment, and a network of lifetime friends.

Just because you are going to stay home doesn't mean you can't keep abreast of what is happening in the large entertainment centers. As a young actor/director/writer in Texas, I made it a point to see every New York touring production that came to town. I was able to absorb lighting and staging ideas I would never have thought of on my own.

Besides staying up to date on the business, it's important to assess what jobs are available and how you can fit into the existing scheme of things.

When I was in high school trying to figure out how one goes from studying acting and being in local plays to making the jump into the big time, I decided to write my MGM musical idols for advice. Among the three people I wrote (who all answered me) were the late Gower Champion and his wife Marge, star dancers for MGM at that time who both went on to choreograph and direct on Broadway.

Ms. Champion wrote me a wonderfully warm and detailed letter telling me that the best thing to do was to stay in Dallas until I had done everything there was to do in my hometown and then go to New York and study at The Neighborhood Playhouse or with Herbert Berghof at The HB Studios. When I got to New York fifteen years later, I had forgotten the letter, but I still followed the advice. She had made a deep impression on me.

Unless you are dropdead beautiful and your beauty is dying on the vine, there is every reason for you to refine your craft in a more protected environment. Then you can enter the bigger marketplace with training, credits, and hopefully a savings account.

Although you may not be able to make a living as an actor on the stage in your hometown (that's pretty hard to do even in Los Angeles and New York), there are many variations on that theme that offer a chance to make money.

Acting Jobs That Don't Look Like Acting Jobs

Most people think of book reviews as being something you read, but there are actors who make a nice living by reading a current best seller, compiling a sort of verbal Cliff's Notes, and presenting it for various service organizations as entertainment. Have various versions of your review prepared so you can easily tailor the material to the needs of the audience. I always wanted to do a book review with a stack of 8x10s of famous actors and cast the parts as I tell the story; "This part should be played by William H. Macy" and hold up his picture, and so on. They would immediately know just what I was talking about.

Acting opportunities can appear from strange places.

✦ *Between regular acting jobs, [Sarah] Blevins works as a standardized patient for medical schools at USC, UCLA, and Western University of Health Services in Pomona. Medical facilities nationwide are using actors who portray patients in one-on-one encounters to help medical students develop a better bedside manner. Actors make an average of $15 to $20 an hour for their work. UCLA's School of Medicine uses a core group of about a hundred actors in its program according to program coordinator Liz O'Gara, whose office shelves hold sixteen burly three-ring notebooks filled with hundreds of head shots and resumes, labeled according to age and ethnicity.*

"I hire actors like anybody in Hollywood hires actors," she says. "People send in head shots, and we audition them."

Laurie K. Schenden, *Los Angeles Times*[40]

The article went on to say that almost every school in the country has a standardized patient program. This acting assignment obviously requires an actor who is good at improv since obviously he gets no script. He does get the patient's background, character bio, attitude about doctors, and what the patient's expectations are.

Call your local stations and ask what the possibilities are for employment on the air. If there is no one to talk to there, look in the Yellow Pages under advertising agencies and call them. Ask who hires on-camera or radio talent, note the name and ask to speak to him. Say something like: "Hi, I'm Mary Smith. I'm an actress and I'm interested in finding out who hires actors for commercials."

When you get that person on the phone, reintroduce yourself and say that you would like to come by and meet him. If you have a picture and resume, mention that. If you have done any jobs that might impress, mention those.

When you call, do so late in the day. Frequently the secretary is gone and your future employer will pick up his own phone. Be up, personable, brief, energetic and specific. Arrange a meeting. Go. Be on time. Be professional and be strong. Don't play like-me-like-me, but do indicate that you are willing to learn and are a hard worker. Show that by arriving a few minutes early. Center yourself in the hall before you enter the office. Just take time to collect yourself. Make sure you have read the morning newspaper so that you can have something to talk about other than yourself.

If that person can't help you, ask him for advice on who else to speak to or what to do next. People love to give advice.

If all else fails, offer to work as an intern. Say you could spare one day a week to work for free. You want to learn the business and they can have free help. Say you'll do anything and mean it. File. Run errands. Just get into the system. You'll learn so much.

In every marketplace, there are locally-produced cable television shows. You don't even need a camera to produce your own program. There was a bargain shopper on a major local news show in Los Angeles whose career started when she produced her own weekly cable access show. She went on to write a weekly *Los Angeles Times* news column. A young comic I know produced a funny restaurant guide show that became a part of the CBS nightly local Los Angeles news.

Teach/Start Your Own Theatre

It's not that difficult to get a job teaching acting at a local school or at the YMCA/YWCA. Decide whether you want to teach children, teenagers, or adults, or all of the above. You can put notices up in your local supermarket, church, or post office announcing your classes.

Teaching is not only a source of revenue and fulfillment, it can also focus your thinking and improve your acting. Academic credentials are helpful, though by no means essential. We all have encountered teachers without heart, empathy, insight, and passion who had very impressive degrees but were not inspiring in any way. Great teachers (and great directors) arouse the actor's passion and motivate him to resonate in ways he never thought. If you feel you don't know how to teach, pattern your work on the best acting teacher you ever had and read books by great teachers like *A Passion for Acting* by Allan Miller, *Respect for Acting* by Uta Hagen, or *Intent to Live*, by Larry Moss. Michael Shurtleff's book *Audition* contains so much acting insight that I read it at regular intervals.

Whatever teaching method you choose, find a way to present your students before the public. Write or find plays that have to do with the holiday of the moment and produce something short. It's more fun to study acting when you know you'll have a place to show off your new abilities.

Start your own theatre and teach acting on the side. That way your students can have the possibility of auditioning for your own productions. Chambers of Commerce and other civic groups like to have theatre in their community and might be enlisted to help you bring your plans to fruition. Choose a play you love that has a small cast and one set. It's not that hard.

Wrap Up

✓ check your hometown options
✓ evaluate the big marketplaces
✓ choose worthy livable goals
✓ be open to all local opportunities
✓ become your hometown's celebrity
✓ act, write, produce
✓ lots of acting jobs aren't onstage

≈ 6 ≈

Making Plans

Whenever civilians (people who are not in the business) ask me questions about being an actress, they never ask questions about how to act. Some may want to know how an actor remembers all those lines, but they all seem to think that, of course, they would be able to act. The thing that totally eludes them is how one translates acting ability into gainful employment. It's the question actors ask continually.

There is no big mystery. Translating dreams into reality simply entails being businesslike, focusing on the goal, and marching toward it. It's sort of like building Will Smith's wall. Some people possess business skills naturally and others have to learn them. Some need to refine those skills, while others just need support.

Business Plan

Get a pencil and a substantial book for your business plan. A scrap of paper is not enough. You are going into business, so make sure your plans are stored appropriately. You will be referring to your notebook/journal frequently, so make it user-friendly. Let it reflect your style so it can bring a good price after you are famous and they auction it off.

Resist the temptation to use your computer or typewriter. The visceral force unleashed by the hand forming the words takes thought one step closer to reality.

Write down your fantasies, but make sure they are attainable. You're not going to look like Tom Cruise, be ten years younger or a foot taller no matter how hard you work. Stick to the realms of possibility.

Do you want to win an Oscar? Own a Rolls? Speak French? Write it down. Live in the best part of town? Marry the person of your choice? Live happily ever after? Have three kids? No kids? Think. Dream. Write everything down. Edit later. Let yourself go.

Don't forget to write down those things you are willing to do in return. Delay starting a family. Live frugally. Give up desserts. Study. Spend hours researching parts. Read at least one script a day. See a play a week. Know the name of every casting director in town. Cultivate writers and directors.

List everything you need to do. Consider all the options.

Goals

Do you want to be a classical actor? A film actor? An actor who does television? Soaps? Theatre? Do you intend to pursue your craft in your own hometown? Do you intend to go to Los Angeles or New York? Can you make a living as an actor in Rapid City, South Dakota? Can you make a living in show business in Wilmington, Delaware? Can you be happy with the options available in your own hometown?

If you live in a small town and your goal is to be a respected actor, your first goal might be to get a part in a play. If there is not a theatre group, start one. If there is a theatre group, join it. Get a part if you can. If not, stage manage, help build sets, be the property master; just become active and demonstrate your reliability and your creative powers in whatever job is available. Your time to act will come. You will figure out how to make it happen.

Whether or not we realize it, we are constantly setting goals. I recognized this recently when an old college friend reminded me what I did with our first assignment in Public Speaking class: to introduce ourselves in some way to make people remember who we were. I was alternately thrilled and mortified to hear him report that I had said: "Remember my name because someday I am going to be famous and you are going to want to come swim in my pool."

When I moved to New York to finally seek fame and fortune, the subsidized low-income housing I lived in had a swimming pool and so does my home in California although that was not a consideration in choosing either place. From my Texas viewpoint, a swimming pool equated success as an actor. Since I was so powerful, I sure wish I had said: "Remember my name, I'm going to be the world's greatest actor and I will win five Oscars!"

As you conceptualize your goals, be informed and be specific. Focus carefully on what you want. If you commit to your goals, you will reach them.

Immediate Goals

Your immediate goal needs to be intimately related to your marketplace. It's unlikely you'll be able to win an Oscar in Valentine, Nebraska. But you could probably have a career in local radio.

Take the most important thing on your list. Let's say it is to win an Oscar. Put a date on it. Say ten years from now. Then work backwards. What are the steps that would have to be taken before you could realize that goal?

If you wanted to build a house, it would be pretty clear that you would have to do some research. What do architects cost? What style do you want? Victorian? Modern? Country? Which architect designs that type of house? What type of building materials will you use? Do you need the same building materials in Nebraska as you do in California? What's the budget?

What kind of bathtub do you want? In order to answer that question, you would have to go all over town looking at the bathtubs that were available. You would need to price them and check their availability, find out whether you have to order one or they have it in stock. All this just for a bathtub. Can you imagine the kind of detail involved in truly planning a career?

In order to set goals for yourself as an actor, you'll need to answer specific questions to formulate a plan for success. Write about the life you want to lead: where you want to live it and what kind of house you want to live in. Describe the clothes you want to wear and the food you want to eat. Whether you want a cook or want to cook for yourself and your friends in a big family kitchen. Do you live alone? Will you study with Larry Moss? Will you work with Ang Lee? Will you be married? Are you always involved with your current co-star? It's your story. No one else will read it.

Some ideas about how to chart your goals follow. Construct yours however suits you best, but leave a space to check off goals as you achieve them. Set your own timetable. If you manage to achieve some of these goals faster, fine. Some will be slower, but this is a pretty realistic schedule. For every goal, focus on what you are willing to do to accomplish it: lose weight, learn to sing, get a second job, give up junk food, ask for what you want, read a script a day, etc. The key to success is action. Your version of this will be much much bigger.

Identify the roles you want to play. Discuss how you want a typical day in your life to be and visualize these goals on an emotional level. That is what engages the brain, focuses it, and puts the plan into action. Your plan should take at least two weeks to formulate. You are starting a business. Since you are investing your life in this pursuit, protect your investment by doing meticulous research and planning.

5 yr	Jan-Mar	April-June	July-Sept	Oct-Dec
Year 1	train: acting voice dance writing meditate* buy video camera, learn to edit	join theatre company form weekly group to read plays/work on camera together write daily. Read showbiz biographies intern in biz, 60 seconds on youtube every week	get onstage book reviews check ad agencies for commercials write daily showbiz bios become technically proficient online	get name in newspaper for current project write daily read more showbiz bios patience
Year 2	classes bigger part write daily more press make a short film	continue doing plays continue writing, studying, read about the biz, keep getting name in the paper patience	continue plays continue writing, reading about biz patience	write daily showbiz reading patience weekly play reading
Year 3	classes local commercial write daily	more commercials continue writing showbiz reading patience	begin audition tape continue writing showbiz reading patience 5 minutes standup on youtube weekly	1-man show standup write showbiz reading Equity card
Year 4	NY/LA ** fix up your place write daily study patience start film group	get industry-related job or internship showbiz reading read scripts, write learn what casting directors cast what encourage yourself	theatre company pictures showbiz reading read scripts write	onstage research casting directors showbiz reading read scripts
Year 5	commercial agent write daily meditate patience encourage yourself	non-union film student films add to audition tape query casting director write daily showbiz reading read scripts	get another film redo tape begin agent search name in paper radio interview write daily read scripts	theatrical agent continue personal agenting efforts build CD contacts write daily

*   Meditate, write daily, center yourself.
**   Best time to move: Los Angeles/August and New York/Spring.

Your goals may be totally different, this is a just a shorthand template to give you some ideas.

The more you conceptualize acting as a business as well as an artistic venture, the more successful you can be. You will also be less likely to personalize the rejection. Compose a short version detailing your current goals and what you are willing to do for them. Read your intentions aloud first thing every morning and last thing every night. Your thought process will change. Behavioral scientists say it takes three weeks to make or break a habit. I'm more likely to think it takes three months to be securely into a new behavior pattern, but three weeks is a good start.

I read that years before any kind of validation came their way, Sonny and Cher used to drive to Bel Air and sit in front of the gates of one of the swankiest, most theatrically-historic houses in town. They decided they would live in that house one day. They did.

To give you support in focusing your goals, I recommend investing in effective motivational tapes. Napoleon Hill's *Think and Grow Rich* is the original positive thinking book. Hill was saying things in 1937 that Anthony Robbins has made a fortune on today.

Another inspiring book is *The Artist's Way* written by Julia Cameron. The book encourages goal-setting and has exercises to help you discover who you are and what you really want.

Be Specific

Paul Linke (one of the stars of the hit television series *CHiPS*) wrote a one-man show about his own life called *Time Flies When You Are Alive*. In it he told an ironic story about being specific. He said he used to pray to get a part in a hit series, and but for the omission of a single word, *quality*, he might have ended up on *Hill Street Blues*.

I have my own specific story and it coincidentally involves an audition for *Hill Street Blues*. The scene had to do with a woman who was hysterical because her no-good boyfriend had left her. I could not seem to find a way to motivate myself to the tears they wanted using that scenario.

I could motivate myself substituting one of my kids for the love object. I reasoned, tears of rejection are tears of rejection. It worked, and the scene went very well. Only one hitch. After my reading, the producer stopped me and said, "Could you do it again with a different thrust? That kind of seemed like one of your kids left you instead of your boyfriend."

That was scary. They actually got what was going on in my mind although the words were totally different. The mind is a powerful instrument. You can have whatever you can imagine. Decide what you want. These decisions are not written in stone. You can change them. But the more detailed your life script, the less chance of error.

Wouldn't it be interesting to know how Sonny and Cher got from sitting in front of the house to owning it? Do you suppose their first big goal was a hit record? Maybe the immediate goal was just to get to a place where they were hanging around with people in the business they could learn from. Perhaps their next goal was getting a paying job singing.

Targeting signposts that let you know you are moving along will give you courage and inspiration when you need it most. When all seems dark, you can whip out your list and notice that, in fact, you have already accomplished A, B, and C, even though D is eluding you at the moment. It's nourishing to notice when you make progress and celebrate it.

Support Groups/Role Models

Find another ambitious actor to join you in your quest. You can be a team. Try for a team of four and make a commitment to support each other. Meet twice a month to talk about your plans and announce your newest goal. Check each other to see that you are really staying on the track, making timetables and keeping on them. At each meeting, choose a new goal or take the last one further. There is something magic about saying your intention to another human being. The energy gets into the air and becomes concentrated and powerful.

Choosing a role model can also provide guidance. What actor/actress has the career and life you would like to have? You will have your own career one day, but today focusing on another blueprint will help you to have a concrete picture of your goal. Get a picture of your role model and put it where you will see it every day. If you have a hard time choosing a role model, maybe you are ambivalent about choosing acting as your life's work.

Go to the library. Ask the person at the reference desk for all the sources of material written about your role model. Find out how he/she started and studied. If there's a biography, read it.

It's a good idea to give yourself the task of reading one showbiz biography every week. It is fascinating to find out how other people solved some of the same problems you have or will encounter.

You can do all these things even before you study. Set study deadlines. Research the possibilities of teaching. Get a part time job at a theatre or a radio or television station and see what some phase of show business looks like up close.

Start at any point in your life. It may be five years before you can expect to realistically be looking for an actual part, but that's okay. Begin to conceptualize today.

Groundwork

In an actor support group I belong to, my friend George began lamenting pilot season. A pilot is the first show of a proposed television series. Getting a pilot, whether or not it is sold, can make an actor's year financially.

He was upset that he was not being sent on as many auditions as he felt he was due. He wondered what he could do to enhance his chances.

The group concurred that the most important work toward getting a pilot comes nine to twelve months prior to pilot season. Actors chosen for pilots are frequently those actors who have done other interesting (usually less lucrative) work all season that has gotten their agent and/or the casting director excited about submitting them for pilots. You have to get the part before you can get the award. The most effective way to do this is to become an entrepreneur. If you're not going to do that, you must be very lucky. Many are. There's an old saying, "I'd rather be lucky than good." Me, I would rather be lucky and good.

In order to have good luck, one must understand its concept. Yes, you can create your own luck. But even so, life really is like one big poker game. You are never going to get all winning hands and you won't get all losing hands either. The trick is to make the most of the wins while you minimize the losses. Learn to play poker well.

Positive Thinking

One of my favorite show business stories involves Clint Eastwood and Burt Reynolds. Contract players for Universal, they were called in on the same day and told that their contracts were not being renewed. Management said neither of them had a future: Reynolds, because he couldn't act, and Eastwood, because of his unusually large Adam's apple. As they walked together, lost in thoughts of failure, Reynolds turned to Eastwood and said: "Well, I can learn to act. What are you going to do?"

We create our own lives. Successful people invent themselves. The late Albert Hague was a Tony winning composer before his success as an actor on the television show *Fame*. His years on the other side of the table watching actors make major audition mistakes led him to create a class teaching actors how to audition for musicals.

I took that class early in my career. Although he had many valuable things to teach about auditioning and the business, the one thing he said that keeps coming back to me had nothing to do with career: "It takes a lot of creative energy to have an interesting life."

The real focus needs to be on your life. It can have as much excitement as you are willing to create. With all the statistics and casualties and hard work, you still can be that actor who consistently works in the smallest or the largest marketplace.

Wrap Up

✓ make a specific plan
✓ set goals with date
✓ consider what you are willing to do for them
✓ make a commitment
✓ join or form a support group
✓ select role models
✓ be positive
✓ it takes a lot of creative energy to have an interesting life

↣ 7 ↢
Getting Organized

It can get confusing and lonely pursuing goals independently, particularly if you have relocated to a larger marketplace and no longer have your hometown support system. It's difficult to tell if you are making progress since there are so many tasks to accomplish. It's easy to become overwhelmed, run in many directions at once, and accomplish nothing.

Since you are the architect of your career, no matter what else happens you may as well look upon your career as your pursuit of a Ph.D. Inherent in that degree is the ability to initiate your own game plan as well as conceive a unique idea that no one in your field has exploited before.

The saving grace of being a candidate for the Ph.D. is you get your own private major professor: a person who discusses goals, puts you on the right track, and monitors your progress. The bad news is that you'll have to be your own major professor; the good news is that you are going to be your own major professor. Who else would have so many daily insights into your personality and goals? Who else would have such a stake in your success?

Since we are in the habit of assuming other personas anyway, if we conceptualize a part of ourselves as the major professor we can slip into character, become wise, and perhaps even gain perspective.

Sometimes when I can't figure out what to wear, I say, "What would Ralph Lauren say?" and I know what to do. Just like air-conditioning, I don't know why it works, it just does.

First Things First

When you finally arrive in New York, Los Angeles, Chicago, or wherever else you have chosen to pursue your acting career, there are certain basics of life that must be attended to before you should try to get an agent or an acting job.

✦ *Get a job and a nice place to live. Truthfully, you would be amazed. People take years to take care of that problem. In New York, especially, it's so important to have a base. One of our clients said in an interview recently that acting wasn't her life. Her life was her life. Acting was what she did. She loved doing it and didn't want to do anything else. But it wasn't her life.*

Whenever people said they were having problems with their acting and what could they do to change it, her response was always, "Change your life." That's something young actors don't want to believe, but I think it's very true.

So if I just arrived in New York I wouldn't worry so much about acting until I solved the problem of where I was going to live, how I was going to make a living, and how I was going to get by day to day because I don't think you can solve anything else first.

Tim Angle/Abrams Artists, Los Angeles

Surviving on your own without a 9 to 5 job demands great courage and discipline. Nothing demands your attention at a specific moment. You can sleep until noon if you choose. There's no place you have to be. In the abstract, this sounds like heaven. The reality can be depressing and paralyzing.

The structure of a regular job provides some sort of mental health. There are times set for arriving, eating, and leaving. There are tasks to be performed, people to talk to, people to rebel against, and someone to pay you. There's frequently some type of dress code. When you are self-employed (or in the case of the actor, mostly unemployed), the situation can awaken latent insecurities. Don't wait until all those primal needs are screaming at you to create a life for yourself. Start now.

Work Corner

Establish a work center that includes book shelves, desk, computer, a bright lamp, Rolodex, phone, answering machine, a reference library, office supplies, pictures, resumes, manila envelopes, mailing labels, good stationery, and a bulletin board for appointments and calendar.

Don't use this space (even if it is just a corner of your kitchen or bedroom) for anything but work. That way your subconscious will subtly begin to shift into business/creative mode every time you sit at your desk. I have a favorite chair I have endowed as my inspiration chair and I sit in it every time I read a script and prepare for an audition. I fully expect to have great inspiration every time I sit there and it usually works for me in a way no other space in my house does.

Keep a clock and a pad and pencil by the telephone for messages. There should be a pencil and pad next to every telephone in your house. Never keep a business contact waiting on the phone while you search the house for pencil and paper.

Routine Softens the Blows

It is stressful to be constantly rejected. Just as being continually exposed to a virus soon wears the system down, your spirit is vulnerable to attack if you haven't made provisions for rejuvenation by controlling all the things you can.

The familiarity of routine softens the effects of never knowing when you will be making money again, so make a list of things you commit to do daily. Set aside a specific time for each of these activities and stick to it.

Schedule a time for awakening and going to bed. You don't have to be fanatical about it, but the more you adhere to a schedule, the more secure you will feel. We are all comforted by the familiar. It will make a difference.

Schedule errands for one particular day of the week and put a time frame around them. These tasks have a way of eating up energy. No matter how onerous, they are a lot more fun than calling up some person who might end up saying no to whatever we are asking.

My son-in-law Don is right when he says, "Errands are those things we do when we're avoiding our real work."

Spiritual and Physical Health

No matter what, exercise daily and eat nutritiously. If you begin each day with stretching and exercise, you can assist your body's own natural resistance to both physical and emotional illness while keeping your instrument fit and in tune. Get sufficient sleep. If you feel yourself getting depressed, check to see if these basics are being addressed.

It is important to take time for a regular sit-down meal. And even if you can't resist eating self-destructively, counter that behavior by detoxifying your system as much as possible with good food. The famous nutritionist Dr. Henry Beiler teaches that green vegetables (the darker green the better) detoxify the system.

Students at The American Conservatory Theatre in San Francisco benefitted greatly when Los Angeles' famous nutritionist, Eileen Poole, visited regularly on a volunteer basis to advise them on appropriate eating habits. She was so inspirational that the students actually gave up sugar and caffeine.

One of those students, actress Annabella Price, told me that her mental outlook as well as her physical abilities improved dramatically as a result of her diet.

We have already discussed forming a support group for acting goals. It's even more important to have a regular family experience to support your personal life. If you don't have family nearby, form one with members of your acting class or your neighbors or the people from the Laundromat. The operative words here are create a family for yourself. I believe one of the great lures of being an actor is the families we create when we work.

In his book, *The Right Place at the Right Time*, employment consultant Dr. Robert Wegmann states:

✦ *"To help maintain perspective: Exercise regularly...and keep in close contact with friends whom you trust and with whom you can share your experiences."*

Life is problem solving, and challenges are easier to meet with the support of loved ones. It helps to be involved regularly with a group of people who recognize this, offer mutual support, and encourage shared feelings.

If you don't have loved ones in the area, the 12-step groups are invaluable (Alcoholics Anonymous, Overeaters Anonymous, Adult Children of Alcoholics, etc.). They boil down to free group therapy any day of the week.

When we join existing support groups, we are usually in a vulnerable state and we are ready to lay down all our defenses in the hopes of feeling better. I'm not against that in concept, but retain your own persona and way of speaking. Don't throw out the baby with the bath water.

Some people go to church. Others garden, practice yoga, or study martial arts. Los Angeles Lakers coach Phil Jackson set up a program of meditation, tai chi, and yoga for his players. A practicing Zen Buddhist, Jackson believes success doesn't demand the greatest talent, it demands the greatest attention and awareness. He's firmly grounded in the belief that if his players stay competent and focused on the floor, the possibilities to succeed are maximized. Some of his players agree:

✦ *[Rick] Fox: "What I picked up is that having control over myself, having a focus, a growth process translates into being a better basketball player. No coach ever told me that. No coach ever took the time to know me. Look at all the guys who've played on his teams. They seem to be on a greater plane mentally. That's because he gives them a greater understanding of themselves."*

[Brian] Shaw: "When he was having us do yoga and tai chi, everybody kind of looked at each other at first and said, 'He's crazy.' Then you see it's broadening your horizons. Then you get a 16-game winning streak, and everybody's saying, 'Damn, he does know what he's talking about.'"

Elizabeth Kaye, *Los Angeles Magazine*[41]

Of course the Lakers aren't as successful now as they were then. I guess yoga/meditation can't counter personnel problems. Or perhaps they stopped meditating!

Choose whatever might get you in touch with your own vitality. You will be stronger, more vulnerable, and a better actor. The added self-esteem will help put your career in perspective.

Meditation

There are all kinds of meditation. I don't care which kind you choose, but it is vital to take ten to twenty minutes twice a day for yourself. To take stock. To be silent. No music. No eating. No drinking. No talking. Just be with yourself. To train your mind. Not just when you think about it, or if it happens, but establish a regularly-scheduled time for you and yourself. Many people believe these are the moments that allow you to tune in to your own feelings and intuitions. If you don't take the time to do this for yourself, you are shortchanging yourself as a person and as an actor.

It's a challenge to carve out time for nurturing yourself. If that time twice a day spent by myself allows or encourages me to visualize my goals or to be still long enough to hear whatever is going on inside me, I know that's got to help every part of my life. I don't always get it done, but when I do, I can tell the difference.

Class/Study/Teachers/Gurus

When I lived in New York, I went to dance classes Mondays, Wednesdays, and Fridays, had a voice lesson on Tuesday morning, and worked with an accompanist on Thursdays. I also went to acting class on Tuesday nights. Depending on your goals, you should be involved in some version of this. Classes not only improve our skills, but they keep us plugged into the network of actors and help structure our days.

A word here about teachers. I think most of us are looking for the secret of life, the answer or magic ingredient that is going to make life work better. I think actors believe in magic more than most people, so I caution you, if you can find a great teacher who can help you marshal your creative forces, whether you're in Podunk, New York, or Hollywood, do it, but do not give up your own thought processes.

Even very good and very reputable teachers sometimes have their own agenda. Perhaps it is religious or political or maybe their agenda is simply to get laid, but that's their path, not yours.

Since people are defined by their belief systems, don't allow anyone to trivialize yours. Refine your belief system as you grow, but question, question, question. You don't have to be a pain in the butt and do it out loud, but a certain amount of skepticism is healthy. As an actor, all you have to sell is your self, so make sure you are still intact when class is over. Don't blindly follow anyone.

Acting is greatly entwined with our psychological well-being. That does not mean making our psyches vulnerable to just anyone who displays an interest. If you need help, get a reputable shrink and deal with your emotional problems there. Don't let acting teachers play in your mind.

If a teacher is opposed to anyone with other thought processes, watch out. If you stay with people who do not encourage you to question, how will you ever nurture your imagination and exercise your own creativity? Give yourself credit. A friend of mine left her acting class not long ago when the teacher declared: "You have really become a better actor since you began working with me."

Maybe that was true. Also true was the fact that my friend didn't get a single job during the entire time she was in that class. I think the teacher just meant, "I like your acting better because you are getting to be so much like me."

Focused Analytical Viewing

Study includes more than formal classes. Your education includes viewing the work of others and noting what works and what doesn't.

Evaluate. Greet each experience as though you were going to have to write a paper on it.

That attention to detail will keep you focused and in the present. Say to yourself before every meeting, even lunch with your friend, "What do I want from this experience?"

If we all took the time to consciously think of our goals before our actions, we'd be less likely to get off the track, take a disagreement personally, and get bogged down in negativity. If the goal is to make things work (not to be right, make points, or show someone the error of his ways), things do work and everyone has a better time.

I studied briefly with Stella Adler who used to strike terror in the hearts of students when she pointed at us and screamed: "Untalented!" Of course, we were all pretty happy when she pointed at us and beamed: "Talented." It took me a little while to gain enough perspective to understand that what she was saying was: "That is an untalented choice. This is a talented choice." We make choices every day in the way we choose to view things.

For instance:

Untalented Comments	Talented Comments
I hated that movie.	The movie needed faster pacing.
That play was no good.	The play needed focus.
That actor stinks.	The lead needs more flamboyance.
What a waste of time.	She's usually so good. It's comforting to remember that we can all stumble.

Begin to think in a problem-solving way. Not only will you be more interesting to be around, since you will be looking for a solution, but you'll be sending out positive energy. It takes more effort to be positive, but it pays off 100%. Become a problem solver instead of a critic and you'll be more fun to be around.

As part of your education as an actor, get a job working in the business in some area other than acting. Be an usher in the theatre or work in an agent's office or at a television station. Be a gofer. You will begin to get a clearer idea of the lifestyle. It may not be as appealing up close. If that is the case, think of all the time and heartache you have saved yourself.

When I was interviewing agents for *The New York Agent Book*, I met a young woman who was assisting a famous agent. She was an aspiring actress who had come to New York from a small town. After spending two years seeing firsthand how it really is, she no longer wants to be an actress. She perceives the rejection as too depressing. She now wants to be a producer and have power and a decent lifestyle.

Reference Library

You should have your own library of showbiz reference books which list the credits of actors, writers, directors, producers, and casting executives along with biographies that give you another peek into the actor's lifestyle. There have been some candid books in the recent past which delineated the real scoop on what goes on behind the scenes.

Here is a list of books that will give your library a good start:

Actor's Audition, The/David Black
Actor's Script: Script Analysis for Performers, The/Charles S. Waxberg
Actors Turned Directors/Jon Stevens
Adventures in the Screen Trade/William Goldman
AFTRA Agency Regulations
Artist's Way, The/Julia Cameron
Audition/Michael Shurtleff
Big Picture, The/William Goldman
Born Standing Up/Steve Martin
Equity Agency Regulations
Film Encyclopedia, The/Ephraim Katz
Filmgoer's Companion, The/Leslie Halliwell
Final Cut/Steven Bach
Halliwell's Film Guide/Leslie Halliwell
How I Made 100 Films in Hollywood and Never Lost a Dime/Roger Corman
Hype & Glory/William Goldman
Indecent Exposure/David McClintock
Intent to Live/Larry Moss
Los Angeles Agent Book, The/K Callan
Making Movies/Sidney Lumet
My Lives/Roseanne
New York Agent Book, The/K Callan
Next: An Actor's Guide to Auditioning/Ellie Kanner and Paul Bens
On Sunset Boulevard: Billy Wilder/Ed Sikov

Reel Power/Mark Litwak
Ross Reports Television/Television Index
Saturday Night: A Backstage History of Saturday Night Live/
    Doug Hill and Jeff Weingrad
Sayles on Sayles/John Sayles
Screen Actors Guild Agency Regulations
Screen World/John Willis
Season, The/William Goldman
Wake Me When It's Funny/Garry Marshall
Which Lie Did I Tell?/William Goldman
Wired/Bob Woodward
Working Actor's Guide to Los Angeles/Kristi Callan

If you know of any books that belong on this list, let me know and I'll include them in future editions. Books like *Wired, Indecent Exposure,* and *Saturday Night* detail the costs of becoming famous. Keeping them on your bookshelf and reading them from time to time will encourage you to keep your values in perspective.

It's easy to get caught up in the glamour, publicity, money, and power of this fairytale business. These things can leave as quickly as they come. Success won't fix you. You may feel better for a while, but you're always you just with a different set of problems.

I cannot stress strongly enough the need for a good reference library.

Read Tony Randall's *Which Reminds Me* for fun and Carol Burnett's *One More Time* for inspiration. Charles Grodin's *It Would Be So Nice if You Weren't Here* talks about more bad luck than you will ever have. Roseanne's instructive book *My Lives*, speaks candidly of the behind-the-scenes intrigue involved with her show. Garry Marshall's book, *Wake Me When It's Funny* shares some great attention-getting ideas for everybody in the business.

There are many other helpful books. These are just ideas for a starting library. Schedule time each day for business-related reading. Whether this means browsing your local newspaper for audition announcements or noticing who just took over an ad agency or when the local Kiwanis Club might need a speaker. Do it regularly.

Even if you don't live in New York or Los Angeles, you can begin to learn to read the trade newspapers online — *Variety* and *The Hollywood Reporter.* You won't get all the stories, but you'll get a taste at *www.variety.com* and *www.hollywoodreporter.com.* The trades most helpful for newcomers are Los Angeles' *Back Stage West*, the New York counterpart *Back Stage*, and *The Ross Reports* (*www.backstage.com*) plus New York's *Show Business* (*www.showbusinessweekly.com*). These newspapers cover information about classes, auditions, casting, etc. *Ross Reports* lists names and addresses of advertising agencies, production companies, and agents. All are available at good newsstands or by subscription.

In other marketplaces, check any university or school where students are involved in film. Read the classifieds. Be alert. When you go to the theatre, go backstage, let people know you are looking for opportunities.

Money Wisdom/SAVE!

There's no guarantee that a prestigious acting job will enable you to pay your rent. Off-Broadway and chorus jobs don't pay much and decent showcases (for which there is great competition) don't pay anything at all. But sometimes a job paying a lot of money can end up being a trap. It's very seductive to work every day and make good money. If you are on a soap opera or a television series, you are lucky to be employed for several years, but you only get to play one role. Many actors in this position have yearned to leave those jobs for what they felt would be more artistically challenging work, but big money can make any artistic decision hard to make and regular jobs are hard to come by.

Other actors, who do not have as visible or lucrative careers, are frequently more fulfilled though much less regularly employed because they choose to have the opportunity to play varied parts.

Though actors who are currently making money refuse to believe it, money seldom continues in an unbroken string. It's never wise to live up to your highest earning level without providing for the day when those bucks either shrink or disappear completely.

The third year after I entered the business in New York, I made a lot of money in commercials. When I visited my accountant, he cautioned me about changing my lifestyle. "It won't last. Take your children on trips and enjoy it, but don't get a new apartment. I prepare actors' income tax returns all the time. It won't last."

I'm conservative anyway, so I was fiscally careful, but I secretly thought he was wrong. I was different. I was just going to make more money every year. Only two years later my income was down 66%.

Pretty humbling, but you know what? When I get a string of work I still think there will be no more dry seasons. It's part of the human adaptive mechanism. Hope springs eternal.

How Much Should You Get Paid?

During that early flush time, I had dinner one night with the producer of a soap on which I was guesting. The unspoken purpose of the dinner was for the producer to ascertain whether or not I was interested in joining his show as a regular before he would go back, find a place for me, and make a real offer. During my first two years in the city, I had dreamt of such a job, but by that dinner I was already making enough money via commercials that the idea of being tied to a soap no longer appealed to me.

The producer wanted his information and I wanted mine. I was curious to know how well my agent had negotiated for me. I had no way to measure whether the money she got for me was good, better, or best.

The producer did me a big favor. He not only answered my question honestly, but he gave me a little education as well: "Part of being an actor is having that information yourself. You have to tell your agent what to ask for. You have to know what people are getting paid. You must know all the business ramifications as well."

From that day forward, I've discussed money with other actors. Pay scales are now on the net, so it's easy for me to remind myself what the going rate is for any kind of work. I make it a point to share information regarding what I am making and what others in the marketplace are making. If an actor never knows that his peers are capable of getting $1,500 or more for a day of work, he will never press for it.

Enhancing the Merchandise

Another part of your education includes knowing everything required to make you look good. It seems pretty astounding that when Cher won an Academy Award, the makeup and hair people were the people she thanked, but a large part of Cher's appeal is her visual impact. Cher's great style and single-minded focus on fulfilling that style emanates from her constantly in the form of charisma.

Successful movie stars know camera angles and understand everything about how they are lit in a scene. If you plan to make your living in front of a camera, get one and photograph everybody you know. Study the photos intently to see why one is more appealing than another. Get your own video camera or use your phone, set it up, and photograph yourself. Do a scene and see how your face looks from different angles and in different light.

A story that demonstrates how successful this approach can be involves an actress named Sara Purcell who became successful hosting the magazine show *AM Los Angeles*.

The road to Sara's success was predictable if you knew Sara. While working in a department store in San Diego, she got a chance to audition for the *AM* show. She found out on Friday about the audition for the following Monday. Luckily, she was then married to a man who directed local television commercials, was enormously creative, talented, and supportive, and owned a video camera in a time when most folks didn't.

All weekend they taped Sara interviewing their friends. They would tape, then sit back, look, and critique. What worked? What didn't? How did she look when she moved a lot? A little? What was visually interesting? Sara not only got the job, but an ongoing career.

Besides being very smart and enormously resourceful, Sara also has an innate sense of fun that's always apparent in her work. Those are the traits that she expanded upon to become a performer with a consistently successful track record. The stars I know dedicate themselves single-mindedly to their careers. Are you prepared to do that?

Relationships

Don't forget about the people in your life. Actors have a reputation for being totally self-involved. It's hard not to be. We have to sell ourselves, assess where the next job is coming from, indulge our uniqueness, and deal with how our changing physicality is affecting our marketability. As a result, sometimes we get engrossed in ourselves and miss out on the really important things in life: family and friends. It takes creative energy to live a balanced life; it doesn't just happen.

All we have is today. Since the really successful people say the most fun was getting there, make sure you and your family enjoy the trip.

Wrap Up

✓ get a day job
✓ organize your personal life
✓ make your living space comforting
✓ make a schedule
✓ establish and set aside workspace
✓ create and maintain physical and spiritual health
✓ provide for emotional needs
✓ form and nourish friendships
✓ choose a mentor/role model
✓ join or form a professional support group
✓ get in classes
✓ find a teacher not a guru
✓ retain your own belief systems
✓ practice informed viewing
✓ get a job in the business
✓ read books about the business
✓ read the trades
✓ educate yourself about handling money wisely
✓ learn union minimums and how to negotiate

❦ 8 ❧

Self-Knowledge

People who are not working in the business are fond of saying: "It's not what you know, it's who you know." I think I might rephrase that adage to say, "It's not what you know, it's how well you know your self." If you are your product, you'd better know all there is to know about your strengths and weaknesses.

✦ *Successful actors have an accurate image of what they sell. Unsuccessful actors don't. That's the sign. If you're getting the job, then you know who you are. If you're going out and you're not getting the job, then something is wrong. And you can't say it's talent. In this town, talent doesn't mean a lot. If you are the right type, you will get the job. I'm not saying you are going to get a Hallmark Hall of Fame signed contract, but you will be getting work.*

You must always show your most commercial quality. They may or may not be looking for that essence that day, but one day they will and they will have already seen the one person who could do this better than anyone else in the world.

Martin Gage/The Gage Group, Los Angeles

His East Coast counterpart Phil Adelman said it another way:

✦ *I had a funny-looking lady come in, mid-thirties, chubby, not very pretty. For all I know, this woman could be brilliant. I asked her what roles she could play; what she thought she should get. She saw herself playing Sandra Bullock's roles. Amy Adams' roles.*

I could have been potentially interested in this woman in the areas in which she would work. But it was a turn-off because, not only do I know that she's not going after the right things, so she's not preparing correctly, but she's not going to be happy with the kinds of things I'm going to be able to do for her. So I wouldn't want to commit to that person.

Phil Adelman/The Gage Group, New York

It's easier for us to conceptualize that writers bring a certain voice to the proceedings. Actors frequently think their job is to give a face to the scriptwriter's voice. The actor may not realize that he has been chosen to be the face of the material not just for his physical presence, but for his innate character and spirit.

Being Liked vs. Having a Voice

When you are so engaged in pleasing the prospective employer that your task becomes intuiting what he wants and seeking to give it to him, you mute your instrument. Until that material passes through you and comes out processed by your own life experience, you have not added your contribution to the collaborative effort.

If you have no views, no life experience, and no body of knowledge, you are restricting your potential. I can still get in my own way at an audition. I hear what the buyer is looking for. The casting person gives me a direction (it may be a good one), but the instinct to please gets in the way of my evaluating it and making it my own before I take it. The result is not organic.

Meryl Streep, interviewed on *Inside the Actor's Studio*, said she had forgotten how to act and could not even remember her lines when she had been given a direction to emphasize this word instead of that. I had to smile. Of course she forgot her lines; she was no longer playing the through line, she was worrying about a word. Even Meryl Streep can get burned trying to please a director.

What Do You Like?

The more you perfect your own persona and trust your instincts, whether it is for what constitutes a really great pair of socks or a superb jump shot, the more you become the one you are. Neither may be great by someone else's standards, but what you are searching for are your socks and your jump shot.

If you can particularize your socks and your competition's socks, you'll have more understanding as to why one actor is chosen over another. Analyze the people in your acting class. Try to perceive what they have to sell, not just what part they should play. What are their strengths and weaknesses? Try to imagine how they are going to approach their next scene. The more you are able to examine others, the more perfected that skill becomes for your own use.

Once you begin to successfully isolate your strengths and develop them, these attributes will take on a life of their own. There is an esoteric law of attraction: focus on your goal, do the work, live your life, and the goal becomes yours.

Thoreau said it best:

✦ *"If one advances confidently in the direction of his dreams and endeavors to live the life which he has imagined, he will meet with success unimagined in common hours."*

Henry David Thoreau, *Walden*[42]

When I moved to New York, I did everything I could lest I be mistaken for the middle-class lady from Texas I was. I wanted to be a sophisticated New Yorker.

What I didn't realize, Texas accent not withstanding, was that my very middle-classness is what I had to sell. I have played women who went to Vassar, but more often, they can and will get someone who actually went to Vassar.

I'm an authentic lady from Texas who has raised three children and had various life experiences before, during, and after. There is nobody else who has all of my particular components. If I don't prize what is uniquely me and find a way to tie that to a universality of the life experience, not only will I not work consistently and honestly, but my life will be a mess as well.

✦ *All my mistakes in my roles and my life and all my self-explorations have put me in a good place. What I can bring to a part that no one else can is my life, my past. That's why I don't change my face or pretend to be younger. What I bring is what no 22-year-old can bring.*

Susan Sarandon, interviewed by Bob Campbell, *Sunday Republican*[43]

In another feature on Susan, she reiterates the value of experiencing real life.

✦ *I don't know how full a cup you can bring to a project if you're not living a life. If you're not drawing from real life, then all you're doing is rehashing images you've seen in films. Even the images of yourself. And all that doesn't interest me.*

Gene Seymour, *Los Angeles Times*[44]

Andre Braugher (*Homicide: Life on the Street*) is another who has taken heart from life's painful lessons and learned from them.

✦ *A graduate of Stanford University and Juilliard, Braugher received rave reviews for his performance as a rebellious slave in the hit 1989 film, "Glory." In 1991, the New York-based actor was told to come to Los Angeles because he was hot. Braugher waited and waited for the phone to ring. It didn't. So by year's end, he moved back to New York and soon got "Homicide."*
...Braugher learned a lot from his L.A. experience. "This business is not going to keep me warm," Braugher says. "This business is not a priority. My priority is being a husband, a father, a son, a brother, and a citizen. The lesson I learned back in 1991 was that I am not an actor. I am a man who acts. So consequently, everything that I need, everything important to me is about being a man."
Susan King, *Los Angeles Times/TV Times*[45]

Getting To Know You

Independent LA agent Martin Gage (an ex-actor) and manager John Kimble shared insights regarding self-discovery and distinctiveness:

✦ *Anything you can do to give you more of an idea of who you are, whether it's therapy, talking to people or looking in a mirror, that's valid. There's an exercise I used to give my class when I taught actor therapy. I would tell them to get stark naked in front of a mirror and sit and look at themselves for an hour. Just sit and look at yourself. Look at how you look when you talk. When you move. Look at how your face changes. Look at how your body moves.*
The smart actor will study himself until he can see what it is that he has that is unique, special, commercial, saleable, acceptable in him that he can develop and magnify and use better than anybody else.
Think of you and your four closest competitors. If someone sat and talked to each of you for twenty minutes, what would they see that was different? What is it about you? Why should they hire you instead of the other one? She may have more credits or make more money. Why should I hire you?
You have to go in with the qualities that are the most accessible of you to make those people buy you. When you walk in a room, you have about four seconds while people decide to hire or not hire you. It's your vibes. They may call it your nose, but it's your vibes. You have to go in with the qualities that are most accessible of you. You've got to get those people to buy you.
Martin Gage/The Gage Group, Los Angeles

✦ *I believe every person on the face of the earth is unique. If I had a set of identical twins who were in touch with their uniqueness, I could sell them separately because once they are in touch with their own uniqueness, there is no such thing as competition.*

A person's ideas dictate his uniqueness. What I believe about homosexuality or what I believe about any major subject is my uniqueness because it comes from my experience. So you can't compare it. Many times you will be in the minority. The greatest people in the world have normally been in the minority.

John Kimble/Manager

✦ *This is what I am. This is what they want me to be. Can I put them together and find out what I am capable of being? They want me to be a nerd. I want to be sexy. Maybe I can be a sexy nerd. Then you have to convince your agent that this is who you are, because if your agent doesn't see it, you're out again.*

If the agent sees you and thinks he can make money on you, but not in the same way you think, then you have a problem. You and the agent must have the same vision. You might change his vision or he might change yours. If you both have the same vision, you'll be successful. The level of success may vary, but if you know who you are and the agent knows it, accurately, that's the recipe for success.

And remember, what you are at twenty-five is not what you are at thirty-five. Things change and your perception of yourself must change, too.

Martin Gage/The Gage Group, Los Angeles

Martin said the key words: develop and magnify.

The film *Stage Door* features several star actresses at the beginning of their careers before they developed and magnified their respective uniquenesses. It's fascinating to see Katharine Hepburn, Lucille Ball, Eve Arden, and Ginger Rogers in such an early stage of development

Perhaps these women are not as familiar to you as actors you routinely see on television, but if you do know their later work, gleaning the kernel of what became their ticket to stardom is an instructive process.

Dan Faucci shared an exercise for getting to get to know yourself.

✦ *Spend ten minutes communicating with yourself in the mirror. Do it by the clock. Just look at your face. Don't look for anything. You can look at your eyes, nose, lines, skin. See what you focus on. Don't judge it. Experience it. Take it in. If you start getting itchy at eight minutes, you're probably getting ready to feel something that is beginning to make you uncomfortable. Be brave: spend the full time and see what feelings come.*

Dan Faucci/Producer

What Makes You So Special?

Let's focus on what about you is special. What do you want to say? You can't be someone who says "I don't know" when you are asked which restaurant you want to go to. You can't say "I don't care" when someone asks where you want to sit in the theater. Have an opinion and know what you want.

People should be able to answer a lot of questions just by looking at you. If you don't know the answer, you can't communicate it. They don't pay the big bucks for averageness, unless you are so average you can be the prototype, as Ron Howard was in *Happy Days*. The people who will work in the business are those who can communicate a particular essence in the dramatic sense.

In Sidney Lumet's illuminating book *Making Movies* he speaks of the importance of self-knowledge.

✦ *In "Murder on the Orient Express," I wanted Ingrid Bergman to play the Russian Princess Dragomiroff. She wanted to play the retarded Swedish maid. I wanted Ingrid Bergman. I let her play the maid. She won an Academy Award. I bring this up because self-knowledge is important in so many ways to an actor.*

Earlier, I mentioned how improvisation can be an effective tool in rehearsal as a way of finding out what you're really like when, for example, you're angry.

Knowing your feelings lets you know when those feelings are real as opposed to when you're simulating them. No matter how insecure, almost all the stars I've worked with have a high degree of self-knowledge. They may hate what they see, but they do see themselves. I think it's self-knowledge that serves as the integrating element between the actor's natural persona and the character he's playing.
Sidney Lumet[46]

Assets and Liabilities

Make a list of all your skills. Your acting-related skills, your entrepreneurial skills, everything you do well. Include making friends and staying positive if that's in your repertoire. These insights may take you further in your exploration.

How you work on the tasks we are speaking of delineates who you are. Your whole life is a laboratory to keep on looking at your way of working. If you procrastinate about your pictures and resumes, you are going to procrastinate about learning your lines.

Napoleon Hill's message in *Think and Grow Rich* is that every person has to conquer procrastination. Start now to do all your tasks the moment you think of them. As you work on the details of any project, you will work on every facet of your life. Begin to practice what you want your life to be.

Make a list of your liabilities. As you list drawbacks, perhaps you can formulate a plan to overcome them. If you think they're unsolvable problems, Carol Burnett's biography *Just One More Time* will make you think otherwise. There's no one in this business who could have been more disenfranchised than she was. If she could become successful against those odds, believe me, you have a chance if you can become that focused.

Veteran actor Hector Elizondo (who finally became visible as the hotel manager in *Pretty Woman* and is now seen as Pancho Duque on *Cane*) has compelling things to say about hardship.

✦ *You can't really have style unless you've been someplace. I mean, you have to have been down. You have to have overcome something to have something. If you've had everything all your life, then you've never been tested and I don't think you're really the genuine article.*

You have to have come through something because that's how a sword is made. It's made from a piece of iron from the ground, and it's forged and beaten that's the great metaphor for a human being. If you're born a sword, you aren't a real sword. But if you're forged from this iron ore then comes this beautiful sword.

Hector Elizondo, interviewed by Elias Stimac, *Drama-Logue*[47]

Jim Carrey is another example of tremendous success arising out of more than talent.

✦ *I look at stuff that's happened in my life like it's "The Grapes of Wrath." You know you'll always win in the end if you don't let the problems make you angry. I've been through some wild times. When my father lost his job and I was 13, we went from lower-middle class to complete poverty, living in a Volkswagen camper.*

My father was not good at business because he was too nice. I learned not to be too nice. I definitely have an edge because of all that. But nothing made me go, 'Life sucks, people suck.'

I now want to make sure that my daughter Jane's financial future is as secure as I can possibly make it. That I'll be able to look after myself when I'm old. That drives me. Definitely.

I've always believed in magic. When I wasn't doing anything in this town, I'd go up every night, sit on Mulholland Drive, look out at the city, stretch out my arms and say, 'Everybody wants to work with me. I'm a really good actor. I have all kinds of great movie offers.' I'd just repeat these things over and over, literally convincing myself that I had a couple of movies lined up. I'd drive down that hill, ready to take the world on, going, 'Movie offers are out there for me. I just don't hear them yet.'

It was like total affirmations, antidotes to the stuff that stems from my family background, from knowing how things can go sour. Still, I've had times that, when I'd walk down the street, I'd look at the street people and feel like, 'I'm already one of them. I'm already there.' I mean, I can scare the shit out of myself.

... I've always believed that everything I've wanted, prayed for, will come to me in one way or another. I'm real careful about what I ask for. I asked God when I was young to give me whatever I need to help me be a great actor-comedian.

So, okay, it's like now you're going to be poverty stricken, now you're going to go through a divorce. I've always seen these things as, 'This is a rock in my way for me to learn how to get over. Like, I expected to get on "Saturday Night Live," do that trip, but that didn't happen. But I got on "In Living Color." You may not always get where you expected but, so long as you're somewhere, who cares?

Jim Carrey, interviewed by Stephen Rebello, *Movieline*[48]

Maybe you must come from a background of great pain to have that kind of drive. My personal bias is that a balanced person wouldn't have the drive to be a star in any field because he would not have that desperate need to prove himself.

Debra Winger thinks success is about being available:

✦ *In a word, openness. Openness of the heart, of the soul. The camera is open. Many people are not. A director can spend a whole day setting up a shot, getting the angles just right, the lighting perfect; but visually, if the actor isn't open, it's a dead end. It's got nothing to do with physical beauty either. You can shoot identical twins; if one is open and one is closed, the one twin will resonate on film and the closed one won't.*

Debra Winder, interviewed by Tom Robbins, *Esquire*[49]

Focusing on What You Have to Sell

Knowing what you have to sell does not necessarily mean always preparing yourself to play the same part, but preparing to focus on the energy that will alert the casting director to your strength.

If you consistently play banker types, it's probable that you have an innate fastidiousness that is associated with detail-oriented people. If you exaggerate and develop this trait, you might be the first thought for any casting executive who is casting these roles.

Check to see how you fit in with actors who are being bought. In situation comedies, there is usually a next door neighbor who is zanier and less pretty/handsome than the lead. Frequently there is an acerbic, scratchy quality to contrast the lead. The lead needs to be more bland than the supporting players in order to create the perfect balance.

When you make a cake, flour (bland) is the chief ingredient followed in quantity (but not importance) by the liquid (the binder) and the spices. The flour holds it all together and the spices add zip, but too much vanilla or sugar or salt, without which the project or cake would be inedible, would render the effort useless as well.

In adventure/detective shows, there's usually a hard-boiled chief that is at odds with the hero. And of course, there are always exotic bad guys and white trash bad guys and corporate bad guys. If you can come up with a new twist on the bad guy, you can really be in demand. Commercials feature the dumb one (with the problem) and the smart one (who solves the problem).

We don't ever finish changing and there is always something more to learn about acting. No professional ever finishes growing. A brain surgeon learns a particular procedure one day, but if he doesn't continually practice and refine the technique, he won't be the brain surgeon everyone wants. If he does not continue to read, search, and study, he will not maintain his edge. Neither the actor nor the surgeon will prosper without enjoying and practicing the continuity of process.

You Already Have "It"

If you are not fulfilled by the now, if your only payoff is a Tony, an Oscar, or big bucks, change jobs. You will miss your whole life waiting for a peace that will never come. If you are unfortunate enough to win the prize while in this mind-set, you will despair to find yourself the same unhappy person you were the day before you got your statue.

I once heard an interview on the radio with Desi Arnaz, Jr., a young actor who at one point appeared to have it all.

✦   *"Yes, it did seem like I had it all. Except that's not 'it'. I had the car, the house, the position and I was terribly unhappy. I got into alcohol and drugs. That wasn't 'it' either."*

"There's really no difference between me and the people who have nothing...who think 'it' is all those things. They, at least, think if they had a big career and all the things money can buy, they would be happy. Imagine how depressing it is to have all those things and still be unhappy."

It's up to you and how smart you are, how you make positive choices, how you focus, how you ask for what you want, and how you don't let yourself sink into negative thinking. It's absolutely self-indulgent to allow yourself to think all those self-destructive thoughts actors leap to given the barest opportunity:

"Oh, I'll never get a job."
"Oh, I'll never get another job."
"Nobody wants me."
"I'm no good."

Not only does nobody want to hear you talk like that and/or be around you in that frame of mind, but that thinking only drains your energy, prolongs your pain, and makes people question, "Hey, maybe he's right!" Don't cut yourself off from your feelings. You don't have to be in denial; acknowledge the pain to yourself and then go for a walk.

Spend time with yourself. Explore. Use the meditation time I spoke about to just be. Gain perspective. This business is a constant test for maintaining perspective. Write about it. Writing is a magical exercise. At my most depressed moments, when I can remember to write about it, the feelings go from my brain through the pencil to the paper and I feel better.

If you enjoy being unhappy, then keep thinking about your pain. You have the ability to turn your mind to something else. If you don't refocus on something else and put your energy into something positive, we have to assume you would rather be unhappy.

Learning about yourself can be a painful experience, but the payoff is worth it. I remember one point in my life when I realized that the one constant in all the unhappy relationships I had ever been involved in was me. That was pretty depressing until I realized that was good news. If the problem was the other people, there was nothing I could do about it. But, if it was me, I could set about changing it.

Wrap Up

✓ know which one you are
✓ assess your assets and liabilities
✓ explore what makes you special
✓ choose mentors and role models
✓ analyze the marketplace
✓ allow yourself to hear your voice
✓ knowing when you change
✓ ongoing depression is self-indulgent
✓ defining oneself is a lifetime process

⚔ 9 ⚔
Stand-Up Comedy/One-Person Shows

Many of today's biggest film and television successes entered the business as stand-up comedians. Jim Carrey, Whoopi Goldberg, Ray Romano, Robin Williams, Billy Crystal, George Lopez, Christopher Titus, and Jerry Seinfeld are just a few of the entrepreneurs who started either as stand-ups or in their own one-person shows.

Claudia Shear's *Blown Sideways Through Life*, Julia Sweeney's *And God Said, Ha!*, Pamela Gien's *The Syringa Tree*, Paul Linke's *Time Flies When You're Alive*, and Spalding Grey's *Swimming to Cambodia* were all drawn from incidents in the performers' lives. Jason Alexander, Julie Harris, and Ron Silver took material from the lives of Harry Truman, Emily Dickinson, and promoter Bill Graham and fashioned them into illuminating evenings of theatre.

Separating vanity One-Person Shows that are really just an excuse get onstage and tell *What I Did on My Summer Vacation Using All the Dialects I Know* from a worthwhile evening of theatre is fashioning material with resonance that deals with issues. If you have the drive, stamina, courage and entrepreneurial ability to put together an evening of theatre, you will not only have a chance to act and a platform where producers and casting directors can view you, but you will also create a source of income on the college and possibly cruise ship circuit.

In case as a would-be stand-up, you skipped right to this page, let me reiterate page 20:

Only 6% of SAG members earn middle-class wages of $30,000 to $70,000 annually. About 71% earn less than $7,500 a year. Many earn nothing at all.

Anyone who goes into the business for the money is buying a very big lottery ticket. You've got to be in the business because you love being in the business rain or shine.

If you were to apply the same amount of time and creative energy pursuing any other kind of work, you would have a better return on the investment. That said, here's the way to begin, if you want to become a stand-up.

Though the idea of putting together material might seem intimidating initially, like everything else broken into small increments, anything is possible.

How to Begin

Start with 10 minutes of material and then look for a place to hone it in front of an audience. The Lions Club, The Elks Club and the library, all look for speakers and performers for their meetings and luncheons. Once focused on finding venues, you'll find not only benevolent associations but corporate gatherings looking for entertainment. You'll not only get a chance to try out your material, but you can probably come up with a stipend as well.

The skills you develop writing, producing, and performing your own stand-up act can move you toward varying careers as evidenced by the number of successful names listed at *www.imdb.com* when you type in *Saturday Night Live.*

Obviously, one is hired by *SNL* if he possess not only acting, writing, and producing skills, but the discipline to focus those elements day after day. The only other show that comes close to producing alumnae that would later shape the business to such a large extent is Sid Caesar's *Your Show of Shows* which spawned Mel Brooks, Larry Gelbart, Carl Reiner, Neil Simon, Mel Tolkin, and Woody Allen.

Put together a stand-up act. If there are no comedy clubs in your area (which seems unlikely), call local service organizations like The Lions Club and The Jaycees. They are always looking for entertaining speakers for their functions. Charge at least $50, and remember, the more they pay you, the more they respect you.

Another way to hone your material is to put you and your routine on *www.youtube.com* and see if you can't build a following. You'll still need to perform live, but this is a way to start. If it's not good no one will probably see it (unless it's REALLY bad), but if you come up with something good, it will begin to be passed around.

Putting together an act is not as formidable as it seems. Just do it one joke at a time. A way to build material is to sit down and make a list of things that make you angry: the guy who parks in the handicapped zone while you obey the rules, people who cut in front of you on the freeway, the guy who steals what would have been your parking place, shoppers who speed up just enough to beat you to the checkout line at the grocery store, etc.

There's a universality of humor in all our pet peeves. Tap into that. Get one minute together, then five. Test the jokes out on your friends (but don't tell them you're auditioning your material), then volunteer to be master of ceremonies at some function and try out your material. When you have twenty minutes, call comedy clubs and get onstage.

Perhaps you could be the weather forecaster on your local television station. Weathermen/women in the major markets are frequently cast from the ranks of stand-up comedians. As a matter of fact, stand-up comedians are considered such ripe potentials for television situation comedies that casting directors from Los Angeles regularly monitor comedy club operations all over the country.

When Jerry Seinfeld appeared on David Steinberg's *Sit Down Comedy*, he told a wonderful story about how he began to focus on his early career.

✦ *I had a part on "Benson" for three episodes. I was excited to get it and then I got fired. The part was so small and so irrelevant to the show, that they didn't even bother to tell me. And so I showed up for work and sat down in my chair for the read through and go "Hey, where's my script?" and this guys gestures me over. The director didn't even bother, it was just somebody who said "Get out of here, kid."*

It was one of the great experiences that I had because they made me so angry that they had the power to just take this away from me that I began to really value my stand-up career in a different way after that.

I started really focusing and writing and working hard. I said, "I'm going to be a comedian because they can't take that away from me." I really resented it.

When it came time that NBC was interested in me doing something, I had my own career which I was very comfortable in, so I said, "This is the way it's going to be or, to hell with it, I don't care."

Jerry Seinfeld, interviewed by David Steinberg, *Sit Down Comedy*

What It Takes

Producing your own stand-up act or one-person show doesn't necessarily take much money, but it does take a sense of humor, writing knowhow, and drive. If you have not perfected your writing skills yet, get on with it.

John Kretchmer was directing an episode of *Lois & Clark* when I tracked his path for my book *Directing Your Directing Career*. His pragmatic approach can teach us all a lesson.

Organized and smart, John set about researching his employment possibilities and learning the business by working in a variety of jobs on the sets of various films and television shows.

He worked as a production assistant, a prop man, and in craft services hustling food for entire sets of cast and crew. Armed with his own firsthand analysis of job possibilities, as soon as John was sure that he wanted to be a director, he made a wise decision. Knowing that a good script is the director's first step and knowing that he didn't have any option money, he determined to take a year off and learn to write.

He learned well. One of his plays was read at the prestigious O'Neill Playwrights Foundation in New York and another was a finalist at the Sundance Institute. Although he didn't get his first directing gig via his own material, that single-minded focus on his goal placed him in fortune's path and Steven Spielberg became his mentor.

My own personal bias is that if you can write, you can cross over many lines. There may be many jokes about the lack of power in the writer's career, but the truth is that if you can write your own material, particularly if you can write your own funny material, you can begin to be in charge of your own destiny. Stand-up is a good place to gather skills and experience without waiting for someone else to choose you.

Comedy Club Salaries

Comics are remunerated in proportion to their fame in a given area.

✦ *"Craig Shoemaker is a phenomenal draw in regions where he's a staple. He can bring in $15,000 in a short week but in places where he has less exposure, he may only bring in $4,500," says Improv booking agent Robert Hartman.*

"Salaries vary according to ticket sales and whether the club can sell tickets on Tuesday, Wednesday, and Thursday," Hartman adds. At 300 seats, for four shows at $20 a ticket, a headliner act can get 50% of the gross [$12,000] and maybe bonuses too. A name act who plays a five-show weekend at the Los Angeles Improv negotiates a salary based on the $17 ticket price and 300 seats, which creates a gross profit of $25,000. Middle-liners can get up to $5,000 a week and are booked for several consecutive weeks, while MCs (who often have the most demanding job in the house) currently only receive $75-$100 per set.

"Salaries on the road peaked about three years ago," according to comic Rhonda Shear, who has hosted 400 episodes of USA's "Up All Night." "A lot

of people who were making $4,000 a week on the road three years ago are only getting $1,200-$1,500," Shear reports. The new club scene seems to be the cruise ships, which pays the same top acts $4,000-$5,000.
Brooke Comer, *The Hollywood Reporter Comedy Special*[50]

It's a long road, economically at least, from the comedy clubs to a hit TV series.

✦   *Ask Paul Reiser. "You started at nothing, coming to the city, then you'd work your way up to $5 a night, $20 a weekend, $50 for a gig here and there. With luck, you could put that together and you'd get enough to pay the rent....Certainly no one goes into comedy for the money. You can't make money."*
David Kronke, *Los Angeles Times*[51]

It may be a long trek, but what a pay off. Reiser won an Emmy, Golden Globe, American Comedy Award and Screen Actors Guild nominations for NBC's *Mad About You* and, in addition to his film and television work, he wrote *Couplehood* and *Babyhood* which made it to the top of *The New York Times* bestseller list.

Character/A Special Voice

Wherever you establish your developmental beachhead, your goal is not simply to make money, but to create a character that is your own. If you can do that, you will have the option of taking your creation into a larger venue than your own hometown.

✦   *Kim Fleary, vice-president for comedy series development at ABC Entertainment, says that to score big, what a comic needs most is "a point of view and an infectious personality."*
Ibid.[52]

Though the comedy club craze has peaked, there are still venues in which to practice your skills:

✦   *A lot of comedy clubs have closed across the country, but there are still a fair amount in the Northeast so it's easier to keep a comic working there as they start to develop. The more stage time they get, they better they become. We encourage them to get into acting classes, not to become actors, but just to start. We want to know*

what their long-range goals are. In order for a comic to become popular, he needs television exposure. If you can support that with a strong act, you're going to have a good career.
Tom Ingegno/Omnipop, New York

✦ *We've definitely steered toward a very personality-oriented comic. A charismatic style comic. "The Tonight Show" might use a comic because they're a very good comic in terms of their writing, a structural comic who writes a perfect setup and a punch line. Some of those comics wouldn't cross over into a sitcom because they might just be joke tellers. We want somebody who is a very full-bodied character a la Roseanne, Tim Allen, or Seinfeld. The development and casting people are looking for that. They are already walking in with a character. Some comics have stronger skills in that area.*
Bruce Smith/Omnipop, Los Angeles

✦ *A comedic person has to have the backing of theatrical training, otherwise you're looking at a personality-oriented project. Many stand-ups came out of theatre and did stand-up as a means of survival.*
Steve Tellez/CAA, Los Angeles

✦ *I wouldn't assume that just because you are a comedic actor that you can do stand-up. Soap opera people try to do stand-up. Most of them, since they are so pretty, have not lived that angst-ridden life that comics have. It becomes a frivolous version of comedy.*
The first thing you want to establish with an actor that is going into comedy is: Do they have a natural feel for it? Do they have comedic rhythm for it? There are many actors who are wonderful with comedy, but can't do stand-up. You need the stage time.
Bruce Smith/Omnipop, Los Angeles

Jim Carrey might appear to be an overnight success, but he has been perfecting his talents for fifteen years in an extremely focused and businesslike way:

✦ *A native of the Toronto area, Carrey went professional in 1980, ultimately developing a reputation for his ability to do impressions, with a repertoire of 100+ characters. After moving to Los Angeles, he became a regular at the Comedy Store, where he honed his skills. In 1982, he landed the lead role in the NBC midseason sitcom "Duck Factory," a show that was quickly pulled. He then took a two-year sabbatical from stand-up to take acting lessons:*

"I saw where it was going. I was going to end up some kind of comedy phantom in Vegas, doing some kind of tribute show. It was so confining creatively, because I had all these weird ideas that I could never use, because it didn't fit into the act. I just got tired of it. I wanted to be an original. That's all."

David Pecchia, The Hollywood Reporter, 1994 Comedy Special Issue[53]

The personal appearance agents that I spoke to in New York and Los Angeles supported what I have learned from theatrical agents and scriptwriters' agents: established agents are mostly not interested in one-shot representation. Many unrepresented actors (directors, writers, etc.) think that if they land a job on their own (even a development deal) and call up an agent to handle it for them, that the agent will welcome them with open arms. The agent is going to make money, right?

That's not how it goes. The agent is interested in a client with a body of work that shows growth and development, not what might be just a lucky incident in a young career.

If you lived in New York and got a guest shot on *30 Rock* and called an agent with that shot as an entree, he would probably take your call, but if you don't have a track record of credits the credible agent would not be interested. Ten percent of an episode is not enough for him to put you on his list to share all his introductions and hard work.

If you have written a one-person show and Disney is interested, that may or may not be interesting to a stand-up agent. Development deals go south with regularity and if you don't already have a stand-up career going for yourself, personal appearance agents won't be interested. They want people who have been playing clubs in and out of town and have done the stage time.

This is Wendy Liebman's 10th year as a stand-up; she moved to Los Angeles four years ago to pursue it full-time. This year, she was a nominee in the best female stand-up category of the American Comedy Awards.

✦ ...*I've always done things in my own time. When I moved out here, I just knew I wasn't ready. I wasn't that anxious either. I knew I had to get some acting classes under my belt. The thing about stand-up, I know I can go into Caesar's Palace and open for Julio Iglesias or Ann-Margret and feel comfortable doing it.*

I feel like I could do any stand-up anywhere because I've done it. But acting, it took me a while to feel comfortable there. To say out loud that I'm ready is the first step. From there, people can say yes or no, but I'm ready.

Wendy Liebman, interviewed by David Kronke, Los Angeles Times[54]

A career as a stand-up is a bonafide way to get up in front of people quickly, but there are no short cuts to acting or comedic maturity. You gotta do the time.

Several companies and studios are pioneering a way for young comics to be seen once they are ready.

✦ *As a way of providing a showcase for their clients and perhaps offering a glimpse into the future of programming, several companies and studios have turned to alternative outlets like cable. CAA launched a weekly series ("Limboland") featuring its clients on cable's Comedy Central. Others are following suit, most notably Messina-Baker Entertainment.*

Its program "Small Doses" is being funded by Viacom in exchange for options on the talent and concepts. The sketch-like format, featuring a collection of mini-programs that are prototypes for would-be series, is being made at low costs.
Rick Sherwood, *The Hollywood Reporter/Comedy Special Issue*[55]

Since successful comedians breed successful and visible comedy clubs, smart club owners in Los Angeles are known to give a helping hand to developing comics.

✦ *Club owners such as Jamie Masada (Laugh Factory), Mitzi Shore (The Comedy Store) and Budd Friedman (The Improvization) don't just book comics; they also help them with their acts. "We work them out and place them and watch them grow," the Comedy Store's Shore says. "It's like a gym."*

"We're obligated as club owners to keep feeding the industry with talent and train them and make them ready," adds Masada, who co-manages Harlan Williams, the thirty-two year-old star of the WB Network's sitcom "Simon" about a Forrest Gump-like character.
Connie Benesch, *The Hollywood Reporter/Comedy Special Issue*[56]

Comedian Referral Service/Rent a Comic

The Comedyzine Referral Service is a free online listing for comedians, agents, managers and publicists. Each listing links you to their site. If you need to hire a comedian for a corporate, college, or other function, you can select the comedian by going directly to their site, or their agent's site. *www.e-zine-list.com/ezines/082/778.shtml*

If you are a comedian, agent, manager, or publicist, and wish to be listed, you can E-mail your URL address to: *listings@comedyzine.com* including your city, state/province, and country. There is no charge, but you must have a web page for them to link to.

One-Person Shows

If you don't see yourself as a stand-up artist, but have the drive and ability to produce a one-person show, you can only grow from the experience, whatever the outcome. Even if you don't attract someone who sees your act as a pilot for a situation comedy, if you have a point-of-view and are well produced, you might well have an annuity that can be booked across the country into college venues.

It's not a new idea and it's not reserved just for new talent trying to break in. Lynn Redgrave's *Shakespeare For My Father* has been playing across the country for several years and Patrick Stewart's production of *A Christmas Carol* has become a seasonal Broadway attraction.

As successful a venue as stand-up has been, some feel one-person shows may be the way to go.

✦   *With the economic trouble the stand-up world has found itself in, people are taking their act and shaping it into one-person shows. The industry is now looking to solo performers as artists who are not only funny but have also fashioned a way to present that theatricality in an entertaining way. Claudia Shear, whose hysterical one-woman account of her working world struggles, "Blown Sideways Through Life," is now inundated with book and feature film deals.*

While Shear noted that the solo show is nothing new, she was completely unprepared for the 'tsunami of publicity' that followed when "Blown Sideways" opened off-Broadway in the fall of '94. "It's become more acceptable to hear the one voice. It's a very elemental connection with people saying, 'This is what happened to me tonight,'" explains Shear, who does not consider herself a solo performer nor a comedienne, even though her show has been widely perceived as such.
Rachel Fischer, *The Hollywood Reporter/Comedy Special Issue*[57]

Filling the Stage

It's so hard to get into the business that actors forget that agents, producers, networks, cruise ships, colleges, film companies, and anyone else who hires, all really need the performers as much as the performers need the bookings. There are many stages to fill, whether that stage is on a sound stage or at a comedy club. If you are any good at all and have the creativity, drive, reliability, and stamina to move forward on your own, there will be someone who will see your energy and try to attach themselves to it.

Assuming that you plan to make the necessary investment of time, energy, and entrepreneurial spirit, decide now to take yourself seriously. Resolve to grade your work as you would any other performer's. Just because you get a job, don't assume that it means your cake is baked; it only means you have a job.

✦ *"The danger comes when the comedian isn't ready but he thinks he is because they put him on a contract," says the Laugh Factory's Masada. "He thinks he knows it all, and instead of developing his comedy, he's relaxing, living in a dream that they're going to make him a star."*
David Kronke, *Los Angeles Times*[58]

✦ *But even getting the order for a network series does not mean that a stand-up comic has cleared the final hurdle. For many reasons like a difficult time slot, a mistranslation of comic persona, or a lack of acting skills, even the most highly touted vehicle can flounder.*

For instance, the Korean-American comic Margaret Cho's "All-American Girl" was a huge disappointment for ABC. Industry consensus is that Ms. Cho, still in her twenties, had nowhere near the show-business savvy or corporate support needed to turn her sassy observational humor into the ground-breaking sitcom that critics and viewers were expecting.
Andy Meisler, *The New York Times*[59]

That was 1994. Margaret Cho learned some hard lessons.

✦ *One thing she learned, she said is that "artists, including actors and comics, must honor their own opinions above everyone else's and not take what people say too personally."*
Margaret Cho, interviewed by Cassie Carpenter, *Back Stage West*[60]

You are the one who is going to make you a star. Because there is such a fine line between the kind of arrogance it takes to get up and believe in yourself and the kind of arrogance that blinds itself to criticism, you can't afford to sip the drug of self-satisfaction. Your focus has to be about fulfilling the work; otherwise, when the money people want to change you, you won't have the strength to stay true to yourself. A true picture of your contribution only emerges over time. Take the time to become.

Indeed comics' and networks' expectations can be exasperatingly at odds. Comics are hired because of their distinctive outlooks and perspectives, but then the networks usually try to shoehorn them into premises antithetical to their nature and saddle them with writers and executive producers who don't understand their appeal.

✦ *"The nature of TV development is that there is this tremendous ambivalence on the part of networks; they want something new and different, yet they feel most comfortable with what's tried and true," [Paul] Reiser says. "Had 'Seinfeld' not had the process it had, going through NBC's late-night division, it never would have gone. They'd have just said, 'What is this about?'"*
David Kronke, *Los Angeles Times*[61]

Craig Shoemaker is a successful stand-up who spent much of the 1980s on the road. In the late eighties, NBC signed him to a development deal and he found himself auditioning in the office of Brandon Tartikoff.

✦ *"All of a sudden, I couldn't act to save my life," Shoemaker says. "I was supposed to do a scene on the phone to someone. When I'd rehearsed it, I'd pantomime the phone, but this time I picked up the real phone that was sitting there. There was someone on the line and he was yelling at me to get off.*

"...The wrenching experience served as a dividing line," he says. Shortly afterward, Mr. Shoemaker swore off alcohol and drugs, blaming them for his lack of focus, and became more serious about his comedy: "I realized that I'd been so involved in the results, I hadn't been into the work itself."
Andy Meisler, *The New York Times*[62]

Roseanne's book, *My Lives*, details the battles she had to fight in order to get her work onto the television screen, and in a *New York Times* interview, Brett Butler made the same points:

✦ *...unless you're willing to put yourself on the line every single day you're doing this, you might as well just stay home.*
Ibid.[63]

Margaret Cho is smarter now:

✦ *Be really stubborn. Know as much as you can about what you want, because you'll be pulled this way and that...Stick to your guns, even though it's really difficult.*
David Kronke, *Los Angeles Times*"[64]

Margaret's advice is pertinent no matter what you do. Learning how to get along with all the other collaborators but being able to hold onto your voice at the same time is an art. If you're just doing stand-up with a stool and a microphone, you don't need anyone else except sound and lighting to make an impact, but when you venture onto a larger stage, you and your collaborators must be in sync.

There are many doors and windows into the business other than having an agent, casting director, or producer call and invite you in. Making the commitment to work in the business is far different than saying you want an acting job.

I'm convinced there is a job for anyone who commits to action instead of waiting.

Wrap Up

✓ successful stand-ups get the key to the bank
✓ patience and work ethic are necessary
✓ most stand-ups don't make money
✓ the road is long and challenging
✓ writing ability and sense of humor are essential
✓ character and viewpoint are necessary
✓ one-person shows can have a big impact
✓ need to be strong, flexible, and have a unique voice

☆ 10 ☆
Children in the Business

Children have no business giving up their childhoods to be actors. They are not in a position to make such a costly judgement about their lives. You only get to be a kid once. If you don't experience childhood at the appropriate time, you will never get a legitimate shot at it again.

I urge any parent who is considering letting their child earn what looks like easy money to pay for their college tuition with a few commercials now and then, maybe an episode or two on television or maybe even a play, to think again. Management pays a child as much money per day as an adult and expects the child to behave as an adult, no matter what.

And what if things get out of hand and your child becomes the new Haley Joel Osment? Can you or your child turn your back on all that money and adulation just so he can play football and be a normal kid?

To parents who tell me ardently that it's the child who yearns for the career, I say, "Children are in no position to make such a decision. They want to stay up all night and eat candy too, do you let them do that?"

That said, my interview with successful stage mother/manager (now children's agent) Judy Savage pretty well refutes my point of view:

✦ *Kids who have problems in the business came from dysfunctional families in the first place. It's not necessarily that the business goes to the children's heads, it goes to the parents' heads. I don't think the number of showbiz kids who become messed up is any greater than the general public, but you hear about them because they are so visible and they have a little more money for drugs.*
Judy Savage/Judy Savage Agency, Los Angeles

Judy's philosophy explains why her clients and her own kids ended up not only working, but being productive grown-ups as well:

✦ *I think it's a great business and that you can pay for your braces, your caps, your car, your wedding, your house, and hopefully go on in the business or in some other aspect of life with a good start.*

Treat it as a hobby that you are lucky enough to get paid for, it's not going to go on forever. You can count on your two hands the number of actors whose careers go on for 40-50 years. The average career is five years for all members of The Screen Actors Guild.

Judy Savage/Judy Savage Agency, Los Angeles

Jodie Foster seems to have graduated from child actor to power adult actress with no real problems, but she also seemed extraordinarily mature.

✦ *My way of being well-adjusted at a young age was saying, "This is a really weird world, but it's nine-to-five." When I come home, that's when my real life starts. I had to know that as a kid or they would have eaten me up. When you're eight years old and a camera crew follows you into your third-grade class, you learn very quickly to say, "Oh, no, that will not be my life." I also knew if I didn't put my foot down and say that I was going to college, my life wouldn't have been mine. But when I was a kid, we didn't have long lenses, and kid actors didn't make $10 million.*

Staff Report, *The Hollywood Reporter*[65]

Even so, Elizabeth Taylor's early life as a child actor is not one she recommends.

✦ *"Looking back, I think I missed not having a childhood, not going to a regular school. I had a lot of fathers and avuncular friends on the set. They were great.*

They used to throw me around and play baseball with me and sneak me candy and comic books. But it wasn't the same as having peers, and I think I would advise parents of child actors not to push it. It's a hard life for a child not to have a childhood. It's rough."

Charles Champlin, *Los Angeles Times*[66]

Look at the Big Picture

If your child is serious about pursuing a career in show business, in addition to studying acting, I would encourage him to exercise his entrepreneurial skills, so that when he gets out of school, he will be truly prepared. The newspapers are full of the stories about the troubles of ex-child stars who will never get their lives back because they did not prepare for their future.

If you are a kid and want to work in the business, take note. Your life expectancy in the business is five years, ten years tops. While you are on the set missing growing up like a normal kid, playing ball, having dates, and going to the prom, you are getting a lot of attention, money, and perks. You get to go special places and people ask for your autograph.

Once you hit the later teen years, it may well be all over. Carrie Fisher (daughter of Eddie Fisher and Debbie Reynolds) wrote and narrated a special on A&E called *Carrie Fisher: The Hollywood Family.*

It was an illuminating hour about many aspects of life in the business. There was nothing more upsetting than the segment dealing with child actors.

Paul Peterson spent his childhood on *The Donna Reed Show.* When parts stopped coming his way, he got into trouble with drugs and the law. Today, he is clean and has dedicated himself to helping kids whose careers didn't make it past age eighteen.

On Carrie's show, you see Paul visiting Anthony Thompkins, a former child star from the show *Diff'rent Strokes.* He visited Anthony in prison where he is doing time for drugs and burglary. Anthony said:

✦ *Nobody sat me down and said, 'Well, look out. You are twelve years old now, but when you're eighteen, you'd better watch out, because work is going to dry up.' If they'd told me that, I would have been prepared for it.*

By not accepting the fact that I could expand, that there was something else I could do, that's how I ended up here.

Anthony Thompkins, interviewed by Carrie Fisher on *A&E Television*[67]

I'm not sure that anything other than experience teaches us anything so it's doubtful to me that Thompkins would have believed his career might be short-lived. Rejection and unavailability of parts for people in his age range played an important role in the downward spiral that put him in jail.

He's not the only one. His fellow cast members Todd Bridges and Dana Plato followed a similar path, though Bridges is clean now and sports a string of credits on imdb.com as well as a regular role on *The Guiding Light.*

What's the window of opportunity for child actors? Five years? Ten years? How long are you an adult? Forty years? By pursuing something so limited in time, you're foreclosing your options for professional achievement for forty to fifty years. That a bad deal. And all of this comes at the expense of homework and socialization skills. Carrie

Fisher closed the show saying:

✦ *Celebrity can never be a career, it's too fleeting; but by the time that the kid actor realizes that learning lines is no substitute for learning, it's too late. They have nothing to fall back on when Hollywood gets sick of them and drops them without even a gold watch.*
Carrie Fisher, *A&E Television*[68]

And then, there's Jodie Foster who it seems was always wise beyond her years.

✦ *But I think the truth is, I didn't think I'd be an actor when I grew up. Everyone told me, "Child actors are done at seventeen, so what do you want to be? A doctor? A lawyer?" The good thing is it made me develop other sides of my personality. I'm still shocked I'm an actor. I have a new backup plan every ten days.*
Staff Report, *The Hollywood Reporter*[69]

If you are a parent reading this, the following information regarding child labor laws as specified in the California Labor Code may be helpful to you. If you live in another state, you might want to use this as your guide. It is up to you to protect your child. All management cares about is getting the film in the can.

Working Hours

✦ *The number of hours minors are permitted at the place of employment within a twenty-four hour period is limited according to age. Travel time must be considered working time.*
Babies under fifteen days old are not permitted to work. Babies fifteen days to six months old may be on the set no more than two hours, but may work no more than twenty minutes.
Babies six months to two years may be on the set for four hours, but may work no more than two hours, the balance of time reserved for rest and recreation.
Children two to six years old may be on the set for six hours, but may work no more than three hours, the balance of time is reserved for rest and recreation.
Children six to nine years old may be on the set for eight hours. When school is in session, they may work only four hours and must receive three hours of schooling with one hour for rest and recreation. When school is not in session, they

may work six hours, the balance to be used for rest and recreation.

Children from nine to sixteen years old may be on the set for nine hours. When school is in session, they may work five hours and must receive three hours of schooling with the balance to be used for rest and recreation. When school is not in session, they may work seven hours, the balance to be used for rest and recreation.

Children from sixteen to eighteen years old may be on the set for ten hours. When school is in session, they may work six hours and must receive three hours of schooling with the balance to be used for rest and recreation. When school is not in session, they may work eight hours, the balance for rest and recreation.

All minors under sixteen years of age: A studio teacher must be provided and has the responsibility for caring and attending to the health, safety and morals of the minor. For babies fifteen days to six weeks, a nurse must be present. A parent or guardian must be present on the set or location for all minors.

All minors under eighteen years of age must have a permit to work issued by the Labor Commissioner and their employers must also obtain a permit to employ. These permits are not required if the minor is sixteen or seventeen and is a high school graduate or has a certificate of proficiency.

California laws apply when a California employer takes a resident minor out of state. The hours at the place of employment as shown above may be extended by no more than one-half hour for meal periods.

Twelve hours must elapse between the minor's time of dismissal and time of call on the following day. For purposes of the California labor code, the entertainment industry is defined as: Any organization, or individual, using the services of any minor in: motion pictures of any type (film, videotape, etc.), using any format (theatrical, film, commercial, documentary, television program, etc.), photography, recording, theatrical productions, publicity, rodeos, circuses, musical performances and any other performances where minors perform to entertain the public.

David Robb, *Variety*[70]

If you live in Los Angeles, the Screen Actors Guild holds a special Young Performer's Orientation that occurs the third Tuesday of each month at 7 p.m. in the James Cagney Room on the first floor of the Guild headquarters at 5757 Wilshire Blvd. Current labor laws and contract provisions pertaining to minors are reviewed.

Actors' Equity

Although Actors' Equity (the union for actors working in the theater) oversees the contracts of many children working in shows like

Miss Saigon and *The Sound of Music*, not only in New York City but in cities all over the country, the union has no provisions in their contracts for young performers.

They do, however offer seminars on topics such as: Touring and the Family; Interaction with Agents, Managers, and Financial Advisors; Careers Behind the Scenes and The Transition from Child to Adult Performer.

Managers

There's a full treatment of the pros and cons of having managers in Chapter 15. If you are prepared to be your child's manager, then you must learn everything about the business you can. How to get work permits, the right teachers to study with, etc. If you have no idea how to start, getting a manager might a good idea. Agents are sometimes reluctant to sign child actors whose parents know nothing about the business as they end up spending so much time educating them.

If you've got the skill set to be your child's advocate and learn enough about the business on your own, you can act as your child's manager yourself. If you don't, it's likely you could use some guidance concerning pictures, resumes, proper training and set behavior.

Managers also have a pulse on the agents in the area, know the demands of the marketplace, and can arrange meetings with various agents and oversee those relationships. It's not necessary to have a manager, but it can save you time. If your child is marketable, you can easily act as his/her manager. Just send good snapshots to a children's agent along with a letter telling them about the child. If they feel the child can work, most will be happy to educate you.

Managers are not licensed or franchised, nor do they have any rules governing them. Just like agents, there are really good managers and really bad ones. Many managers charge a 10%-15% commission on top of the 10% charged by agents.

Some managers coach their kids, nurture them, help choose appropriate classes, and go with them on the interviews.

Do not do business with any manager who charges a fee to be listed with them. Not only is that unethical, that usually means the manager has no access and doesn't expect the child to make money.

Set Behavior

If your child does work in the business, it is your responsibility to make sure the he does not dominate the set. Neither the director, the assistant director, nor the other actors are responsible for parenting your child. If your child acts like a child and is obnoxious from time to time, it is not the responsibility of the creative staff to keep him in line.

You might feel that if the director or the assistant director disciplines your child, he might be more likely to respond. Don't give up your place with your child. It's up to you to make sure he behaves not only professionally, but as a happy addition to the set.

If your child is going to be on the set, he should be on time, attentive, respectful and as focused as possible. This is why I don't think it's a good idea to make a child conform this much until he is an adult. He is being paid as an adult and it is extremely rude and unfair to the adults on the set (who are trying to be accommodating, but also have their own jobs to attend to) when he is allowed to absorb everyone else's time and energy.

Jodie Foster, Elizabeth Taylor, Mickey Rooney, Shirley Temple, and Ron Howard are the only mega-famous child stars I can think of who seemed to have made it to adulthood intact. Few are able to balance showbiz success with a successful adulthood beyond the business.

Ron Howard's father Rance says that one reason Ron never lost his perspective was that Rance and his wife (both actors) made sure that they never used Ron's money to upgrade their standard of living. As long as they were still supporting Ron and the family, they retained their parental position in the family and Ron was able to stay a little boy.

It's hard to come down hard on someone who is paying your rent or who has enough money to leave at the first cross word.

Sacrifices for Everyone

Rick Schroder was Ricky Schroder, three months old and living on Staten Island, when he started going out on photo shoots in Manhattan. He had made sixty commercials by the time he was six. His parents both worked for the phone company and his mom quit to stay at home with Ricky and his sister. What started as a way for the family to make extra money soon took over everyone's life.

✦   *Schroder's success in "The Champ" led to other movies and then to "Silver Spoons" which required him to move to Los Angeles. "My father kept his job in New York and flew back and forth every weekend," he said. "My parents weren't together five days a week. They really sacrificed for my career."*
Tom Seligson, *Parade Magazine*[71]

Although Rick's mom made sure that he retained the right to act like a kid, it was still difficult.

✦   *My mother was the best mother. I remember when I was doing "The Champ," I was playing on the ground, getting grass stains on my pants. The wardrobe person told me to sit down and behave, that I was in wardrobe.*
   My mother rushed over and said, "Well you better get three changes of pants for him, because there's no way he's going to be expected to act like a little robot. He's a little boy, and if he gets dirty, so be it." That was her attitude; she protected me and tried to keep it all as normal as possible.
Ibid[72]

Even though his mother protected him, Schroder has no thoughts of allowing his own kids to become actors.

✦   *"If they want to become actors when they're a lot older, then I'll support them, but not before," he explained. "It's difficult being a child actor. I don't think everything beautiful has to be exploited. Some things can be beautiful and left beautiful."*
Ibid[73]

Kids/Money

So, after all the classes, coaching, auditioning and missing baseball games and Brownie meetings, what are the possible financial rewards?

✦   *"On most shows, kids start around $5,000 an episode," says one executive. "They tend to have built-in raises [like adult actors] that are 5% or, if they're lucky, 10% per year. They sign seven-year contracts; virtually no one will hire a performer without that. With breakout characters, I'd say renegotiation is the norm*

by the third or fourth year on a successful show. But you only give more money in return for something else."
Stephen Galloway, *Hollywood Reporter Showbiz Kids Special Issue*[74]

Before you put those numbers into your calculator, understand that even though there are usually twenty-two shows in a season, not all performers on a show are signed for all shows. A usual contract can call for seven of thirteen shows or ten of thirteen. That formula translates to twelve of twenty-two and so on.

The contract that confines the actor does not bind the producer. Every year when/if the show is picked up, management has the right not to exercise the option on the actor's services. No such alternative exists for the actor unless you can negotiate for that.

Minorities/Girls/Boys

Just as in the adult world, there are more jobs for little white boys than for anyone else. In the Special Showbiz Kids Issue of *The Hollywood Reporter,* casting directors Jane Jenkins and Janet Hirshenson (who have cast youngsters in *Mrs. Doubtfire, My Life, Jurassic Park, Dennis the Menace,* and many other films) were interviewed concerning the discrepancy in the numbers of parts for girls and boys.

✦   *I think it's largely a similar situation for little-girl actresses as it is for big-girl actresses. The majority of the scripts that are written are written by men and they write about their own childhoods. And the majority of men are directors and producers, and so they pick material that has some personal meaning to them.*

There are just very few projects that really feature strong women, although there are a few more now than there used to be.
Stephen Galloway, *The Hollywood Reporter Showbiz Kids Special Issue*[75]

Kim Fields played Tootie on NBC's hit sitcom *The Facts of Life*, the only black actress in an all white show. She also starred on Fox's *Living Single*. She was asked if it was tough overcoming the obstacles of being a black woman.

✦   *I didn't look at them as obstacles, just non-changing facts. My sex wasn't changing, my race wasn't changing. So it just became a part of the package.*
Michael Arkush, *Los Angeles Times*[76]

We all have to find a way to think positively about unchanging facts. One of those rare kid actors who has managed to translate her earlier success into adult employment, Kim has worked to expand herself. She earned a degree in telecommunications from Pepperdine University and is not only directing for the theater, but has produced her own 35-minute short film. She talked candidly about her own rough times:

✦ *Just knowing I had something to fall back on helped. The work ethic didn't just disintegrate. The doubts fueled positive motivation that I needed to learn how to do something else, so I wouldn't be sitting around waiting for my agent to call. I would have gone crazy sitting in my apartment doing that. I learned how to direct and produce. I got my education, so that validates me.*
Ibid[77]

Gullible Parents

In every business, there are unscrupulous characters seeking to separate the vulnerable from their money. No one can guarantee your child an audition, a job, or a career. All an agent or manager can do is promise to introduce your child to buyers. Some agents and managers have more ability to do that than others, but none of them should be selling photographers, classes, or coaches.

If you are encouraged by an agent or a manager to pay to see them, to pay to be listed with them, to use their photographer, or to pay them for acting lessons, beware.

✦ *Two operators of a Beverly Hills talent agency who claimed they could turn children into actors and models have been ordered to spend thirty days in jail for making false promises to parents, who sometimes paid thousands of dollars up-front.*

"Most of the parents had been enticed by telemarketers to bring their children to auditions sponsored by West Coast Talent," Lambert said. "After the auditions," he said, "the agency pressured clients to pay fees for acting classes, photo portfolios, and the chance to audition in front of casting directors."

Sandy Bosnich, one of the original claimants, said she paid $6,000 to West Coast Talent after she was told her three daughters all had the potential for success in commercials. She said the company provided photographs and acting classes but never fulfilled the promise of work. Lambert said the families never got such auditions.
Kurt Streeter, *Los Angeles Times*[78]

A Final Word to Parents

Think carefully before exposing yourself or your child to showbiz. It's a heartbreaker for adults and even harder for people who have not yet reached their own personhood and therefore cannot really make an educated decision.

Obviously money is the lure that seduces parents to not only give up their own free time, but their kid's childhood as well. If it's just a little money and a little time, if a career in showbusiness can be seen, as Judy Savage suggests, as an alternative to dance class or Little League, maybe that's a good tradeoff. However, when there is a lot of money at stake, that's a trap for all involved. And you never know what will happen.

Currently advertisers are concentrating on younger and younger children as customers not only for toys, but for every kind of entertainment. That means casting directors for commercials, film, television, and print modeling are constantly looking for the newest, cutest, most unusual, most precocious, most normal, weirdest kids they can find.

The whole child actor market has become so lucrative that even the conglomerate agencies have opened departments for young actors.

Money-making potential is also the thing that makes your child attractive to agents and managers who might like to usurp the parents' place in the child's life.

Be careful.

Wrap Up

✓ you only have one shot at being a kid
✓ your child receives adult pay and should behave as one
✓ know the Child Labor Laws of your state
✓ make your own code if your state has none or if it's inadequate
✓ don't live on your child's money
✓ be informed/not gullible
✓ there is no free lunch/don't be greedy

☇ 11 ☈

Ways into the Business

Other than having a father as a studio head, there is absolutely no better way to enter the business than by graduating from one of the preferred conservatory schools. Although there is nothing like experience to teach actors about acting, training should make you a better actor and give you confidence. If you go to a status conservatory, you can enter the marketplace on a higher level than you could in any other way.

You may still not be one of those fortunate actors who walks from school into a job, but many doors will open to you that the rest of us can only dream about.

Determining the hot school at the moment demands up-to-the-minute research. Just as an agent's fortune rises and falls with the success of his clients, a university's fortune is tied to the faculty that produces graduates who become distinguished in their field.

There is a wealth of information available if you just do the research. When Rutgers University was recommended, I checked their webpage and found the names of successful actors that the highly regarded chairman of the graduate department, William Esper, had trained.

On your quest for information, evaluate the background of the faculty and the curriculum. Make sure there is a full-time program that includes training in speech, voice, and movement.

One of the reasons that top schools are able to produce successful actors is not only the quality of the faculty, but the quality of the students they are able to attract. When you screen 600 women and 400 men to find the eight women and twelve men you will admit for your program, your chance of choosing winners increases.

This article from *Yale Herald* is over ten years old but I see nothing that makes me think things have changed.

✦ *Last year, 1,270 hopefuls applied to the Yale School of Drama. Sixty-eight got in. That's a five percent acceptance rate. And you thought getting into Yale*

College was hard.

A look at the bare facts of Drama School admissions is daunting: Out of the thousands of hopefuls who request information, out of the hundreds who actually apply, out of the dozens who are granted interviews or auditions, a mere fraction actually make it past the final cut and spend three years learning in what is arguably the finest Master of Fine Arts (MFA) program in the country.

Admissions is "an enormously difficult process," Earle Gister, director of the acting department, said. Gister sees approximately 900 actors every year, in New Haven, Chicago, and San Francisco. He picks sixteen. Gister has been teaching and auditioning actors for thirty-four years, seventeen at Yale, and his criteria haven't changed.

Siobhan Peiffer, *Yale Herald*[79]

Although requirements for admission into conservatory programs are rigorous, the applicants are usually chosen solely on their auditions. Some actors, writers, and directors who attended these highly-touted schools tell me they don't feel their education is necessarily superior, but that the network of achievers they encountered was worth the tuition.

There is a list of schools whose acting graduates instantly alert the antennae of agents, producers, and casting directors and are perceived as the next Paul Newman and Meryl Streep. If nothing else, the buyers realize that the screening process (in addition to the demanding course of studies) enhances the students potential for stardom.

The list of schools whose graduates are anointed for brilliance varies slightly depending on whom you interview. No one wants to take responsibility for saying one school belongs and another one doesn't. So based on hearsay and research, these are at least thought of by more people than others to be the schools for actors at this moment in time. You'll be able to get an overview of the school and its curriculum from their web pages.

Who's Cool?

Whether or not a school should be included in the connected list depends on who you talk to. Andy Lawler was an still an agent at DGRW in New York when he fearlessly spoke these words of wisdom on schools:

✦ *The two best musical theater programs in the country belong to the Cincinnati*

Conservatory of Music and the Boston Conservatory of Music. Each year, these schools' industry showcases attract almost every agent and casting director in New York City. Their graduates probably have the highest employment percentage of ANY drama school, musical or otherwise, graduate or undergraduate.

Juilliard is, of course, one of the two or three best drama programs in the country, but does not specialize in musicals. Nonetheless many Broadway musical stars have gotten their start there, including Patti LuPone and Kevin Kline.

A number of other schools offer good programs as well, although they lack the prestige of the above mentioned three: Carnegie Mellon, Northwestern, and, to a lesser extent, Michigan and NYU. Questions you need to ask are:

Does it offer a Bachelor of Fine Arts or a Bachelor of Arts degree? Aim for the BFA, as that's the sign of an actual professional training program. Does it offer a showcase in NYC or LA? There's little point investing in a degree if the industry doesn't see you at the end of it. What sort of performance options do you have? How recently have the faculty actually been participating in the biz?

A note of caution to close. Remember that everyone auditioning for these programs has been the star of their schools. Stature at your high school rarely guarantees success beyond. However, don't be intimidated by a lackluster resume either. What gets people into these schools is their audition and their look, and nothing else will really matter.

Andy Lawler

Here is a list of other schools, based on hearsay and research that are thought to be the chosen schools at this moment in time. The best way to judge is to check out the curriculum as well as the track record of graduates via their web pages.

American Conservatory Theater, Carey Perloff
30 Grant Avenue, 6th Floor
San Francisco, CA 94108
415-834-3200
www.act-sfbay.org/conservatory/index.html

Carnegie Mellon, Drama Department/Elizabeth Bradley
College of Fine Arts/School of Drama
5000 Forbes Avenue, Room #108
Pittsburgh, PA 15213
412-268-2392
www.cmu.edu/cfa/drama

Columbia University in the City of New York, Kristin Linklater
305 Dodge Hall, Mail Code 1808
2960 Broadway
New York, NY 10027-6902
212-854-2875
www.columbia.edu/cu/arts

Harvard University, Richard Orchard
American Repertory Theater/Loeb Drama Center
64 Brattle Street
Cambridge, MA 02138
617-495-2668
www.amrep.org

Juilliard School, Kathy Hood, Director of Admissions
60 Lincoln Center Plaza
New York, NY 10023
212-799-5000 Ext. 4
www.juilliard.edu/splash.html

New York University/Drama Department
Arthur Bartow, Artistic Director
721 Broadway, 3rd Floor
New York, NY 10003
212-998-1850
www.nyu.edu/tisch

North Carolina School of the Arts, Gerald Freedman
Post Office Box 12189, 1533 Main Street
Winston-Salem, NC 27117-2189
336-770-3235
www.ncarts.edu

Northwestern School of Communications, Dean Barbara O'Keefe
Frances Searle Building
2240 Campus Drive
Evanston, IL 60208
847-491-7023
www.communication.northwestern.edu

State University of New York (at Purchase), Dean Irby
735 Anderson Hill Road
Purchase, NY 10577
914-251-6360
www.purchase.edu/academics/taf

Yale School of Drama, Yale University, Lloyd Richards
Post Office Box 208325
New Haven, CT 06520-8325
203-432-1505
www.yale.edu/drama

As long as you are wishing, if you have the time, money, and visa to study abroad, it seems to me that attending London's Central School, alma mater of actors Judi Dench, Julie Christie, Peggy Ashcroft, Claire Bloom, George Rose, Vanessa Redgrave, Alice Krige, Mary Ure, Harold Pinter, Natasha Richardson, Kristin Scott-Thomas, Zoe Wanamaker, and a zillion others would be very close to heaven.

I'm sure you learn the same things you'd learn at Yale Drama school, but I don't see the same things mentioned on the Yale webpage. I'm excerpting a small part here, but go to their webpage *www.cssd.ac.uk/* for the full story. There are aid packages for US students. When you finish the program, you have full Equity status (probably British Equity) and are allowed to stay an extra year on your visa to work if you can get hired.

If I were just starting out and had the Central School as an option, I'd think about it.

✦ *As well as developing performance skills you will learn self-motivation, self-discipline, and critical thinking. You will be expected to maintain a rigorous code of professional conduct throughout the course - a crucial part of your training for the industry.*

You will develop complementary personal skills in self-motivation, self-discipline, initiative, time management, and critical reflection. You are not just learning performance skills, you are developing as an individual. You will also find that students are required to maintain a rigorous code of professional conduct throughout the course. This is a part of your training for the profession.
Central School of London Webpage/*www.cssd.ac.uk/*[80]

Another exotic option is the Actors Centre in Sydney, Australia where Hugh Jackman trained. Their webpage will enrich your fantasy life, if nothing else. One of the perks that interested me is that when you finish, you have a professional DVD of your work. Why don't our schools do that?

Actors Centre
241 Devonshire Street
Surry Hills, Sydney NSW 2010
Australia
(+61 2) 9310 4077/fax (+61 2) 9310 2891
www.actorscentre.com.au

Don't forgo your education just because you can't afford or can't get into Yale or Juilliard or any of the other status schools. However, if you gain admittance you are in a select group.

Actors from these programs are courted by agents and some even have agents as early as freshman year. The career boost by the annual showcase of graduating students produced specifically for an audience of agents and casting directors in New York and Los Angeles can be priceless.

✦ *Although the leagues may sometimes lead to auditions for immediate employment on a soap opera, in summer stock, in an off-Broadway play, more often it serves as a casting director's mental Rolodex of actors to use in future projects.*
Jill Gerston, *The New York Times*[81]

Conservatory education requires a big commitment of time and money. Choose the school that is right for you.

Even if you are educated at the best schools and arrive highly touted with interest from agents, ex-William Morris agent Joanna Ross told me there is still a period of adjustment.

✦ *When you come out of school, you gotta freak out for a while. Actors in high-powered training programs working night and day doing seven different things at once get out of school and suddenly there is no demand for their energy. It takes a year, at least, to learn to be unemployed. And they have to learn to deal with that. It happens to everybody. It's not just you.*
Joanna Ross

Even if you can't make it to a league school, all is not lost.

◆ *The truth is, a great performance in the leagues can jump-start a career, but if these kids have talent, they'll get noticed. They just won't be as fast out of the starting gate...they just have to do it the old-fashioned way by pounding the pavements, reading "Back Stage," calling up friends, going to see directors they know and knocking on agents' doors.*
Jill Gerston, *The New York Times*[82]

And maybe faster out of the gate isn't the best way to go anyway. I think it's easier to deal with success when it comes to you gradually. If it comes too swiftly, you think it's always going to be that way. I know I did and I'm here to tell you, it doesn't. No matter who you are or where you studied, careers ebb and flow.

Industry Jobs

The next best successful method of entry is to get any kind of job at any studio, casting director's office, or talent agency. Many studios and agencies have temp pools of overqualified people to call when an employee is out. Your assignment could be anything from picking up an actor at the airport and delivering him to the set, to working in the mailroom, being a production assistant, or driving a producer to appointments. I know of several people who worked as drivers and managed to pass their material on to staff writers who became their advocates.

Though there are temp agencies which specialize in providing workers for networks and studios, Ken Raskoff, head of scripted film and television development and production for Mark Burnett, entered the business through temp work as a secretary. He said he got more access to creative people via a regular temp agency. There is more opportunity for showbiz related jobs in Los Angeles, but there are jobs in New York as well.

You don't get to choose where you are going to work if you go through an employment agency, of course, but you can end up working at WMA, ICM, Paradigm, CAA, or any of the big agencies, production companies, or networks. Any destination will be illuminating.

Check the temp ads in the trades or call a studio yourself and ask if there is an in-house temporary employment pool. Many temp jobs work into regular employment if you strike the fancy of your employers and are clearly motivated.

I don't want to imply that getting a show biz job is a piece of cake, but if you apply yourself, you can do it. No matter what city you live in, there is some kind of show biz community of work. Check out your local opportunities.

Internships

If you can't get an industry job, an internship is also a great beginning. There is a lot of competition for the choice spots, but someone gets them so it might as well be you. Many universities post industry internship possibilities on their bulletin boards. If your school doesn't or if you are not in school, it's still possible to track down your own internship. A good place to start is through the Academy of Television Arts and Sciences who sponsor an annual summer internship program.

The Television Academy's internships are designed to provide qualified full-time graduate and undergraduate students and recent graduates with in-depth exposure to professional television production facilities, techniques, and practices.

✦ *Internships exist in 27 categories: Agency, Casting, Animation-Traditional, Animation-Non-Traditional (computer generated), Broadcast Advertising & Promotion, Business Affairs, Art Direction, Commercials, Children's Programming/Development, Cinematography, Costume Design, Development, Documentary/Reality Production, Editing, Entertainment News, Episodic Series, Movies for Television, Music, Network Programming Management, Production Management, Public Relations & Publicity, Sound, Syndication/Distribution, Television Directing/Single Camera, Television Directing/Multi-Camera, Television Scriptwriting, and Videotape Post Production.*

There is no application fee. Last year, out of approximately 1,000 applicants, 28 were selected. The Princeton Review has recognized the ATAS program as one of the top ten internship programs of any kind in the United States.

If you are currently enrolled as a full-time student in a U.S. college or university (undergraduate or graduate) or you graduated after January 1 (of the current year) you are eligible to apply for the Summer Competition. (Taking extension courses does not make one eligible.) Foreign students are eligible if they meet the above requirements.

Most internships begin during mid to late June or early July depending on the schedule of the company which hosts the internship. Each internship ends eight weeks *after the start date. (The music category, however, starts in late July or August.) All positions are full-time. All internships are located in the Los Angeles area. Each intern receives a stipend of $2,000. Interns whose permanent residence is outside Los Angeles County will receive an additional $400 to help defray travel/housing expenses.*

Academy of Television Arts and Sciences/*www.emmy.org.*

Flyers are mailed to Career Resource Centers and TV/Film Departments nationwide. Check the webpage for the current guidelines. They will send you information if you call their office, 818-754-2830.

There are no job guarantees, but a good internship experience can put you ahead of the pack. Academy interns learn a lot about how the television business works and definitely access the system, at least for that moment in time.

Although it would be ideal if your school set you up with internship entree, a selective mailing to places that interest you would certainly get you some phone calls.

Sara Dulaney Gilbert's excellent resource book *Internships* (an Arco book by Macmillan USA) lists many more and would be worth adding to your list of resources.

Industry Classes

Whether you came from a League School or don't have a degree at all, a way to not only broaden your entertainment industry education, but to gain access to some of the most successful writers, directors, and agents in the business is to take an extension class at UCLA and USC. The regular faculty at these schools is pretty terrific with Jason Alexander dropping in to teach acting at USC and *Variety* editor Peter Bart and entertainment lawyer Mark Litwak often teaching extension classes at UCLA.

The creme de le creme of the business side of the business allows its resources to be tapped for UCLA extension classes, so take advantage of the opportunity. USC's program is not as accessible nor as extensive, but still, if you might run into Steven Spielberg on campus, it might be worth thinking about.

The Learning Annex also sponsors such classes. The classes are usually very small (if they're not taught by casting directors or agents) so you have a chance to get up close and personal with the instructor.

With an industry job, connections, good energy, and a growing education about the business, the next most logical thing to do is to produce. Even someone with connections, visibility and great credits like Michael Douglas came to that conclusion a long long time ago.

In the seventies, Douglas was a success on a hit television series, *The Streets of San Francisco*. Many actors might have banked that money, considered themselves a success, and waited out the overexposure and lack of work that frequently comes after such high visibility and hoped for the best.

But Douglas wanted a film career. When no one appeared to be interested, Douglas (being the entrepreneurial person that he is) figured out a way to become a force in the business. Fourteen years earlier, his father had bought the rights to a property in which he hoped to star. Michael rescued the orphaned material in 1975 and found a way to make *One Flew Over the Cuckoo's Nest* into an Academy Award winning film.

Once he was a successful producer, he had the attention and respect of the film community, but still had no interesting acting offers. So in 1979 he produced *The China Syndrome* before producing and starring in *Romancing the Stone* in 1984. Douglas' career has changed now and he's more focused on his family, but his accomplishments stand.

It's true he had a rich, powerful, and successful father. Because of his background, he obviously had a close-up view of how business was conducted in the film community. It's also true that not all star offspring manage to translate this largesse into brilliant careers. The bottom line is that Michael Douglas went in and created his own professional life.

Actress Illeana Douglas (no relation) had a breakthrough experience in the film *Café Fear*. The following year, she shared a page in *Film Comment* with John Leguizamo, Brad Pitt, and Samuel L. Jackson as *New Faces of the Year*. But, as Douglas wrote in *Premiere*, just as Brad Pitt was signing at CAA, she was at yet another audition.

Taking her career into her own hands, she took the money she had made from the movie *Alive* and decided to produce her own movie.

✦ *... Shooting a movie in two days has its drawbacks. While the actresses showed up for Day Two the crew did not. But the greatest thing about such disasters is that* *there's no turning back. "In the end, I was able to accomplish two things: use personal material (making fun of women as victims, mainly myself) and do in ten minutes what most major studios can't do in two hours: give thirty women a job. Much to my surprise, 'The Perfect Woman' took on a life of its own. It traveled the festival circuit (including Sundance, Aspen and Edinburgh) and closed the New York Film Festival, sharing the bill with 'The Piano.' It played on Bravo and was picked up by Miramax to be distributed with 'Camilla.'" So an actress who just wanted to work ended up being a director to find work for herself.*

... Gus Van Sant gave me a picture he had painted. The inscription on the back reads, 'Be your own flying saucer...rescue yourself.' And you can do that anywhere.

Illeana Douglas, *Premiere Magazine*[83]

That pretty much says it, doesn't it?

Wrap Up

Ways in

✓ father owns the studio
✓ connected conservatory schools
✓ industry job
✓ internships
✓ industry classes

Best Resource

✓ yourself
✓ produce
✓ be your own flying saucer

⚔ 12 ⚔.
Actually Pursuing Work

The best way to look for work is to work. Since you can't be in the union until you get a job, but you can't have a job until you are in the union, how are you going to scale the castle walls?

Actually, you can find work, just not union work. I know you want to join the union and become a professional actor as soon as possible, but have patience; it's not wise to join the union until you have amassed a few impressive credits and (in LA/NY at least) have some film to show. At that point, when you are actually marketable, then it's time to join the union.

Otherwise, you not only pay a considerable fee to join, but take yourself out of the non-union marketplace (where you might actually find work) to join 120,000 Screen Actors Guild members who have more credits and experience than you in pursuit of a minimal number of jobs. Check out Chapter 17 for more information about unions.

Pictures and Resumes

Before you can really follow up on anything, you'll need a picture and resume. No matter what market you are in, you are going to have to come up with pictures and resumes. You will need pictures for the newspapers, casting directors and producers as well as to introduce yourself to the various organizations in your community.

When selecting a photographer, check other actors' pictures to see what appeals to you. Check all your own pictures, including snapshots, to discover what is most interesting about the best ones. If you feel you can't analyze them appropriately, consider taking a photography or art class to develop a more discerning eye.

One of my favorite New York photographers, Van Williams, knows how anxious actors can get about having their pictures made, so he encourages them to go through a warmup routine of exercises to relax themselves. I think stretching as you finish putting on your wardrobe is a good idea. If you can make time to meditate for a few minutes before your pictures, that would also be a help.

The most important aspect of any photo is that it look exactly like you. It's self-defeating to choose a photographer who takes glamour photos if you are a regular person. If a casting director calls you in expecting to see Halle Berry and you are Kathy Bates, he is not going to be pleased. Ditto the other way round.

Forget about trying to change people's minds; casting directors are busy. They have their orders from on high, and they are trying to fill them.

Analyze every picture you see. Look at the pictures your friends are using, but don't let those pictures make your decisions; just use them for research. Make up your own mind. When I am choosing my own pictures from a contact sheet, I try to decide which of the images is the person I would want to approach and speak to at a party. Then I check to make sure all parts of the picture are sharp and clear and that the top of my head is not cut off. These things seem elemental, but you would be surprised what some photographers get away with when actors are just concentrating on their faces.

If you have an agent and/or a manager, it is always wise to get his input regarding these decisions since he will be selling you via the pictures. He will have concrete ideas about what is best. Learn more by asking him how he made his choices.

It's usually not a good idea to let photographers choose. Their criteria for a good picture is not yours. They are not necessarily in a position to know what is the best representation of you relative to selling yourself as an actor.

With Photoshop or its little brother, Elements, you can doctor photos yourself if you put your mind to it. Maybe a friend with a digital camera can look at pictures that interest you and take some photos that will get the job done.

Wardrobe

Consider the purpose of the photos when you are choosing wardrobe. Commercial casting directors usually like to see you in plaid shirts/blouses and sweaters. Theatrical pictures need to sell you in a more formal way. Musical performers require a trendier approach. Study pictures of people in your field for ideas. Make sure your photo fulfills the appropriate criteria.

In general, buyers are interested in a full-front representation of you.

No hands up to the face; it's too distracting. Choose clothing that is relatively plain. You're not selling clothes; you want them looking at you.

Your resume is stapled to the back of your 8x10 color matte print so that when you turn your picture over (like the page of a book) the resume is ready to read. You can have your picture printed with or without a white border with the name printed on the front.

Constructing Your Resume

The buyers see hundreds of resumes every day. Yours should be simple and easy to read. Not only is it not necessary to have millions of jobs listed, but when prospective employers see too much writing, their eyes will glaze over and they won't read anything. Choose the most impressive credits and list them.

There is a prototype on the following page for you to use as a guide for form. If you have nothing to put on your resume, list your training and a physical description. Lead with your strong suit. If you have done more commercials than anything else, list that as your first category; if you are a singer, list music.

Choose a font for your resume that is easy to read. When casting directors, producers and agents are reading resumes, they want to be able to read quickly and comfortably.

You may live in a market where theatre credits are taken very seriously. If so, even though you may have done more commercials, lead with theatre if you have anything credible to report. Adapt this prototype to meet your needs. If all you have done is college theatre, list it. That is more than someone else has done and it will give the buyer an idea of what you can do.

If you do book reviews, list places where you did them. If you sing, list where. Note that you were master of ceremonies for your town's Pioneer Day Celebration. Whatever. As you have more important credits, drop the less impressive ones.

My own opinion is not to put your union affiliation (Screen Actors Guild, Actors Equity Association, American Federation of Television and Radio Artists) on the resume. Writing down that you are a member of the union makes me think you just got accepted into the union and/or have nothing else to write on the resume. There are credible people who disagree with me on this, so make up your own mind.

Mary Smith/323-555-1212

5'4" 115 lbs, blonde hair, blue eyes

Theatre

Paradise Lost.	Boston Court Theatre
The Adding Machine.	LaJolla Playhouse
A Little Night Music.	South Coast Repertory

Film

The Jane Austen Book Club.	directed by Robin Swicord
Knocked Up.	directed by Judd Apatow
The Ten	directed by David Wain

Television

Boston Legal.	directed by Ellie Kanner
The Closer.	directed by Gloria Muzio
'Til Death.	directed by James Widdoes

Training

Acting.	Larry Moss, Allan Miller
Singing.	Suzanne Kietchel
Dialects.	Joel Goldes, Jessica Drake, Paul St. Peter
Dance.	Valentina Oumansky, Lula Washington

Special Skills

guitar, horseback riding, martial arts, street performer, British and Spanish dialects, gourmet cook, have British passport, etc.

The most important thing on your resume is that your name and contact number be prominently displayed. If you have an agent, use his phone number instead of yours. If you don't have an agent, list an answering service or phone mail. It's safer and more professional not to list your personal number for business phone calls.

Located in both Hollywood and in Studio City, and online, Ray's Photolab makes beautiful copies. A photographer I know won't let his clients go anyplace else. When I got my pictures, I knew why. They are terrific. Color prices are great: $42 for 25, $52 for 50, $79 for 100, etc. Set up fee is extra. 323-463-0555 and 818-760-3656. *www.raysphotolab.com*

Two Los Angeles resources for putting your reel together and/or getting it copied are EditPlus.tv and uptodatereels.com. Edit Plus (formerly Phaze-L) provides every kind of service from shooting your reel to assembling the pieces you already have to uploading it to your webhost. Their prices are great. *www.editplus.tv*.

Partners Denton Heaney and Josh Orenstein's backgrounds in agenting and production give Uptodatereels.com an inside track at producing DVDs that both your agent and casting directors will love. Their demo/speed reels feature all your clips with a menu to select just what the CD needs. *www.uptodatereels.com*

Online Databases

Not counting *www.imdb.com* (where it's free to list all your credits) and *www.imdbpro.com* (which costs but you can add your reel), the top three online databases for actors are LA Casting (aka Casting Networks), Breakdown Services (aka Actors Access), and Now Casting (which includes Players Directory).

These companies provide online billboards for your resumes, headshots, and demo reels and offer a variety of marketing tools and services for actors. The fees for casting submissions and demo reel maintenance vary from company to company. It's advised to be at least listed in all three databases.

LA Casting is Los Angeles based and almost exclusively handles online commercial casting. Breakdown Services and Now Casting cover the world with casting data for film, theatre and television. Breakdown Services, the oldest, most established company, currently handles the bulk of information between casting directors and agents. Now Casting, the innovator of online actor submissions, has entered into an agreement with Baseline Studio Systems as provider of actor data.

Go to Baseline's webpage to learn about their services, register for their free newsletter and enter your own data.

LA Casting/*www.lacasting.com*
Breakdown Services/*www.breakdownservices.com*

Being Available

We are in a business where nothing happens at all for days and weeks and then your agent calls and someone wants you ten minutes ago. Make sure you are always ready for that call. Have call waiting on both your home line and your cell. Make it easy for a buyer to reach you. Have a reliable answering machine and/or beeper. Make sure your agent has all your phone numbers. If you give him your cell phone number, make sure you have it turned on. Check messages on both your machine and cell phone religiously.

In the meantime, stay connected in other ways. Read the trades. Read the popular press. See what's happening. Notice who is working. Know what's playing in town. See everything that's playing in town. Read a play a day.

If a theatre group is casting, go there. Audition. Find the play and read it. If you are right for a part, select the scene that shows that character best and learn it. Get a friend to read it with you and be prepared to read that scene when you arrive.

If management wants you to do a different scene, don't be afraid to suggest the one you are familiar with. They will probably let you do it. If not, ask for a few minutes to work on the alternate scene before reading. Do not read cold. You will never do as well as if you had prepared the material. No matter how well you think you are able to cold read, it will never be the work you could do if you were able to prepare ahead of time.

If you sing, offer your services at church or at a Lions Club Dinner even if you're in Los Angeles, New York, or Chicago. We all have to start somewhere. First appearances are probably not going to be all that successful. You don't have to invite anyone to see you fail, but get the failing over with so you can get to the good stuff.

There seems to be a certain no to yes ratio. Some actors say they get ten nos to every yes they receive. There are some periods of one's career when it certainly seems like you need fifty nos to get one yes. It's part of the business. That being the case, you may as well get started. The only problem is, every time you get a yes, there will still be fifty more nos lined up there someplace in your career waiting for you.

My brother is a salesman who seemingly thrives on abuse. Whenever a prospective customer keeps him waiting or treats him rudely, Jim just smiles to himself. He believes that people basically do feel guilty about bad behavior and he makes sure he capitalizes on that guilt by getting an even bigger order.

Focus

Producer Dan Faucci told me that when he was an actor, he met with two other actors three times a week for two hours to work on-camera, reading commercial copy and evaluating each other. I asked him if it helped him and if he began booking jobs. His answer:

✦ *Yes. We did book jobs, but I think it didn't matter whether or not we had the camera. It was the fact that we met three times a week focusing on what we wanted.*
Dan Faucci

Wherever something is happening, become a part of it. Be the master of ceremonies at the charity auction or be the host who greets everybody. Take every opportunity, no matter how menial, to get up in front of people and you'll find that with experience comes heightened self-esteem as well as skill. People will begin to think of you as the person who helps make their event work. If nothing is happening, find a way to stimulate some activity. If you get tired of being the one who always starts the merry-go-round, you are in the wrong business.

Whether you are in Podunk, New York, or Los Angeles, you have to make your own opportunities. Actress Nia Vardalos' *My Big Fat Greek Wedding* was a long-running show in both New York and Los Angeles well before Rita Wilson saw it and conscripted husband Tom Hanks to help her produce it.

✦ *Vardalos wrote and starred in the pic and also starred in the pilot after writing it with Marge McCall ("Just Shoot Me"). "It's the first time we've done a low-budget indie feature, and it has been a purely word-of-mouth movie that has connected with its audience and is being fueled by old-fashioned word of mouth," Goetzman said.*
Michael Fleming, *Variety*[84]

"Bob King, Saxophone"

My friend Bob King doesn't really act anymore, but when he was an actor pursuing agents, casting directors, and jobs, there was no one with as much wit and ingenuity. He started his attention-getting ploys as a young musician, playing the saxophone.

The way musicians got jobs at that time was to go to the hiring hall and wait to be called. Someone who needed a piano player would come in, stand up, and yell out "John Smith, piano," and John would get up and walk out with his new employer.

Even though Bob was young, he was mature looking enough to be considered. Instead of just sitting there waiting to be called, he walked in, cupped his hands and called out "Bob King, saxophone," and then appeared to see someone and walked out. After several weeks of that, one day a prospective employer asked who he was. Bob answered, "I'm Bob King. I play saxophone." The man replied, "Oh yeah, I've heard of you. Come on!"

That is absolutely one of the best stories about getting work I ever heard, topped only by a later story of Bob's. After his career as a musician ended, Bob became very popular in commercials. A casting director ran into him one day and said, "Oh, Bob. You are becoming the 'George Jenkins' of commercials." Bob didn't know what that meant, so he went to George Jenkins and asked. George replied, "Oh, that means you are getting ready to be overexposed. You'd better develop a voice-over career or something fast. I got overexposed and couldn't get an on-camera job for two years."

Like most of us in those days, Bob worked through many different agents for commercials and often had several auditions in a single day, so the next time an agent called him, he put a new plan into action. When an agent said, "Be at Y&R at 10 am for Lipton's Tea," Bob said, "Oh, could it be at 11:15? I have a voice-over booking." He continued to change every single appointment he got for the next two weeks until finally an agent said, "Well, who in the hell is getting you all this voice work?" Ever shrewd Bob answered sweetly: "Not you," and a big voice-over career was born.

Actors have been using their creativity for centuries figuring out how to get people to notice them. Post card campaigns. Balloon deliveries. Presents. Candy. Strip-O-Grams. These ideas have been used on agents so many times that they engender little more than a smile or a shake of the head coupled with eyes rolled heavenward.

I know an actor who did something extremely clever, only to have his agent (who had supported his idea initially) turn on him when the casting directors became offended.

The actor invested a lot of money, time, and imagination creating a milk carton filled with candy which he had delivered to the casting directors. The gimmick was that his picture was on all the milk cartons. Under it was written the word missing. The actor had been out of work for some length of time and was looking for a way to get himself back before the buyers. The milk carton also listed his description, credits, and agent's phone number.

As it turned out, some of the casting directors became offended with the milk carton idea. They felt that the whole idea of missing children and milk cartons was too important to be joked about. Well, of course, they're right. The actor had been so caught up in his own cleverness, he had not taken in the whole picture.

Good Work Demands Attention

Call yourself to the casting director's attention without seeming desperate and/or unemployed by doing good work. If you have to produce it yourself, do it. If you are good, the material is right, and you are ready, agents and casting directors will find you. In the meantime, be a good agent for yourself, read all casting notices, submit yourself for everything.

Take every job, be in every play, get up in front of people at every opportunity. This is part of your training and part of your life. People don't become actors to be shrinking violets.

The other part of this equation (which I cannot stress too strongly) is that one must get out of the business of being chosen and into the business of acting. It may be even more valuable to mount your own vehicle and act in it than for somebody else to hire you.

Gretchen Cryer and Nancy Ford, writers and composers of the Broadway show *I'm Getting My Act Together and Taking It on the Road*, say they only began being taken seriously when they began to produce their own material. Earlier productions had been noticed, but when they put their money on the table, they became part of the system in New York theatre.

I know how easy it is to be caught up in the madness of "I am only valid if somebody else chooses me," but if you indulge that kind of thinking, your life will be a nightmare. If you are constantly focused on being chosen, you can never become a valid person: you will always be second guessing what someone else might want.

Do they want me to be funny here? Uglier? Prettier? They don't know. When you go shopping you don't always know exactly what you want, but when your eye catches something, you know that was lingering in your subconscious the whole time: Yes, this is what I want, I didn't even know it existed, but I must have it.

Contacting Casting Directors

Most beginning (and even experienced) actors wouldn't dream of trying to call on a casting director personally, but casting directors are not as inaccessible as your fantasies might lead you to believe. I know an actor who had been quite successful in commercials in New York. For some reason (he now doesn't know why either), he had the idea that when he moved to Los Angeles, agents would be waiting for him with open arms. Of course, anyone who has spent any time in Los Angeles (or New York) will be happy to tell you that being a commercial actor or even a soap actor doesn't mean much to film and television people. It is a whole different part of the business.

My friend, a business-oriented and determined type, decided to do for himself what agents would not. He would get himself in to see the casting directors. He made a list and every day he targeted five casting directors to call. He sent a picture and resume. When he made the follow-up call, he always found out to whom he was speaking and noted the name and date.

Invariably, the casting director (or assistant) would say he was not seeing anyone right now. My friend then asked when he would be seeing people again. If the casting director said three weeks, the actor would note the date and call in three weeks. This went on until he actually got an appointment.

His feeling was that people begin to feel guilty after a while, and will finally see you just because they can't handle saying no again. He got a lot of jobs that way and eventually landed an agent.

So, if a casting director tells you to call back in three weeks, do so. Always call the person by name, "Hi, Mary? This is Kelly Smith again. How are you? What did you think about the Academy Awards

(Dodgers, earthquake, etc.)? Well, here I am again. Just wondering if you have any time for me to come meet with you. I'm going to be over in that direction tomorrow anyway."

Elizabeth Peña (*Resurrection Boulevard, Tortilla Soup*) got her first job in a feature by being relentless. After several fruitless months in Los Angeles, she read that *Down and Out In Beverly Hills* directed by Paul Mazursky was being cast. Undeterred by the fact that she had no agent, Peña began bombarding the film's casting director with photos, letters, and resumes. She finally persuaded a studio guard to deliver a demo tape and eventually wound up with the role of the sultry maid, Carmen.

✦ *I believe you should just go for it. There's no door thick enough; if it's too thick, you blast it open. If you have to get through, you have to get through.*

Elizabeth Peña, interviewed by Libby Slate, *Premiere Magazine*[85]

Kathy Najimy had already spent time doing stand-up, improvisation, and political theatre when she teamed up with Mo Gaffney to create a cabaret act that ran off-Broadway, won several Obies, and was made into an HBO special. From that exposure, Kathy was cast in six movies in two years, and she and Gaffney got a two-picture writing assignment with Hollywood Pictures and the CBS development deal that put her into *Veronica's Closet*.

Gary Sinise is another actor who took matters into his own hands.

✦ *I can honestly say that I've done everything I've wanted to do, always. Not without difficulty. But every time I wanted to do something, I just did it. From the age of eighteen when I started my own theatre with my friends. When I decided I wanted to act, I just bit the bullet. It's terribly difficult out here. There were plenty of times when I wasn't working.*

Gary Sinise, interviewed by Virginia Campbell, *Movieline*[86]

Action breeds success; go get things, go make things happen, go do the work. Once you become a force financially, there will be agents and managers who will want a piece of that and though they may want to initiate work for you, your vision still needs to fuel the engine. Sharon Stone has managed her career beautifully; I love what she says about taking risks:

✦ *I think risks are terribly exciting. I'd rather lose than be timid. After all, we're just the amalgamation of the experiences we've had. If you don't take risks,*

eventually, you're nothing.
Sharon Stone, interviewed by Virginia Campbell, *Movieline*[87]

Getting and Taking a Meeting

Pictures and resumes may sit in a pile by the door waiting until it's Look at the Pictures and Resumes Day, so sending a note first might get someone to actually open your picture and resume when it appears. Letters are opened immediately. Particularly those that are on good paper and are typed.

Last year I met a lovely young actress. I saw her work a time or two and thought she showed some promise. One day she showed me the letter she was sending out to casting directors. I knew immediately one of the reasons she was not getting their attention.

The paper looked like the cheapest dime store note paper and her handwriting belonged to someone in primary school. While it is not a sin to have substandard handwriting and cheap paper, it does not demand you be taken seriously. Use your computer and invest in good paper or go to a copy center and pay to have the letter typed.

When you actually do get someone's attention and have a meeting (as opposed to an audition) there are several things to attend to in addition to spiffing up your resume and praying.

Make sure your shoes are polished. Your clothes don't have to be expensive, but they should be clean, well-pressed, and in good repair. The care you take with your person projects the care you take in general and will be the key to how you are perceived.

When men dress casually they lose some of their authority; when women do the same, they lose most of theirs.

✦ *Even within the confines of casual dress, the folks in charge figure out how to display their rank and power. Maybe it's linen slacks and $800 Italian loafers on dress-down Friday, or a crisp jacket over that snazzy sleeveless dress. Walk into any company on casual day and chances are you'll have no trouble figuring out who runs the show.*

No matter what the dress code says, the old rule of thumb still applies: Don't dress for the job you have today, dress for the one you want tomorrow.
Marla Dickerson, *Los Angeles Times*[88]

Make sure your handshake is strong and that you have something to talk about. If there's a bowling trophy on a table, mention that your father bowled. Don't lie, but find an authentic way to connect with the other person.

Sit back in the chair, don't slump. They may be buying an actor who is going to play a bum, but they want to know that the actor is strong, has his own ideas, and is unafraid.

Employers are putting a property in an actor's hands. It is a huge responsibility and demands a great deal of energy. If you are playing the leading role and you are frightened and don't have a vision of how to do it, they do not want to know that. This is as true for an executive at IBM as it is for an actor.

After the meeting and/or audition, sit down and make a list of all the things you did well and all the things you could have done better. Review this material before the next meeting. It will pay off.

Taking Care of Business

Keep a Rolodex of business contacts. In New York and Los Angeles, this might mean casting directors, producers, directors, agents, etc. In a smaller town, it might mean ad agencies, radio personnel, newspaper people, or whoever buys talent in your marketplace.

Note every contact: when you met, spoke and/or wrote, what the contact was about, results, etc. Record the person's physical description and where he sits in his office so you will be sure to recognize him next time. Note something the two of you talked about as well as any personal information you might have on him.

Go through your Rolodex at least once a week to see who you need to call. Keep in touch even if there isn't something specific to talk about. Remember those AT&T commercials: you never know what will come out of a phone call.

It's not easy to do these things. It takes energy and sometimes it's scary. Even though it may appear fruitless, it isn't. All the energy you put out will come back, maybe not today or tomorrow, but it will come back. Practice using your imagination, creativity, and courage every day. It will get easier. After all, these people are your business partners. You all need each other.

Respond to Good Work

Everybody likes to know their work has been recognized. Call or write a note to a casting director that you have worked with and tell her what a good job she did on a specific project. Directors and producers you have worked with will also appreciate recognition.

Anne Archer tells a wonderful story about working with Glenn Close. As the star of their film, *Fatal Attraction*, Glenn saw the first rough cut. She immediately sat down and wrote a detailed letter to Anne citing her best moments, scene by scene. Could you ever forget that kind of generosity?

Many years ago, I was fortunate enough to be cast in the film *A Touch of Class* starring Glenda Jackson and George Segal.

By the time I joined the cast in Spain, the cast had already bonded in London with a month's prior shooting. The second night, we all sat in a crowded hotel dining room looking at dailies. It was uncomfortable and close, but in the middle of the screening, someone crawled all the way across the dark room, through a tangle of chairs and legs, and tapped me on the knee. It was George Segal telling me he thought my work was good. I'll never forget how that made me feel.

Early Success Isn't Necessarily Pretty

You aren't going to believe me, but I have to say it anyway: early success can be the kiss of death. With success comes visibility and judgement. Everyone waits to see if you are a flash in the pan and can live up to your early promise. You no longer have the luxury of anonymity in which to refine your art; therefore, it's much more expensive and scary to change anything.

What if no one likes your work when you change directions? So now, not only are you afraid to experiment, but you may get an unrealistic picture of the business. Seem unlikely? Let's assume you get to Los Angeles and because you are cute and adorable and young and new, you luck into a part on a television series.

Whether it runs two years or ten, the following things have happened: you've made more money than ever before and probably adjusted your lifestyle accordingly. You are now recognizable or semi-recognizable (depending on the status of the show). Production assistants call you Miss or Mister and get chairs and food for you.

Producers and directors treat you with great respect and listen intently to your ideas and complaints (whether or not they act on them).

Regardless of the tenure of the show, you have had one job and played one part. Unless you've gotten a TV movie during your hiatus (and only really visible players on top ten rated shows usually have that option) or scored a play during that same time span, you have not grown as an actor at all. But while you were regularly employed, you never noticed and no one seemed to care. You may be surprised and hurt when the show is over and you now have to fetch your own coffee and no one wants to know you. You are now considered over-exposed and have to sit out a few years while the public stops identifying you as that character.

Hector Elizondo spoke of other hazards:

✦ *The danger, of course, is in insulating yourself, especially if you become popular. You lose sight of the rest of the world. Luckily all this commercial attention has happened at this time of my life, [Hector struggled for years before he became visible] because I've seen what it does to folks who are not ready for it at a very early age. And it's devastating because you have a tendency to slip into the illusory world of believing that you are important, and believing that what you are doing is valuable and terrific.*

The biggest danger is compromising your standards of work. Because everyone is patting you on the back, you lose sight of your limitations, your objectives, your growth, suddenly showing up is enough.

The problem is that if you're too young and it happens too soon, you get buried under the illusion of it.
Elias Stimac, *Drama-Logue*[89]

Harrison Ford is an actor who has managed to keep himself together in spite of great success.

✦ *Unlike a lot of actors, Ford doesn't ever refer to himself as an artist, preferring to engage in a rear-guard campaign of reductionism, describing himself variously as a "worker in a service industry" and an "assistant storyteller." He deflects all attempts to correlate the success of his films with any underlying personal affection that audiences might feel for him.*

"I think that that's a result of a relationship not to who I am, but a degree of satisfaction with the product that I am part of," he says, sounding strangely like a vacuum cleaner salesman. "I make audience movies. I work for them, and I think they have a sense that I am a loyal, and to whatever degree, capable employee of

theirs."
Bruce Newman, *Los Angeles Times*[90]

Get Used to It

The constant selling is never over. You may as well face the facts now as later. Your whole career is going to be spent making people think they must employ you. Yes, there will be those times when you are semi-regularly employed, but the bottom line is that you are a self-employed person. You are responsible for keeping the momentum going once you get it started.

Careers go through moments of heat when they appear to sustain themselves, but don't lose your fire-starting skills; as night follows day, cold follows heat; you'll be in the momentum-starting business again.

Doing Your Own Publicity

On any given day, in any given city, where there are theatrical agents, you'll find disgruntled actors who will tell you their agents never get them any work at all. And they may be right.

I believe that the best agent in the world can't sell you if you are not a marketable product. It's still up to you to create that product and to keep making it marketable. One of the ways to do that is with publicity.

It's amazing how much publicity you can actually get for yourself. One follows the same procedure no matter where you live. Although you can just send information addressed 'To the Editor,' you will have better luck if you will do a little research.

Target a periodical and read it for a bit to digest a couple of names. When you are ready to submit material, call the editorial department and ask to speak to the person at the publication that your research has uncovered as most likely to be interested in your type of information. This will usually be the entertainment or theatre editor, but you might be able to slant your story toward general features if you can tie in another element. In any event, make sure you ask for and send to the appropriate person by name.

If I were publicizing this book, I might call the entertainment editor or the books editor. If I slanted the story to include not only the information available in the book, but how I happened to write it in the first place and how this is my twenty-ninth successful book, then the story would appeal to a larger audience.

If you are appearing in a play, you can send a blurb when you are cast and later, when you are opening, send another. If anything interesting or funny happened during rehearsal, you might get a few lines recounting the incident. Send in the information; they may have some space to fill that day.

Make a Phone Call

Call and attempt to speak to the writer before you send material and then follow-up to see that your information arrived. On the first call, say something like, "Hello, Jane Smith? This is Laura Adams, I saw your piece on Performing Pigs and really thought it was funny. I cut it out and sent it to my mother (chit-chat/chit-chat). The reason I'm calling is that I'm producing a play and I have an idea about it that I thought might interest you. Since it's turned out that everyone in the cast was in the first grade together (or whatever else you can dream up that might be unusual or interesting and make a news story) I thought this might make a nice feature. May I send you some information?"

She'll either say "no" (in which case you have saved postage and can now call up another newspaper or dream up another hook) or she'll say, "yes." If she does agree to your plan, verify the exact address whether you send it snail mail or attach it and send it over the net. Confirm receipt of packet no matter how you send it.

I called the *Los Angeles Times* and *Variety* in Los Angeles asking general questions regarding whether one needed a publicist in order to get coverage. I asked if actors were looked down upon if they were calling for themselves. On the contrary, the editors informed me, they would prefer to talk directly to the actor. Perhaps more to a celebrity than you or me, but they did say they would, so put them to the test. If you have something truly newsworthy or funny, they will be thrilled to have it.

If you are trying to get material in a special column, call the columnist, introduce yourself and ask if he accepts material directly from actors. If he does, ask if you might send something. Drop it by personally if possible. If you don't get to see him, follow up with a phone call to make sure he got the material and thank him for his help. Be careful with his time, but take the time to be personal.

Following up takes more time and energy, but you get out what you put in. If you take the easiest route, your rewards will invariably not be as great.

In all cases, take time to make a professional looking presentation of your material and slant the material in a unique manner. Make sure the story is typed, double-spaced and includes a contact name, address, and phone number. In a small town, it's a little simpler to get space and maybe even a picture.

Television and radio are not that difficult, if you can think of an angle. The media has space and time to fill every day, so if you can make your project visually interesting and unique, you'll not only meet with success, but they'll soon be happy to hear from you. If you are just appearing in a play, that is probably not newsworthy, but if the play deals with some relevant topic or if you researched it in an interesting way, people will find it entertaining.

If you are directing or producing a play, consider dedicating the proceeds from one performance to a local charity. That way you and the charity both benefit from the publicity. Arrange a contest within the theme of the play. Have a look-alike contest. There are all sorts of ways to get the media interested, particularly in a small town. Imagine each program you are contacting as if it were your own. If you were the host of that show, what would appeal to you?

Various radio stations in Los Angeles give away theatre tickets provided by producers who give the tickets in exchange for the publicity. Become aware of what's going on in the media in your area and some way of fitting in will occur to you.

Fans

No matter where you live, you will begin to collect some fans along the way. Don't discount them. Fans are a symbol of your growing visibility. When I was in high school, actors answered my letters giving me advice, so I make it a point to always respond to actors asking for guidance. I stopped responding to requests for free autographed pictures after I saw some of them for sale on the net for $25 each.

Many actors have mailing lists and send e-mails to fans when they are in something. If you can get someone interested enough to be your fan club president, they can do those things for you. If you are ever involved in an endeavor which needs support from the public to prove to your employer it is important to keep hiring you, your fans are there to take on the challenge. That's how *Once and Again, Designing Women, Home Front,* and innumerable other television shows kept themselves on the air in the past.

Going In

Once you have done all your homework and feel ready to begin, set goals and begin being businesslike about creating your own work. It's time to call on advertising agencies, television stations, film companies, promotional organizations, casting directors, directors, and/or producers.

We've already discussed taking meetings and how to talk to people when you call. You might want to review that.

Perspective

It's difficult to know when you are working on a project whether it and/or you are very good. You have to believe in your work in order to invest your energies 100%, so sometimes we develop a little myopia along the way. That's why it's always good to invite at least one friend, whose judgement and taste you trust, to see your work before you invite an agent, manager, or casting director. You're only new once. Since people tend to remember first encounters, do your best to make sure yours is a good one.

My young friend "John" recently tripped. After being in town three years studying at a local "conservatory", he had the good fortune to meet an Industry Professional who began acting as a mentor of sorts, answering questions, inviting him to events. About that same time, John was invited to sign with a manager.

He asked advice of the IP on this decision who validated the manager and encouraged the actor to sign. The actor was sent out on all the usual things for a non-SAG actor in his position: independent films, non-SAG commercials, plays, etc. Finally after a couple of years with the manager, John got the lead in an independent film that would pay for his membership into Screen Actors Guild. He was overjoyed and his IP friend was pleased and impressed at his progress.

The movie kept getting delayed and though the IP still had never seen John work, he felt he was "sufficiently far along" and asked if John would like to be introduced to a successful mid-level agent.

Overjoyed, John counted the days until the meeting. Shortly after he returned home from the meeting, the IP called to ask how the meeting had gone. John said he thought he had done okay and that the agency seemed to like him. "I stumbled a bit in the monologue and I think the head of the agency might have noticed."

John was surprised when the IP told him that the agent had called the minute John left the office demanding to know why he had been recommended.

"I told you I had never seen his work, did he not do well?" the IP had inquired.

"He's a nice enough kid, but he was awful. He started the monologue and then just stood there at one point because he had forgotten it."

"Did he know he was going to have to do a monologue?"

"If he didn't have a monologue ready, he should have said so and asked to come back when he was more prepared."

Dumbfounded and embarrassed, John apologized to the IP. His mentor then proceeded to point out to John all the positive things to be learned for this unfortunate event.

- John needs to develop a more informed approach to evaluating his work and his effect on people.
- In a meeting if someone asks him to do something for which he is unprepared, he not only has the right but is much better off saying, "I'm sorry, I didn't know I would be asked to do a monologue today, I don't want to waste your time unless I can do my best, may I come back?"
- He should never never go to any kind of meeting unless he is totally prepared for any eventuality.
- He needs to get into a high quality acting class, not the string of casting director showcases he's been involved in, and commit to those classes 100%.
- He needs to enlist the help of that teacher in evaluating any monologues the actor intends to show as examples of his work.
- And although he blew this one opportunity, he now has a valuable piece of information: he is not as far along as he thought.

If you can step back from the actor's point of view to the other side of the desk there is something else valuable to learn. What if the IP were an agent who had met the actor and had liked him (as the IP did) and though he had never seen the actor's work (as the IP had not) had a Breakdown on his desk with a part for which the actor was perfect, expended his credibility to get the actor an audition and *then* the actor was unprepared at the audition?

That agent put his own taste and credibility into question and now the casting director might be wary of taking future suggestions.

This is exactly why most agents are not interested in seeing an actor that has either not been referred by an industry professional or whose work he has seen.

If you digest that information, it will be easier for you to persevere in being your own agent. Getting yourself work in plays or independent films will begin to build your body of work and your experience in the audition room making decisions like this will improve your acting as it reduces your anxiety.

Acting is about so many things that are not acting. In this situation, John allowed himself to look bad because he didn't perceive that he had a choice. The agent asked for a monologue and John never stopped to think that he hadn't worked on that material for a long time. It never occurred to him to ask to come back. These are the things we learn over time. It's part of the "becoming" process of becoming an actor.

An actor who wants to be successful should always have a monologue in his head and a picture, resume, and reel in his car. You may only be new once, but you don't have to make the same mistake twice.

Hopefully, you've made a decision by now to take things as they come: acting, directing, producing, casting, etc., and in following these roads, you'll find fulfillment in show business.

You've organized your life, your home, your business space, and your way of thinking. You have a specific plan about how you are going to go about creating work for yourself. You now know how to research your marketplace for showbiz jobs of every stripe. You know about agents and unions. You have a support group.

Use that feedback. Knowing your strengths as well as your weaknesses gives you power. Monitor your progress regularly. Make a list with a numerical point system. Over time, you'll be able to see your progress in various areas. Reviewing the check list when you're feeling down will enable you to see how far you have come.

Wrap Up

✓ take care of business
✓ respond to good work
✓ have patience
✓ enjoy the process
✓ deal with rejection constructively
✓ keep perspective
✓ generate publicity
✓ cultivate relationships with the casting community
✓ cultivate relationships with fans
✓ get pictures and resumes
✓ check for phone messages often
✓ learn how to look for work
✓ realistically evaluate your work before inviting scrutiny
✓ be open to whatever comes your way
✓ utilize your support groups
✓ monitor your progress realistically

ᴁ 13 ᴂ
Researching Work Opportunities

You'd be surprised by the amount of job listings you can actually come up with if you are focused and take the time. It's all about research. I remember how cranky I was when I was a freshman in college and a course called Library Science was required for freshmen. How was I going to fit that dumb class into my schedule?

It only turned out to be the most important class I ever took.

Perspective tells me now that what college is about is teaching you how to find and organize information for the entire rest of your life.

Now I imagine that though very few young people have library skills, they all know how to research online. If you type film + casting into Google, you'll find a huge number of online casting pages. Almost every state has a film commission, so typing in your state + film commission should bring up whatever is current or upcoming.

The centers of film and television employment are, of course, Los Angeles, New York, and Chicago. More filming takes place in the Los Angeles area in a day than occurs in most other cities in a year. Except in Vancouver and Toronto, of course.

New York is still the consummate theatre town while Chicago is also a viable working environment for actors both in theatre and film and is the third largest production center in the United States. While less work is available across the land, film companies go on location and cast smaller parts locally.

Chicago

Chicago is the third busiest city for an actor in the country. In 2006, they shot *The Break-Up*, *The ½ Life of Mason Lake*, *He's Such a Girl*, *D.O.A.P.*, *August Rush*, *Grace is Gone*, *Tapioca*, *Butterfly on a Wheel*, *Providence*, *Fred Claus*, *Diacritical*, *Arithmetic Lesson*, *Actually Adieu my Love*, *Counting Backwards*, *Ossobuco*, *Quebec*, *Stash*, *Black Mail*, *License to Wed*, *The Strip*, *Grudge 2*, *The First Breath of Tengan Rei*, *Love*, *Blood Cryptonite*, *Beau Jest*, *Sketches*, and *Fred Claus*.

Chicago's best known theatres are The Goodman, The Chicago

Shakespeare Theatre, The Pegasus Players, Steppenwolf, The Victory Gardens Theatre, and The Powers That Be.

Since Chicago's respected theatre scene produces a large pool of extraordinary talent, film companies are more likely to cast non-star parts from the local talent pool. The Chicago Film Office webpage has reference material plus a list of film organizations in the Chicago area. Their webpage tells all – *www.cityofchicago.org*

Andy Lawler, who was an agent at DGRW in New York, has an extensive webpage on many facets of job-hunting for actors and has a comprehensive listing on theatre, teachers, and all things Chicago. You should visit his site: *www.geocities.com/sams0n/chiinfo.html*

Austin

For the past seven years, *MovieMaker* magazine has named Austin among the top moviemaking cities in the country. In 2004, the Capital City topped the list of "Top 10 Cities for Moviemakers" and took the #3 spot this year, just behind New York City and Philadelphia. More than 350 major features and made-for-television movies have been filmed in Austin over the past twenty years, not including hundreds of commercials and independent projects. *www.austintexas.org/film/*

The presence of locals like writer-director-producer Robert Rodriguez, writer-director-producer-actor Richard Linklater, star actress Sandra Bullock, and attractive tax subsidies make Texas a good location choice. Austin's growing professional crew base and beautiful scenery also adds to the attractive production site.

The Texas Film Office website told me that there were twelve films of one kind of another shooting in Texas when I checked them out. *www.governor.state.tx.us/film/hotline/*

Juicy roles may not be part of the equation.

✦ *As far as the benefit to local talent, Francesca Talenti (radio-television-film professor and independent filmmaker) said that it hasn't been really obvious yet. "I think there's a lot of talent in Austin," she said. "There's a lot of interest and love of film but I don't know many people who are employed consistently."*
Michael Taylor, *The Daily Texan*[91]

Talenti's words, of course, would be just as true in Los Angeles or

New York.

In the late 1950s, a television series named *Route 66* shot all around the country. When they came to my hometown to shoot, as an actress with solid local credits, I was immediately called in to audition and more than elated to qualify for my Screen Actors Guild card in my own hometown on network television as a result of that show.

Although at that point in my life I thought I was going to spend the rest of my life as a homemaker in Dallas, the experience did give me the idea that I might have something to sell in the larger marketplace. The validation gave me courage that I could make the big move to New York when my life changed.

North Carolina

Like almost everywhere else, Wilmington, North Carolina isn't as busy as it once was, but it's still a credible center of production boasting Screen Gem Studios, the largest studio east of Hollywood with nine soundstages. The town is awash in professional crew talent and it's rich in opportunities (if not in $) for actors.

Their webpage lists their credits. *www.wilmington-film.com/home.asp*

✦ *Wilmington's one drawback may be the town's lack of actors. But a SAG East deal allows productions to hire out-of-state thesps from as far away as Atlanta or DC without paying travel expenses.*
Tim Swanson, *Variety*[92]

Los Angeles and New York

Most of the dramatic series shown on TV are produced in California, while sitcoms are primarily produced on Hollywood sound stages. Indeed, while California doesn't track the state's number of TV production days, it represents 85% of the episodic TV market.

While stats on New York's TV production days were unavailable, local shoots currently include *30 Rock, America's Next Top Model, Art Damage, Canterbury's Law, Car Wars with Funkmaster Flex, Cashmere Mafia, Cinematherapy, Cool in Your Code, Criminal Intent, The Edge with Jake Sasseville, Extreme Jobs, Gossip Girl, Grease My Ride, Green Apple, Law & Order, Lipstick Jungle, Live from Lincoln Center, Make Me a Supermodel, Matt Titus: Matchmaker/Date Doctor, Metropolitan Opera Live in HD, Naked*

Brothers Band, The Return of Jezebel James, Special Victims Unit, U-Haul, Watching the Detectives, Yumemachibito plus many cable, news, daytime, late night shows and films. *www.nyc.gov/html/film/html/index/index.shtml*

Other Markets

Television commercial production revenues are also spread into other markets. I recently shot a film in Roswell, New Mexico. More and more states offer tax subsidies for local filming and local hires. That means if you do your research, you might have a better chance of working close to home with your competition there than by moving to New York or Los Angeles and bumping up against people with much stronger resumes than you will have if you are just starting.

A working actress friend moved to Oregon to raise her daughter in her old hometown. Because of the amount of location shooting there, she has now worked more jobs in both film and television than she had in the previous three years in Los Angeles.

She doesn't make as much money per show as she did in LA, but those days at scale plus 10% add up and the pleasure of working at her craft has produced a happier lifestyle than she had in Los Angeles. It doesn't cost as much to live in Oregon, either.

Nick Searcy is another actor who got work when he left New York:

✦ *I lived in New York City for seven years, working on stage but not on film. I never got a film acting job until I moved back to North Carolina in 1989. After a few small parts in films like "Days of Thunder" and "Love Field", I read for a small part in "Fried Green Tomatoes" and (director) Jon Avnet thought I looked mean and stupid so he read me for the larger part of Frank Bennett.*

I got that role, and I count that as the point when my career was launched. I have had no other job but acting or directing since then. If it had not been for the North Carolina market, I would never have gotten the shot at the role in "Fried Green Tomatoes."

Nick Searcy, interviewed by Julie Balter, *Screen Actor*[93]

Ready?

If you are trained, have a picture, credible resume, phone, Rolodex, space, daily schedule, have exhausted your hometown possibilities, have moved to either New York, Los Angeles, or Chicago, have an industry job, are working as an intern, or are just ready to look for acting jobs, you must tap all available resources.

Researching the Internet can be rewarding. Actors Equity's reliable job board is open to all. *www.actorsequity.org* and Google came up with an impressive list of theatre pages when I typed in "casting information." You'll find more on your own, but here's a beginning.

www.actorspost.com
www.actorssummit.org
www.ohiotheatrealliance.org
www.aact.org/
www.americanmusicals.com
www.americantheaterweb.com/
www.artslynx.org/theatre/
www.bakersplays.com
www.bw.edu/resources/bst/
www.BroadwayOnLine.com
www.Broadway.com
www.curtainup.com/
www.ukans.edu
www.fynsworthalley.com
www.groundworksdance.org
www.halleonard.com
www.outtolunchevents.com
www.huntingtonplayhouse.com
www.writersinsight.com
www.lipschtick.com
www.lindaeisenstein.com
www.livebroadway.com/
www.londontheatre.co.uk
www.musicalheaven.com/
www.newschoolacting.com
www.oac.state.oh.us/

www.originalworksonline.com
www.theatercleveland.org
www.elsinore.net/pts/index.html
www.csnmail.net/~parkgoist
www.performingarts.net/
www.playbill.com
www.playersguildtheatre.com/
www.playhousesquare.com/
www.porthouse.net
www.theatre.com
www.rsc.org.uk
www.bigwits.com/
www.sperlman.com
www.scriptseeker.com
www.showbizwire.com/
www.stageplays.com
www.stratfordfestival.ca
www.talkinbroadway.com/
www.theatrechannel.com
www.theatermirror.com
www.theatre-link.com
www.evertdance.com/
www.variety.com/
www.weathervaneplayhouse.com
www.seattlerep.org
www.berkleyrep.org

Living the life of a repertory theatre actor can be quite rewarding. One of the best rep theatres in the country is in Costa Mesa, a community southeast of Los Angeles where a core group of actors have worked together since producers Martin Benson and David Emmes created South Coast Repertory (SCR) thirty years ago.

These actors have played hundreds of parts. They make a decent wage, are highly thought of within their community, and make a living doing what they love. SCR won a Tony for Distinguished Achievement by a Regional Theatre in 1988.

At Equitys' website at *www.actorsequity.org/*, I found information about artists' grants from Theatre Communications Group (TCG), general actor news, as well as specific casting news for all across the country including audition hotlines for NY (212-869-1242), Chicago (312-641-0418), LA (323-634-1776) and San Francisco (415-434-8007).

Entertainment Auditioning Centers

There are several theatre conferences around the country that hold annual auditions for actors. One of the best known is StrawHat. They provide a collective for non-Equity actors to audition for theatre jobs on both coasts in February and March. Their webpage says it best.

✦ *You're a non-equity actor. Maybe in school, or just finished. Now what? You need to meet people in the business. Build a resume. Get known. In short, you need to work.*

StrawHat gathers theatres, production and entertainment companies, casting directors and even TV shows looking for actors to fill roles in plays, musicals and other media. When you apply to StrawHat, your picture and resume are put in StrawHat's Online Casting database, and you get access to the information on the members area of the site. If you're accepted for an audition, your picture and resume will be published in the StrawHat directory, distributed to all attending theatres. You'll audition and most likely get called back by many of those theatres, all on the same day. And most likely, you'll be offered a job. Or two. Or more.

Last year, over 85% of our actors got callbacks. This is our twenty-ninth anniversary. That's the way it works at StrawHat.

Webpage StrawHat Auditions / *www.strawhat-auditions.com / actorap.htm*

The New England Theatre Conference features fifty-six Equity and non-Equity theatres holding March auditions. NETC routinely receives 1,200-1,500 applications and chooses 500. Membership costs $30. Auditioning fees are extra. Even so, affiliation with this group is worth the money. The NETC provides too much information and opportunity for employment to list here. My advice is to become a member and get their newsletter. NETC has opportunities and information for actors and technicians on every level.

New England Theatre Conference (NETC)
North Eastern University/c/o Theatre Department
360 Huntington Ave.
Boston, MA 02115
617-424-9275
www.netconline.org/

The Southeastern Theatre Conference (SETC) in Greensboro, NC conducts annual Spring Regional Professional Auditions.

✦   *Approximately 900 actors and actresses (Professional and Screened Pre-Professionals) will audition for over ninety theatre companies for both summer and year-round employment.*
SETC Webpage/*www.setc.org/auditions/spring.asp*

The Southeastern Theatre Conference/ SETC
PO Box 9868
Greensboro, NC 27429
336-272-3645
www.setc.org/

Voice Work/ADR

More voice-over work in films is done by celebrity voices, but becoming part of an ADR Group (doing voices in animated films and/or television commercials) is a burgeoning career path for actors.

✦   *The commercial business has changed in that it's no longer the announcers that dominate commercials, it's the actors, the people who can 'be real.' Advertisers have become much more honest in their approach and don't want to have charactery voices unless the particular character in the commercial calls for the character voice.*
If you listen to the voices stuff out there now on TV and radio, it's much more real. But you have to be an excellent actor, so you can give them the range of emotions they are asking for, be it comedy, understated, etc.
Sandie Schnarr/Sandie Schnarr Talent, Los Angeles

Audio Dialogue Replacement (ADR) refers to adding voices to an already completed film, looping, localization, or unintelligible hub-bub or the walla-walla sound of background conversation.

You'll frequently be called upon to loop some of your own dialogue on a film or television show, so this is a skill you are going to need whether you get to do further voice work or not. Just like everything else, watching visuals and listening to beeps to lay in a voice within given time parameters while maintaining character requires practice and experience, so either get into a class or spend some time watching a film that you can rewind so you can acquire this skill.

Walla work is a specialized area of replacing existing dialogue with other voice tracks. It is done frequently in movies after the film is shot because the sound during the actual take was not clean. Walla groups also replace preexisting foreign language tracks with American speech.

There are Voice-Over Workshops in New York, Los Angeles, or Chicago, where you can usually study with someone who is already working in the field. If you don't have that option, you can still learn. Record and transcribe radio and television commercials and emulate the style and delivery of the already working voice artist. You'll learn a lot from them and your own style will develop as you hone your skills.

✦ *If you want to get an agent's attention, you better sound like those people who are booking the national TV spots. That's what gets our attention because those are the people who make the money.*

That man who books the national Toyota spot will teach you how to read that copy. So, there's a free workshop running 24 hours a day. Then take workshops with casting directors who know what the advertisers are currently looking for.

Sandie Schnarr/Sandie Schnarr Talent, Los Angeles

Los Angeles Voice-Over Casting Directors

Carroll Voice Casting
Carroll Day Kimble, Susan Cheico, Aleta Braxton
6767 Forest Lawn Drive #203 (just off Barham)
Los Angeles, CA 90068
323-851-9966

The Voicecaster/Bob Lloyd, Pat Lloyd
1832 Burbank Boulevard
Burbank, CA 91506
818-841-5300

Elaine Craig Voice Casting
6464 Sunset Boulevard #1150 (just W of Cahuenga)
Hollywood, CA 90028
323-469-8773

Kalmenson & Kalmenson Voice-Over Casting
Cathy Kalmenson & Harvey Kalmenson
105 S Sparks Street (Olive and Verdugo)
Burbank, CA 91506
818-342-6499
www.kalmenson.com

Comprehensive Voice-Over Casting Directors lists can be found at *www.voicetraxwest.com/casting.htm* and *www.voiceoverresourceguide.com*.

Knowledge Is Power

The more you know about the business in every area, the better equipped you are to handle it. Any job you can get in any city that is industry-related will hold you in good stead as you progress along the route to your goals.

If you are not computer savvy, get that way. Not only will computer skills enhance your marketability in any job-seeking within the industry, the ability to access the Internet and make it work for you opens the door to knowledge and possible jobs.

The Hollywood Creative Directory publishes the most extensive guides to agents, managers, and other industry information. Their hard copy guides are expensive and worth it. They also maintain an informative free website that, in addition to providing the most up-to-date list of agents' names, phone numbers and addresses, also maintains a free Hollywood job board.

Their website services job seekers in any showbiz area you can name including internships. *www.hcdonline.com/jobs*

Websites/Information

The websites of Screen Actors Guild (*www.sag.org*) AFTRA (*www.aftra.org*) and Actors' Equity (*www.actorsequity.org*), The Writers Guild (*www.wga.org*) and The Directors Guild (*www.dga.org*) all provide current guild news as well as information on joining, fees, and upcoming events.

Although the *DGA Monthly* no longer appears to be online, the archives of director interviews are available. You can learn about many directors from these interviews, as in the excerpt below.

✦ *Usually in an action movie, the actress only knows how to scream and yell and run scared. I liked Samantha Mathis because she looked different. I think she stands for a strong character, always independent. Not a scared girl who needs protection. I usually put the actors photos together, to see how they fit, and when I put their pictures together it looked like a golden boy [Slater] and golden girl. That's how we cast.*

John Woo, interviewed by Ted Elrick, *DGA Monthly*[94]

It would be worthwhile to read a *DGA Monthly* director interview every day. *www.dga.org/news/mag_inter.php3*

Excerpts from the WGA Magazine, *Written By...*, are available at *www.wga.org/writtenby/writtenby.aspx*. Their interviews are recommended reading also.

Other essential sites are the Internet Movie Database; *www.imdb.com* which answers movie questions concerning plot, characters, actors, actresses, directors, writers, etc. on probably every movie in existence, and the trade papers *Variety* (*www.variety.com*) and *The Hollywood Reporter* (*www.hollywoodreporter.com*). There are some effective actor support groups online that function not only as an information resource ("Hey, does anyone know a good reasonable hair cutter?" "What's a good class?") to a place for actors to just bond with someone else in misery.

Sherwood Oaks Experimental College

If you are in Los Angeles, I highly recommend the seminars at Sherwood Oaks Experimental College. Slanted toward writers, it's a wonderful place to begin relationships with writers and directors who are at the same place in their careers as you as well as rub shoulders (literally) with giants in the business.

You'll also hear some terrific industry leaders talk and get to meet them. Gary Shusett, who runs the place, always provides time at the end of the sessions for the audience and the panel members to interact. I have been invited to chair several panels there and I'm always impressed by the people I meet. *www.sherwoodoakscollege.com/*

Actors generally don't think to spend their money on these kinds of weekends, leaning more toward acting, voice and dance lessons and those expensive 8x10s; however, I think money is well spent on almost any kind of industry seminars.

The extension courses at UCLA also expose you to some amazing people you would not normally meet. An ongoing class affords the opportunity to make real relationships not only with your teacher, but with your fellow students. *www.uclaextension.edu/*

Independent Feature Project

IFP is the leading resource of the American independent film movement. More than 10,000 filmmakers and industry professionals participate year-round in the activities of IFP to make connections and to find out the latest on who's who, who's buying, who's financing and who's making what features, shorts and documentaries.

The Independent Feature Project members include writers, actors, grips, sound technicians, and literally anyone seeking involvement in independent film. Their five chapters are located in Chicago, Minnesota, New York, Phoenix and Seattle. Membership fee is $100. *www.ifp.org*

This national non-profit group sponsors seminars, classes, screenings, producer series, and an eclectic collection of industry resources. Though it's not necessary to be a member in order to attend events, the monthly newsletter listing free screenings, get togethers, resources, and notes from people wanting scripts is only available to members.

IFP/Los Angeles distanced itself from the other five IFP chapters and is now known as Film INDependent/FIND. The organization rents cameras and casting rooms, maintains a resource library with computers, sample budget and business plans, and every conceivable film periodical. They offer members over 120 free screenings and 150 educational events every year for the $95 membership fee. FIND maintains a casting file for their members. Even if you are not a member, they would be happy to have your picture and resume.

www.filmindependent.org/

Actors in Playwrighting Groups

The life blood of the theatre is new material, so many NY/LA theatres offer developmental possibilities for new playwrights and since writers are the very people you want to get to know, you can support them by volunteering to read material at their meetings. Here are some of New York's best known.

Playwrights Horizons is one of Manhattan's most prestigious off-Broadway theatres and presents new playwrights on a regular basis. *www.playwrightshorizons.org*

Ensemble Studio Theatre's devotion to playwrights is clear from the number of new plays produced, ongoing playwrighting groups, new play festivals, and summer workshops that produce opportunities for playwrights and EST's core group of actors. *www.ensemblestudiotheatre.org*

NY's most famous off-Broadway theatre, *The Public,* continues to develop new voices with ongoing playwright groups. Connected and fearless. *www.publictheater.org*

Repertory Theatre Websites

Google searching for "repertory theatre websites" brought up more addresses than I can print here. I'm listing a few for you, but if you are looking for a job, I'd check out all these websites and see what all is going on. Some of these sites list internship possibilities.

Actor's Theatre of Louisville, KY
www.actorstheater.org

The Alley Theatre, Houston, TX
www.alleytheater.com

American Conservatory Theatre, San Francisco, CA
www.act-sfbay.org/about/index.html

Denver Performing Arts Complex, Denver, CO
www.denver.sidewalk.com/link/10881

Providence Black Repertory Company, Providence, RI
www.oso.com/community/groups/prblkrep

Seattle Repertory Theatre, Seattle WA
www.seattlerep.org/

South Coast Repertory, Costa Mesa, CA
www.scr.org/

Spanish Theatre Repertory (Repertorio Español)
www.geocities.com/Broadway/8369/nfindex.html

The Studio Upstairs Theatre Repertory, Goshen, NY
www.studioupstairs.com/

Threshold Theatre Newtonville, MA 02160
www.theatermirror.com/threshold/

Mentors

We could all use a powerful showbiz-connected mentor, but anyone working in the business who will spend time with you is a gift. If you have lucked into a showbiz job, it's possible that your guardian angel will find you and it's possible your acting teacher might fill that role.

Los Angeles' Women in Film has a Mentor Program that helps find advisers for members. One of the assets of UCLA's MFA program for writers and directors is the exposure to industry heavyweight mentors.

The Breakdown Service

Back in the day, agents in Hollywood journeyed daily to each studio to sit and read the latest script, make notes and then submit actors. An enterprising chap named Gary Marsh, who was doing just that for his agent mother, called the studios and said something like, "I think I could make your life better. If you give me all your scripts, I will summarize them and make a list of the types of actors needed for the parts, the size of each role, etc., and provide that information to all the agents. This will save you the nuisance of having all those people in your offices and them the inconvenience of driving."

The much-maligned service costs agents and managers a hefty amount. Though they must agree not to show it to actors, some actors get their hands on it anyway. A woman in Beverly Hills charges actors $20 per month for access. She hides it under a rock behind a gate. Actors drive up, lift the rock, sit in their cars, read the Breakdown and make notes. They return it to its hiding place and drive away. I'm sure there's a New York version of this somewhere.

Whether or not it's a good idea to have access to the Breakdown is debatable. Casting directors already don't have enough time to look at all the agents' submissions. How will they ever be able to even open all the envelopes they could get from actors much less consider them?

◆ *It's just plain counterproductive for the most part [when actors get their hands on the Breakdown]. The casting directors are likely ignoring submissions from non-represented actors. And as far as represented actors go, you better hope you're wasting your agents' office time pointing out what you're right for. Our work is about everything after (and hopefully before) the Breakdown. We continue to talk to casting and find out so much. Often they want a name for a part, or are just looking for back-up ideas if their offer falls through, or change their mind about the "specs" after the first round of auditions, or cut the part, or a myriad of other factors.*

Casting is an activity and that means change, give-and-take, and yes mistakes happen. For an actor to pin his expectations to the snapshot in time of a Breakdown is wrong. Our office's response to an actor quoting Breakdowns is "that's not a mail-order catalogue there."
J Kane/HWA Talent Representatives

Some actors are able to use the purloined information intelligently, others merely manage to alienate their agents. Though invaluable, the Breakdown doesn't include everything. Many roles aren't listed unless the casting director needs an unusual actor for a role.

Frequently, the script is truly not available. More times than not, the audition sheet will be filled by requests, not submissions.

Since not everything comes out in the Breakdown, it is important to assess your agent's other contacts. If your agent is not in a position to have more information than is in The Breakdown, that's still a lot of information if he uses it wisely.

The Breakdown is now not only part of the New York/Los Angeles casting scene, but it is also available via the Internet.

Los Angeles' Working Actor's Guide

Billing itself as a "Yellow Pages for Actors," *The Working Actors Guide to Los Angeles* has over 5000 listings of every kind from casting directors, agents, coaches, and photographers to dentists and plastic surgeons. Until my daughter became its editor, I didn't know much about the WAG except that it cost $39.95 and that it was "that book" that some actors hauled around with them.

It's only when I found myself regularly calling my daughter from my car to give me an address to a theatre or a studio or to Los Angeles City College for a speaking engagement and she told me that she was getting all her information from *The WAG* that I began to carry one in my car along with my *Thomas Bros. Guide.*

Now, I feel *The WAG* is an invaluable resource for almost anything you can think of. You'll want to add it to your list of great resources. You can check it out for free on their website. It's certainly worth a click. *www.workingactors.com/*

Using Information

Whether your information comes from the net, the grapevine, or The Breakdown, use the data wisely. Only present yourself for something you are right for and at the appropriate career level as well. You may look just like Brad Pitt, but no one is going to consider you for his parts. A connected agent or manager might be able to move you from one category to another in an extraordinary circumstance, but you're not going to do that on your own. It's not even a good idea to try to do that without some support.

It's tempting to just send your picture and resume to the world, but be selective. Not only are pictures and resumes expensive to just scatter in the wind, but you really don't want every single job that's out there; it just seems like it when you are hungry. Strive to make talented choices every day, even when sending out pictures. There is no easy way to accomplish anything other than one step at a time; invest your energy wisely.

Wrap Up

Research

✓ actor support websites
✓ casting websites
✓ auditioning centers
✓ voice-over work/ADR
✓ Hollywood Creative Directory
✓ union sites/IFP/FIND
✓ playwrighting groups
✓ repertory theatre sites
✓ mentors
✓ Breakdown Service/WAG
✓ use data wisely

≈ 14 ≈
Auditioning & the Way It Really Is

After all your hard work, you have progressed beyond trying to get someone's attention, to having a meeting with them, to actually being called to audition.

All auditions are different. Sometimes there will be only a casting director who will read with you, but sometimes the producers and directors are also there. In Los Angeles, there might be twenty people in the room when you arrive. At first glance, seeing all those people might rattle you, but if you take the attitude of "Oh boy! It's a bigger audience!" you'll be using the circumstances to your advantage.

In most markets, the casting director holds preliminary auditions, selects those considered most appropriate, and calls these people back to be reviewed by the director and/or producer. Sometimes the preliminary audition is taped and those tapes are shown to the buyers who make decisions regarding callbacks.

Auditions can take many forms. Commercial auditions traditionally entail many, many actors who are called to read for a casting director and/or producers and/or directors, usually in a conference room.

Theatrical auditions are frequently held onstage in a theatre, but are also regularly held in meeting rooms when a theatre is unavailable. It might be important for you to find out before the audition just where it will be held. Your preparation might be different for a small office than a large theatre.

Film and television auditions are usually held in a meeting room. If your work is not already known by the casting director, she will screen you before presenting you to the producers and/or directors.

Two inspiring books about auditioning that you may find helpful are *Audition* by Michael Shurtleff and *Next* by director Ellie Kanner and casting director Paul G. Bens.

Shurtleff's book was so supportive and instructive that I wanted to sleep with it under my pillow. His descriptions of Barbra Streisand's early auditions alone are worth the price of the book.

The Kanner/Bens book not only covers audition behavior, but answers questions about deal memos and being replaced.

Preparation

Prepare carefully. If you don't want the job, don't go. You won't do your best work and there is no way of erasing a bad impression from a room full of people who just saw you do bad work. You never know who is sitting in and when they might have a job that you would be right for. People remember.

A few months ago I got a job for which I didn't audition. I scanned the list of people involved with the project, searching for a familiar name. How had I gotten this job? On the set, the director reminded me that we had worked together seven years ago. I had one scene on a TV movie that I didn't remember. He did.

Each actor has his own way of attacking a project. Even if you are going to read only a few lines, it is worth every effort to get your hands on the script ahead of time and read the entire script at least twice before focusing on your scene.

It means everything to me to be able to read the material aloud with another human being prior to the audition. Sometimes there is no one around to do this with and I just have to take my best shot. I have been known to pay the neighborhood kids to read lines with me. I just pay their babysitting rate. Some people work with other actors and take that actor along with them to the audition.

If you are to provide your own material, choose carefully. Unless specifically asked, do not bring Shakespeare or another classic. These parts will not show your castability. No matter how well you do it, the material makes the primary impression so if you can entertain and charm them with an appealing script, your chances are better. Actors win Academy Awards every year for being lucky enough to get the role that shows them to their best advantage.

When I was a student of Herbert Berghof's at the HB Studios in New York, he used to suggest that the best material for an actor was from novels and plays written by an author from the actor's own geographical region and background. It's not that difficult to choose scenes from a novel and write phrases that bridge the dialogue if it does not stand as is. When you work with material written by an author raised with your same sensibilities, you will bring an unconscious truth that cannot be acted. When you work from a novel, you have material that is more interesting to your auditioners because of its originality.

It's not wise to do memorable scenes associated with famous actors. You may be really fabulous, but while you are doing Robert De Niro's role in *Taxi Driver*, the producers are wishing Mr. De Niro was present.

When you prepare for the audition, make sure you are specific. Whatever is in your mind when you are doing the scene will show. If confusion and fear are your primary concerns instead of the emotion of the scene and the lines are only coming out of your mouth without access to your brain, confusion and fear will be the message your audience receives.

Dressing for Auditions

Although there is a difference of opinion about dressing for the part for an audition, I always do (within reason). I don't do it for them; I do it for me. Dressing in character helps feed my feelings for the scene. As you dress, think about how your character would go about dressing and how the character feels.

Another facet of auditioning (and acting, of course) is character. If you come in with a character over and above what is written, whether it is an attitude, a walk, or a way of speaking, you will stand out head and shoulders from the crowd.

The reason that so many stand-up comedians get work is that most have honed a character that they play in their act. Writers come in, see the act, steal the most interesting characteristics and write them into their scripts and, sometimes, they take the comedian with it.

The late Peter Boyle had been working for many years when he captured the attention of the world in the film *Joe*. The words and basic value system of that character were written into the script, but in fact, Peter had invented a blue collar character that he had been playing for years in various skits at Second City (the famous improvisational group in Chicago).

When he played Joe, he plugged in the character material he had been working on for years. He successfully played another version of the same character on *Everybody Loves Raymond* for several years.

If you haven't worked on creating characters, start now and add dimension to your work.

Auditioning and Waiting

Being kept waiting past fifteen minutes at an audition can not only make it difficult to maintain energy at the peak you need for a good performance, but the resulting anger it triggers can ruin your audition all together. After fifteen minutes with no explanation and/or apology from the casting director, I quietly call my agent and have him deal with it. He may tell me to leave or he may make a phone call that results in some explanations and/or making another appointment.

If you are a member of Screen Actors Guild, the client must pay for your time if he keeps you waiting past one hour. Don't make a fuss, just jot down the names of some of the other waiting actors from the sign-in sheet, call SAG, mention the incident plus the other names (so the client won't be able to single out that you are the one who called), and you will ultimately get a check in the mail. It will be for one hour pro-rated from SAG minimum for an eight-hour day.

Even if you are going to get paid, it's still hard to stay in a good humor, so don't wait so long that you get huffy. If you feel yourself getting testy, go ahead and leave. They're not going to want to hire an angry actor. Only stars can get by with throwing a tantrum.

Explain that you have another audition and that you will be happy to come back. Be sure to address this before you get irritable and when you will still be happy to come back.

The longer you wait, the more your energy is dissipated by holding the anger down. It is a real test of my mettle to put aside the anger at being kept waiting and still do a good audition.

Dr. Spock says that if a child has a tantrum, it is the parent's fault. The parent's job is to notice the signs that precede a tantrum and take steps to head it off. I try to be as caring a parent to myself as I was to my children. Therefore, I walk out of bad situations.

Audition Behavior

You are judged from the moment you enter the audition office. Receptionists are sometimes quite powerful so be sure to acknowledge them. You don't have to be phony, but this is a human being here who doesn't appreciate being invisible any more than you do.

When you enter the audition room, take a moment to adjust to the atmosphere. Don't waste time, but take a few seconds to breathe. Notice who is there and what is going on. Although it's always fun to chat, I've found that for me, I need to focus on the material first and chat afterwards.

Don't be afraid to move around. Set up the room as you want. Go over the scene in your mind as you physically take in the room to visualize yourself in the scene. The casting director will be happy to take the cue from you about when to begin the scene. If she begins the scene before you are ready, just say you need another moment to prepare. Turn your back, get in character, remember what went on in the script in the moment just before this scene, and begin with that energy.

Insecurity

Some actors think they take the edge off their insecurity and humanize themselves by commenting on their fears in the audition room. Trust me, insecurity is not appealing to the buyer. There is too much money at stake. No one really wants to hear about your impending nervous breakdown. They're worried about their own and they want to feel that they have found the actor that is going to solve all their problems, not present new ones.

In her autobiography, Elizabeth Ashley tells a story of a time in her career when she was really hot. She was hired for a film and suggested her old acting teacher, Sydney Pollack, who had never directed. He got the job. Before shooting began, she saw a screening of herself in *Ship of Fools* and decided that her work was bad.

She invited Pollack to lunch and told him her work in *Fools* was so awful that she would need all his help in order to do a good job in their approaching film. Pollack conveyed the information to his agents who also represented Anne Bancroft. Phone calls were exchanged and somehow Ashley was out and Bancroft was in.

Ashley says she never recovered:

✦ *It broke me. And the thing that broke me was not the hustlers and the handlers, and it wasn't the hard, mean way of doing business. It was that I had thought there was some ground where it was safe to tell the truth, to be afraid and say, "I don't know," and there wasn't. I doubted myself and was looking for help and you don't get to do that. There's no place for that. If you don't know, tell the*

bastards you do.
Elizabeth Ashley, *Actress: Postcards from the Road*[5]

Some actors speak of being so frightened at an audition that they didn't do their best. It's all very well and good for others to say "just relax," but it's not that easy. That's one of the reasons it is so important to get up and perform at every opportunity. The more time you spend in front of people, the less you will be frightened.

The best way to give up your anxiety is to be so specific and concentrated in your work that you don't have time for anxiety to creep in. It takes enormous effort to really focus and take yourself out of the audition room and into the material. You can only do this by constantly exercising your muscles of concentration.

Take time every day to visualize something: Either the material you are working on or something that you want. Train your mind to emotionally visit the situation. If you are picturing a job, then see yourself already having it. Feel what you would feel under those circumstances. Then in a pressured audition situation, those tools are ready for you to use.

Working with props is a good example of how effective concentration can take anxiety away. Props require authentic attention to use appropriately; threading a needle, peeling a potato, washing a dish, or repairing a stool have to be done in reality or the task won't work. That reality grounds the actor into the scene.

Memorizing the Material

There are several schools of thought about memorizing the material for an audition. My own personal preference, which many casting directors say is a bad idea, is to commit the scene to memory. It's not that difficult for me to do and I feel I do a much better job if I can free myself from the page. There have been times that it didn't work out, but I'm still not sorry I go for it.

Frequently, I will announce that I am going to attempt a scene without the script and that if it doesn't work out I will use it. And sometimes I have had to.

I would add that writers are very attached to their every word and when you don't say the lines exactly as written, particularly in comedy material, the writer will probably torpedo your audition, if he has the power to do so. My writer friends have told me this, but I continue to memorize material. Sometimes it pays off and sometimes it doesn't, but there are many reasons for you not to get the job, not the least is one's ability to memorize.

If you do not have an easy time memorizing, don't go for it. A few years ago, I was conducting a seminar for The American Film Institute on Auditioning and the Business of Show Business. I gave out audition material on Saturday night for simulated auditions on Sunday. One of the actresses had put down her script for her audition. She failed to impress me in any way. In a later part of the session, I gave her some material that she had only a few minutes to prepare so there was no possibility of her memorizing it. She was a completely different actress when her energy was freed from the obligation to memorize. Do what works best for you.

Casting directors tell me it's not only all right, but a very good idea to stop an audition that is going badly and begin again. Apologies are bad form, just smile and do better.

Although getting chosen is a big step towards a job, it doesn't necessarily mean you are going to work. The next hurdle is negotiation. Money, billing and working rules are laid down.

If you are in one of the performing unions, many details are already addressed in a standard contact. Whatever is not already spelled out must be negotiated. As a beginning actor, one usually is happy to do anything for any pittance, frequently for free. The actor should look upon the free work as graduate school.

When you are further along in your profession, you will find that there are three plums possible in any job: billing, money, and part. You will want to get at least one of them.

If the part stinks and the money is terrible but your billing is going to be better than you have gotten in the past, that might be a reason to take the job. If you are to get little money and no billing, but the part is sensational, for heaven's sake take the job! Maybe all that appeals to you is the money. That's not all bad, either.

Let's talk a little bit about money. Currently scale for a day working through Screen Actors Guild is $759. Weekly (film or television) is $2,634. Half-hour television episodes are usually shot in five days.

Major Role/Top of the Show rate for ½ hour is $4,080, for an hour, it's $7,527.

It's worth mentioning here that a casting director recently told me that although her show strongly resisted paying more than Top of

Show to anyone, she was able to get away with paying just a few dollars more because most actors didn't know the rates and just needed to hear that they were getting paid more than Top of the Show. Please do yourself a favor and be alert to fees and arithmetic. All the numbers are online at *www.sag.org.* Search for "contracts."

Clearly, there are performers who make much more than Top even though the producers swear it isn't so. It is management's way of price-fixing. In any event, salaries are always what the traffic will bear once you graduate past minimum. If you are hot or you don't want the job, you can demand more. Nothing makes an actor more attractive to a casting director than not wanting the job. The longer you say no, the higher the fee becomes.

There is a point beyond which the casting director will not go. If you want to get your price up, judgment is everything. As in poker, you want your adversary to put as much money on the table as possible, but you don't want him to fold. When you really need the job, it's more difficult to take the chance involved in tough negotiations.

Series regulars (with no important credits) usually work their first half-hour series for $5,000 per show. Series regulars who are visible command much more money. One of the reasons the hit show *Dallas* finally went off the air was that (after 11 years) Larry Hagman and the other regulars had negotiated their salaries to such astronomical heights that the show was just too expensive to produce. Marginal shows whose budgets are low are much more likely to stay on the air than a marginal show with a bigger overhead.

Quotes/Money

Quotes refer to the amount of money you were paid for your last job. If you have been paid $5,000 per week on a movie-of-the-week or $1,500 per day on a film, these fees are your quotes. You use your quotes in negotiation citing where, when, and for whom you made this money in order to get paid at least that much again. Be truthful because casting directors will check. Part of their job is to get the best talent for the least amount of money.

All the casting directors know one another and share information. Actors should share, also. It would be important for you to know that "John" made $2,000 for a day on a particular show. When you ask for $1,500 and they say, "We never pay that much" you'd know they're not playing square with you. Never divulge your sources of information, however, or you will lose them.

Though it's much harder these days for anyone other than stars to make more than minimum or Top, if you have been working on a per-day basis at minimum, doing good work and getting good feedback for a period of time, it might be time to start asking for more. If you are unsuccessful in moving your price up, just amass some more good credits and try again. It will happen.

A friend determined that he would no longer work for Major Role/Top of the Show money. Although not a star, my friend works a lot, has a special quality, and felt he deserved more. In fact, he has been able to demand double Top a couple of times, but the number of times per year that he has worked has dropped dramatically. You may have to decide whether you want to work more often or get paid more.

You might be offered the part of your dreams, but the money is terrible. Though you have painstakingly increased your quote, you are now offered the perfect part for very little money. Take the part and ask the casting director to offer you a no quote. This is exactly what it says. If another casting director tries to obtain information regarding your pay on that job, the information is unavailable. It seems to me, however, that if you have a no quote the casting director must assume that you worked for less than your usual fee.

The following is from 1992, but the information is still timely.

✦ *Casting directors are telling agents, "Get me the best actors for the least money. Don't submit anyone who won't work for scale plus 10%." As a result, mid-priced actors have seen salaries drop as much as 50%, with no room for negotiation. Top of the Show pay for TV guest performers is lower now than it was ten years ago, and more name actors are competing for ever fewer guest spots. Series regulars have taken pay freezes and even cuts in order to keep their jobs. Disney just announced that the studio will not pay more than $25,000 per episode to series stars.**

Compiled by Mark Locher, *Screen Actor*[96]

Why People Get Hired

This is not a business of absolutes. As I've said before, there is luck involved. Part of playing this particular poker game is training yourself as consistently and thoroughly as possible. The more skills you have, the more parts you can be considered for.

Training and ability are a given once you are recognized as part of the talent pool. You and your competitors are all good or you wouldn't be at the audition. The decision will be made on a variety of things that you can't control. Elinor Berger was still an agent with Irv Schechter Agency in Los Angeles when she told me:

✦ *It's also a question of the competition. You can send a girl in who's pretty, does a great reading, but a friend of the producer will come in or a nephew of the director or somebody that somebody wants to go to bed with.*

There's 20,000 reasons why you're not going to get the part. And it's not necessarily that you are without talent. It's because there is so much competition. At the end of the week when I see all the people I've gotten appointments, I think, "It's amazing that I did that. I'm just one little person." When I think about all the agents and all the actors, I think we're lucky to get people out on the appointment.

Elinor Berger

✦ *The actor has got to have the creative energy juices flowing and have the right mind set and the right attitudes to have the wins come to him. He needs to have an angle on the role that's going to be different and maybe the director is going to say, "That's interesting."*

If the actor is not in his most creative time, he's going to miss some things. He's going to walk out of the audition and say, "Damn, I should have put this twist on it, or I don't know why I did that; it's so obvious."

If an actress' energies are in the theatre, and she hasn't done a play in a year, it's going to drain her. She needs to be filled up and dealing with what to do about that. Equity Waiver, scene study, comedy workshop. There are choices; not just sit home and stare at the bare walls.

Ann Geddes/Geddes Agency, Los Angeles

✦ *The winning difference between two actors on the same level auditioning for a role may just be that one makes everyone in the room have a better time.*

Barry Freed/Manager, Los Angeles

So much for talent and training.

Factors Involved in Staying Hired

Getting the job and beginning rehearsal is no guarantee you will actually work the job, although, if it is a union job, you will be paid. Years ago, when I was starring on a series and had the opportunity to see how things actually work, I began to realize how lucky I had been in my career. Our cast would frequently meet for the first day of rehearsal read around the table with the guest cast and by the time we got back from lunch, we might be missing two guest cast members.

Management somehow didn't think they were funny enough at the first reading. The moral here is to always put your best foot forward. There is too much money at stake and people are too paranoid for faith. You must always be showing people what you can do.

It's also not uncommon to shoot a pilot and be replaced when the show comes to series. Sometimes the actor they originally wanted has become available. Sometimes their fantasies did not turn out to be the same as your reality. It's childish to take it as a sign that you are untalented and will surely never work again. Examine the situation and see if there is something you might have done differently with either the people or the material. Learn and get on with it; it's self-indulgent and mean to beat yourself up. That's not to say I didn't act that way when it happened to me, but I was very young and had no idea people ever *were* replaced.

People commonly think of professional behavior as being on time, learning your lines, using deodorant and not eating garlic. There are other essential things that no one ever thinks to tell you.

Don't keep people waiting. If you leave the set to go to your dressing room or the bathroom, tell the AD or the second where you are so they won't have to search for you if they need you. If you are on a set, and the director or stage manager calls for you, don't finish the story you are telling. Go immediately. Finish the story later. It is a temptation to entertain on the set, particularly if you know the latest gossip, funniest joke, etc., but three minutes here and five minutes there do add up. If you are on a film or television set, you could be holding up an enormous group of people. Not only is it expensive, it is arrogant to consider that your joke is important enough to keep 150 people waiting.

Don't clown around. Before entering college, I had no experience as an actress except for school plays. When I got to college, it seemed like heaven. I really wanted to be liked and chose to become a real clown at rehearsals. One day, as I was delaying rehearsals doing some funny thing, not saying the line properly to get a laugh, or whatever, I looked across the stage to my friend Jerry Melton. Jerry was an older, more experienced actor than I and I really looked up to him. As I looked at him for approval of my joke, his face said: "No, no. Don't do that. It's not cool."

I got it immediately and stopped. No one had ever told me and I was young and dumb. I found out later that I had not been cast in a couple of plays at an earlier time because I was known as someone who wasted time.

Stay off the telephone. Stay tuned in. I guested on a television show recently and was aghast to see the actresses literally never let go of their Blackberries. When the cameras were ready to roll, the ladies hid their phones behind them on the couch. At "cut" their fingers were already texting.

When your energy is split you not only can't be as effective as those with their full attention on the work, but the behavior is disrespectful to the set.

Before cell phones, I worked on another show that had many young actors as leads. They varied in ages from six to twenty-one. The show was not doing well for a variety of reasons and it was also woefully behind schedule. Every time the camera was ready to roll, one or another of the young stars was away from the set on the phone. It took time to get them off the phone and back to the set.

Others who might have been more conscientious and stayed close to the set saw no future in that since the set-ups were always delayed, so they started straggling about and had to be rounded up as well. Yes, it is up to the assistant directors and stage managers to make sure the actors are in their places when the camera is ready to roll, but it isn't their job to give actors lessons in manners.

It's unlikely that anyone is ever going to take the time to explain to you that you are wasting everyone's time, that your energies are focused on phone calls instead of the work at hand, and that because of these things, the producers just won't be motivated to request you on future projects.

I was able to see myself in these actors and thought of the times that I had rushed to the phone between shots instead of staying tuned to the set and wondered how many people I might have alienated by this behavior and how my work might have been affected as well.

A friend of mine was on a Top Ten television show. She had very little to do and spent lots of time in her dressing room while the rest of the cast was rehearsing without her. When she had three hours off, she never rushed out to shop or took long lunches. She wasn't spending all that time in her dressing room on her script, but she said that if she left the studio she would not be able to be focused on her work. She needed to be there.

I think of another actress I knew on a highly-regarded show. She didn't have much to do, either. The difference is this: she was so angry because she felt under-utilized that she didn't prepare well. Sometimes, she didn't prepare at all.

The result was that the writers perceived this and had no incentive to write for her. She doesn't do what she is given very well, so why give her more? Wherever you are, if you are not part of the solution, you are part of the problem.

Whatever capacity you are working in, the employer wants to know that you care and that you want the whole endeavor to be the best possible product. I am never happy to pay someone to do the minimum, but it's a pleasure to pay someone money I feel they have earned and it's to my advantage to reward them with more work.

Being Right for the Part/Visibility

When a casting director speaks of an actor as right for a part, he is speaking about the essence of the actor. We all associate a particular essence with Tom Cruise and a different essence with Jim Carrey, so one would not expect Jim Carrey and Tom Cruise to be up for the same part.

Another aspect of being right concerns visibility. Visibility means currently being on view in film, theatre or television. In this business, it is out of sight, out of mind. You can be a dead ringer for Brad Pitt, but if you are not as visible as he is, you're not going to get seen for his part. The bigger the part, the bigger the credits you must have to support being seen.

The third element of right has to do with physicality. If you are 6'7" and everyone else in the project is 5'4", it does seem unlikely you will be hired. If they are putting together a family, it is necessary that you look more like the rest of the family than your closest competitor, all other things being equal.

Protocol

Afraid of doing the wrong thing, when I first worked on a set in Los Angeles, I would quietly go to my chair and sit until someone decided to speak to me. As it turned out, I now realize, this is the most appropriate way to behave.

On a film or television set, there is an unspoken hierarchy or pecking order. By and large, an extra does not go up to a star or director and begin a conversation. Neither does a supporting player, unless there is already a relationship. The star and director can approach anyone they choose. Others best wait to be recognized. It's very subtle, but very real.

There's nothing wrong with this. It's etiquette in the business. Just be cool and observe. You will understand quickly. I don't imagine a lowly secretary goes up to the President of IBM and starts a discussion either. When you become the star, it will be up to you to make others feel at home on the set.

Reporting to Work

For those of you who have never had the opportunity to work on a film or television set, let me give you a taste of what it is like. If you guest on a television series, you will encounter a family of actors who have been working together and who have already bonded. In most cases, they will be welcoming and warm and treat you well. You will, however, be a guest and as in any other family, not an intimate member of the group. It is wise to remember this and wait to be invited to partake in whatever their normal rituals might be.

When you arrive, the AD will show you to your dressing room, advise you when hair and make-up will be ready for you and possibly ask what you might like for breakfast. Hair and make-up will have an idea of how you should look since they have read the script, but remember, you know how you look best.

It's best to address things up front. How do you see this character? I normally wear my hair this way, I usually do minimal make-up, I like my eyes done this way, etc. Be tactful in making suggestions. Although hair and make-up want you to be comfortable, they don't like to be bossed around.

You will have already met with wardrobe for fittings or have been advised regarding which of your own clothing might be appropriate. You'll get dressed and either stay in your dressing room relaxing or report to the set. It's perfectly all right to wait to be called to the set. I usually go on to the set as soon as I am ready because I want to bond with everybody, touch the furniture, and become comfortable on the set as soon as possible.

Although I'm gregarious by nature, when I am on a new set I usually wait to be spoken to especially by those on a higher level. I work my way into the system slowly. It works for me. Do whatever works for you.

The prop man will usually show you a chair marked Cast and you'll hang out until they call you to rehearse or shoot. After a shot or rehearsal when you have twenty minutes or more before the next shot, many people run to the craft table for food. Eat as much as you like, but remember the energy it takes to digest that food is energy you can use to focus on your work and harness your emotional life.

The more you can stay focused on the work, the better off you will be. It's good to fraternize with your fellow actors, but remember to focus on your work. It may feel good to be adorable and tell your best story, but when the AD calls you to shoot, it can be difficult to quickly adjust to what's happening in the scene.

Between set-ups and after lunch, hair and make-up will check you. Make sure you are always where someone can find you. If you must leave the set to go to the bathroom or change, speak to one of the ADs to make sure there is time before you are needed again and to let them know where you will be. If you are in the middle of a shot and need to go to the bathroom, try to wait until that shot is complete; otherwise, there may be 100 people standing around waiting for you to return. It may not look that way, and the AD will say "Go ahead and go" but the result is that the shot is delayed.

When you have finished your work for the day, the AD will release you and you will be given a sign out sheet. You should keep a notebook where you note exactly when you arrived, started to work, ate lunch, and wrapped each day. It may be important later. When you go to your dressing room to change into your own clothes, you'll leave your wardrobe in your dressing room. The wardrobe people are not paid to be maids and/or butlers, so hang up your clothes up before you leave.

Situation Comedies

A situation comedy is completely different. On the first day, the entire cast and staff sit around a large table while the cast reads the script. There is usually a table with breakfast type foods available and people are casual. The regular cast can afford that behavior; you can't. So be alert, pleasant and do your best work.

After the read-through, there's a break while the director and writers confer about what worked and what didn't. At that point, the writers and producers depart to begin rewrites and the director usually begins blocking. Most shows do a run-through for the writers and producers at the end of the day. That night the changes will be messengered to your home so that you will be prepared for the next day's work.

On the fourth day of a taped show, you will spend the day walking the material slowly so that the camera people can mark their moves. At the end of that day, there's a dress rehearsal on camera with full wardrobe so the producers can see what is happening. On filmed shows, they will usually begin filming part of the show on that day.

On the fifth day, you will get a later call (since you will be there into evening if there is an audience), report to hair and make-up, put on your wardrobe, and go out in front of an audience and do the show.

There will be a break for dinner. There might be line changes and then everyone prepares for the second show. After the second show, the audience will leave and any pickups (scenes that need repair) will be re-shot. You might get out by 10 pm if the show is organized and has been shooting for several seasons or it could be midnight.

For feature and television films, the drill is much like my description of life on a television series set. If you are lucky enough to have a good part, necessitating several days or weeks of work, you will get to be one of the family and bond with people. Certainly my favorite situation.

Wherever you are working, remember that our work is collaborative and that everyone is doing his best. Cut people some slack if they are less than charming. They may be as frightened as you.

Can't We All Just Get Along?

Actors are just like civilians; they love famous people and feel (rightly) that working with a famous person will give them more prestige. It certainly enhances a resume. Working with stars can be just as delightful (or not) as working with everyday people.

Stars frequently direct you. It never bothers me although it makes some other actors crazy. When I feel the idea is good, I use it. On occasion I have seen stars blatantly give an actor notes that will make his performance worse, so be sure to evaluate the advice before you take it. It does no good to resist, to go to the director or to get cranky about it. Just tell the star what a great idea it is, thank him profusely and do what you want.

I once worked with a well-known actress who must have been upset that the writers had given me a very powerful scene to play. The scene called for tears. Every time we shot my scene, she managed to drop something, flub a line or otherwise ruin the scene over and over.

She assumed the more we did the scene, the less emotional juice I would have to expend. Too bad for her. That day, I was extremely focused. The only thing she accomplished was to cost the producers more money because we had to shoot it so many times.

Some actors (stars or not) will purposely ruin a take if they do not like the way they looked in it. This keeps the director from making the decision to use the scene for someone else's good performance. There's not much you can do about that.

If you are working with a very competitive actor who feels he can only look good if you look bad, your only defense is not to get hooked into it. I have heard lots of one-upping stories. Some actors are able to be quite powerful in offsetting this. They consider it a testing of sorts and don't get cranky about it. It can be disconcerting, but if you rise to the occasion it can also be invigorating.

There are many stories about Marilyn Monroe and the filming of *Some Like it Hot*. She would supposedly not come out of her trailer until the afternoon. By that time, her co-stars had been waiting for her since morning. They were tired, frustrated, angry and no longer at their best. Billy Wilder supposedly told both Jack Lemmon and Tony Curtis that they better be good all the time, because any take that Marilyn was good in, he was going to print.

Who knows if her tardiness was fear regarding her own performance or competition with her fellow actors?

My friend Leslie had one big scene with a more experienced and visible actress. There were long rehearsal periods in New York before they went to the actual location where they were to rehearse the scene once for the camera and then shoot. The scene was a verbal fight where Leslie had all the lines. Her opponent's role was to attempt to speak. As the director called action and the rehearsal began, the other actress slugged Leslie full in the face. The slap was an incredible stimulus for the scene and it played better than ever.

The only problem was that the camera was not rolling. Because no one had called cut, Leslie continued her performance at a high pitch and had nothing left when the camera was rolling. Whatever the motivation of the other actress, Leslie missed her own biggest moment in the film.

Professional Relationships

Networking is a dirty word to many of you. "Oh, I'm not good at all that bullshit," or "I don't want to get a job just because I know someone" or "I'm here for art, not for commercialism." Come on, wouldn't you really rather work someplace where you feel comfortable and with a director that you already know you can trust? Well, management feels the same way and it's their money on the line. That being the case, keep up with directors, producers, writers and casting people you have worked with. And that doesn't mean just sending them a note when you are appearing in something. Keep up with their careers and let them know when they do something you like. They know you're an actor and that you want a job, and if you're good, hiring you will only make them look good. So do your part, keep in touch and keep growing. Besides, when you become a star, you'll want to recommend directors as well as make-up people, costumers and the best of everyone you know and admire.

Many jobs in episodes are given to people who have previously worked with the director in smaller roles. Do as much as you can to stay connected. Keep meticulous notes. If you meet with a casting director and are able to find out that she has a ten-year-old daughter named Diane, then that information should go on a card to help you remember the casting director and to give you something to talk about. Not only will the casting director appreciate your effort, but you will be able to audition better and feel more comfortable. Life is about connecting, being in the moment, and treating people with respect. If you don't take the time to do that, it doesn't matter how many jobs you get. You'll continually feel that something is missing.

Practice connecting. Talk to the people in the grocery store and the people at the bank. Practice remembering and using their names. Find out something about them. Notice what makes one person different from another. Become a student of human nature. You'll not only become a better actor, but a more appealing person as well. The act of networking will simply be keeping up with your friends.

When my son was in graduate school, his major professor always made sure that when a visiting professor spoke on campus, the graduate students met for coffee afterwards with the star and conversed. He brought Dr. Smart to my son saying, "Dr. Smart, I want you to meet Jamie Callan, he is working on thus and such. Jamie, Dr. Smart is an authority on whatever." As a result, when Jamie (a Ph.D. himself, now) reads something that relates to Dr. Smart's project, he can drop that it in an envelope with a note saying that this material made him think of Smart and his project.

It's nice when someone sets up the guidelines for a conversation, but with a little imagination, you'll be able to do that for yourself. The key is to focus on the other person.

Facilitate

Another way of staying in touch with colleagues is by being a facilitator; helping other people. If a casting director is looking for a particular type, don't be afraid to mention the best actor you can think of for the project. Remember the names of producers and directors, costumers and set designers. Be happy to share a terrific person you have worked with and suggest how she might solve somebody else's problem. If you can't remember names, keep notes and use them. What goes around comes around.

The Way It Really Is

Actors who have given up believing in fairytales in real life still have a hard time letting go as far as the business is concerned. Me, too. I know the score and I still believe the movies. I still think that if I got an Academy Award nomination it would change my career. In fact, it would change my social status if only during that voting season. A win is good for a few more months, but not much more.

I love what Dana Carvey said about fame:

✦ *"Fame is really just good for having sex with different women, that's what it's good for. So if you're married, it's kind of like a drag. But that's what it's good for, period. George Clooney, he's living the life that all men want to live."*
Dana Carvey, interviewed by Sean Mitchell, *Los Angeles Times*[97]

I have watched friends of mine win awards with varying results. The plain facts are that awards, by and large, are economic considerations that only incidentally benefit the actor. They were instituted originally to draw attention to the projects of the producers. Today the sponsors of such ceremonies use them not only to promote their industry, but to gain large television revenues for the awards ceremony.

A Tony is very prestigious within the Broadway theatre community and will certainly get you considered for more parts. Two Tonys are worth a lot more than one and three are worth even more than that. They signify that you have become a bonafide member of the Broadway fraternity (notice that I did not say sorority, for it is still mainly a man's game). Employers in Los Angeles could not care less about Broadway awards unless the winners were in some huge international success that gained great media attention.

One Emmy was thrilling for a friend of mine. But it was only after the second win that she moved up the food chain to become a member of the hierarchy. She still finds herself unemployed like the rest of us and she still loses out to performers of more visibility, but her status is forever changed and she can command more money.

The Academy Award is still the most prestigious award, but I can't remember who won last year, can you? I don't care, I still want one.

Because of the vast amount of television product, the members of the Television Academy can't possibly see everything and few take it seriously enough to vote only for those performances they see. I know all these things. Do you really think I will remember them if I'm ever nominated?

The whole awards process mostly puts actors in a cranky mood. When you spend your whole life thinking one of these events is going to change your standing in the business and it doesn't, it's disappointing. Actors tend to think then, that all is lost. Nothing is any more lost than it was the day before.

You are not a better or worse actor because you were or were not nominated or did or did not win. Just think of it as your birthday. If you are lucky, on your birthday, people treat you very well. Then, the next day, it isn't your birthday. You are able to accept that and it's very similar.

Rags to Riches and Back Again

Henry Winkler had to hitchhike to the audition for *Happy Days*. He was, in fact, picked up by one of the people who ended up hiring him. Henry was young and made it big.

Danny DeVito and Rhea Perlman lived in a one room apartment for fifteen years in New York before they began to regularly make money.

As wonderful as it is to finally make it, it's just as depressing when casting directors and producers decide an actor is overexposed. The actor can then go from being a household name to being totally unemployed for years.

Howard Keel, who was a huge star thirty years ago on Broadway and in MGM musicals, told me an interesting story at a dinner party. When musicals went out of business, so did Keel and he spent years unemployed and depressed. He finally gave up and decided to move to Oklahoma City and get into the oil business. He considered himself a failure when he hired the truck and left California. In true Hollywood style, as soon as he had accepted his new lifestyle, a phone call came that put him back to work on the hit television series, *Dallas*. That break not only gave him a lengthy career on *Dallas* but still fuels concert appearances all these years later.

One needs perspective on oneself and the business in order to survive. The point is to have the chance to work. Very few people get to pick and choose, even people as visible and successful as Broadway legend Jessica Tandy. This interview with Miss Tandy's husband, Hume Cronyn, was written at the time of her death. I think it makes a good point:

✦ *"Jessie adores working," Mr. Cronyn said in 1986. "She's more fully alive when she's working." As she got older she seemed to be in ever greater demand, but over the years she took good parts and she took bad parts. "You are richer for doing things," she said. "If you wait for the perfect part or for what sends you, you will have long waits, and you will deteriorate. You can't be an actor without acting."*

Marilyn Berger, *The New York Times*[98]

My own choice of acting was not based in any way on the reality of what the life is really about. Actually, it may have been based on what the life was about when I was five years old, but the business is totally different today than it was then.

It is even different today than it was in 1980. At that time, there was a long actors strike that had profound effects on the industry. Actually, I don't think the strike changed the business. The strike only reflected the changes that had already occurred in the industry and the world. The same thing may be happening even as you read this.

Whatever the outcome of the strikes of 2007-2008, the trend continues. Less work and less money for the middle class actor. The stars and their reps continue to take home the money. The stars are, after all, the ones who attract the audiences and carry the projects. It's too bad it can't be like the old days (that I mostly never experienced) where there was room for some people in the middle. Again, I think this reflects where our country is right now.

Series Stardom Forever — Not

The star and producer of one of the world's most popular shows found out the hard way that television stardom is unpredictable.

✦ *After his "Knight Rider" series was canceled by NBC in 1986, David Hasselhoff couldn't get a job. It didn't deter the brawny, six-foot, four-inch actor, who has repeatedly turned cancellations of series to his advantage. He's the first to admit that four years spent talking to a car, coupled with his good looks, only saddled him with the label "Can't Act."*

"It was a touchy time," he admits. "I couldn't get a job because I wasn't taken seriously after "Knight Rider." Scripts would call for a David Hasselhoff type, yet no one wanted the real thing. But when you think about it, I spent all that time talking to a car and I made it work. So there I was, sitting out on my back lawn thinking, Holy s--t! What am I going to do with all this energy?"

Kathleen O'Steen, *Emmy*[99]

He lucked into another series, *Baywatch*, and though it was canceled after one year, Hasselhoff's success producing his own record album made him realize that he had enormous popularity internationally so he bought the rights to the show and produced additional seasons of *Baywatch* himself before segueing to Broadway to star in *Dr. Jekyll and Mr. Hyde. Hmmn.* Not just a pretty face, after all!

What Have You Been Doing?

There's a wonderful joke about the actor who was found in bed with another man's wife. The irate husband demanded, "What have you been doing?" The actor struck a pose, scratched his head and announced, "A recurring part in *Without a Trace,* two shots on *ER* and a TV movie."

Most of the time, when someone asks an actor that question, they want to know, "Are you working as an actor?" I'm instantly guilty when someone asks me the question and I'm not. It doesn't matter that I might have written four books, gone to China, volunteered at the hospital, and saved four people from a burning building. Nothing seems to count but working as an actor.

I never ask if a friend has been working and I never volunteer that information about myself. If one of us has been working and the other one hasn't, it can be uncomfortable. If it becomes apparent that we have both been working or that we are both not working, then we can discuss the business, but I'd rather talk about something else.

Civilians, of course, do not understand. When I lived in New York, I did a great many commercials, but like everyone else, I went through dry periods without much on the air. During a particularly depressing time, one of the people in my apartment building (whom I didn't know) greeted me warmly and said, "Say, haven't seen you on the tube lately. Have you left the business?" "No," I wanted to scream at him, "The business has left me."

This still happens. If I don't have something to report when some unthinking civilian asks me, "Well, what are you working on now," I need to pause for a deep breathe to center myself or I feel instantly guilty and worthless. Even then, it's hard.

You are not paranoid. Your worst nightmares are true. If you are not currently working (visible), everyone concludes that you are dead and out of the business.

The truth is, if you have any kind of history of working in the business, you will work again. At this moment in time, you have been given a gift of time to study, do your Christmas shopping or get married before your next job. You are neither dead and out of the business nor an unemployed actor who will never work again. The way you choose to think about periods of not working will make a profound difference in your life.

There will be times (sometimes long times) when you will not work. If you opt to stay home and eat, sleep, cry, drink or indulge in any of the many other self-destructive choices available, instead of making your own work and/or getting on with your life, you will be missing out on time that could be productive and happy.

In order to work, it is true that you will have to be a detective to find the job and a press agent to capitalize on your good fortune. You must have the courage and nerve of a gambler to negotiate your contracts and also to take a chance doing something original at an audition. Only a gambler would stay in a business when it seems as though the odds are against you (and they always are).

You must constantly study to refine your craft. You must be an entrepreneur to create your own work, whether you become a book reviewer, a director, a producer, a teacher, or stand-up or any of the other actor options within the field. You must have the character insights of a psychologist not only to break down a character, but to understand basic human behavior (yours as well as the person you are dealing with), and surely you will have to become a philosopher in order to put all this in a proper perspective.

If you are a smart actor, you will not allow success to stifle these gifts. Actors frequently believe that a measure of success brings freedom from the entrepreneurial aspects of the work. When we become concerned with protecting position and status and lose touch with our own action and vision, work frequently dries up.

Remember, stardom is only unemployment at a higher rate of pay.

Systems Dynamics Exchange

My son explained a useful engineering concept to me: It has to do with Systems Dynamics Exchange. The principle can be demonstrated with my furnace. When I turn up the thermostat in my house, it takes a few minutes for the furnace to kick on. It takes even longer for my house to warm up. Therefore, if I'm smart, I will turn on the thermostat before I am cold. So it is with careers; getting lazy frequently means getting left out in the cold.

Wrap Up

✓ there are many kinds of auditions
✓ prepare carefully
✓ choose material that suits you
✓ your behavior is important
✓ insecurity is unappealing
✓ wait intelligently
✓ learn about negotiation
✓ lots of us have been replaced
✓ it's important to get along with fellow actors
✓ getting hired depends on many factors
✓ being right can be more important than being good
✓ professional behavior is always noticed
✓ networking is important
✓ learn to be a facilitator
✓ deal with reality not your fantasies
✓ awards can change your status in the business or not
✓ systems dynamics exchange can help you stay warm

≼ 15 ≽

Agents & Managers

At the beginning of my career in New York, I thought if I got the right agent, he could/would make me a star. I thought agents had the power to make or break your career.

In Texas, I had learned how to call advertising agencies and film companies in pursuit of commercials so I didn't feel so dependent on agents in that part of the business. I already had a commercial career going, at least in Texas; I had a reel and felt like there was a good chance I could translate my Texas commercial success into action in New York. But theatre, film, and television? No, I had seen the movies: you had to have an agent for that.

Although I had no idea how a theatrical agent would receive me, my previous experience had taught me to be businesslike about calling on agents. I told myself I could not eat lunch until I had visited at least one theatrical agent. I would tell myself that if I did not go in and leave a picture and resume I had no chance. But if I left a picture and resume, the agent would be aware of my existence, at least, and my chances would improve.

After all my late lunches, it was through a commercial agent that I got the break that gave me credibility with theatrical agents. A New York talent agency that submits both commercial and theatrical project sent me for a film titled *The Gap*.

I'm pretty sure the agent must have submitted every actor she had who was the right color and within ten years of being the right age. Regardless, that is how Peter Boyle, Dennis Patrick, Audrey Caire, and I came to be cast in a film that was listed on many Ten Best lists for 1970. The movie, also Susan Sarandon's first film, was released with a new title: *Joe*.

After the film and some nice personal reviews, I still didn't choose an agent. In New York it's easy to exist working freelance and I was so frightened of choosing the wrong agent that I didn't choose one at all. Finally, the late Jay Wolfe (a wonderfully kind and talented casting director) said, "K, you have to choose an agent. It just doesn't look good not to be signed."

Though I now had the credits to attract an agent and had reached a place in the business where I needed an agent to maintain credibility, I still didn't know how to intelligently choose one.

Instead of educating myself, I chose a manager and gave away 15% more of my money (even on the commercial business I had built myself).

Having a manager did not increase my business, so I finally gathered my courage, left the manager, and signed with Jeff Hunter, one of the best agents in the business.

Although an agent is important, he can only sell a marketable product. That means that the actor must maintain his physical appearance, deal optimistically with unemployment and aging, and preserve his emotional health in an atmosphere that seems to thrive on pulling him down.

Even though I've been in the business almost 40 years now and know all this, it's still a temptation to place too much emphasis on my agent. I want to believe he is getting or not getting me appointments. That way, when I'm not going out, it must be his responsibility.

It's not.

It's frustrating, but understandable, that credible agencies (who are not in the business of starting careers) don't want you until you have done all the groundwork that demonstrates your employability and resourcefulness by finding a way into the business on whatever level.

You must become marketable so you are able to attract an agent whose contacts coupled with your growing reputation, result in a job or at least an audition for one. The most successful agent in town can't sell a turkey. He might be able to force someone to see you, but why would he want to?

Since one of your goals is to attract an agent or manager, you will want to consider what kind of actor excites them.

The Definitive Client

✦ *My favorite kind of client? I like character actors. I like black actors and Hispanic actors very much. I understand them. I don't know why. We like developing people. We look at backgrounds. I like stage. I love people who do the footwork. When I see a blank resume and they say, 'I'm talented, trust me,' that's the kiss of death in this office.*

I can see when someone has gone through the theater department; someone has

*done a lot of Equity Waiver plays. I appreciate that. When someone tells me they
study a lot, that kind of scares me. I think there's studying and there's practical
experience.*
Daryl Marshak/Daryl Marshak and Associates, Los Angeles

✦ *I want to know either that the actor works and makes a lot of money so that
I can support my office or that the potential to make money is there. I am one of
the people who goes for talent, so I do take people who are not big money makers,
because I am impressed with talent.*
Martin Gage/The Gage Group, Los Angeles

✦ *More jobs are available for certain types of actors than other types so you look
at the physicality, for that look you know can sell. And nine times out of ten, that
look is gorgeous. Men. Women. Beautiful. It's just a fact.*
Ric Beddingfield/Manager, Los Angeles

✦ *I love a good resume. Even if there is no TV and film, if someone has great
training and practical experience, even if it's La Mirada Steak House Dinner
Theater, it's nice to see that. Some people make up video tapes with monologues on
it. It's nice when an actor comes in well prepared. If he's gotten key casting people
to call me and networks his way into the office, I'm impressed with that.*
Daryl Marshak/Daryl Marshak and Associates, Los Angeles

✦ *If they're a character actor, you have to ask yourself, "Do I need another
character actor in my life?" Or, if they're attractive, then you have to start praying
they can act.*
Ric Beddingfield/Manager, Los Angeles

The late New York agent, Beverly Anderson told me about meeting
a prospective client:

✦ *Sigourney Weaver asked to come in and meet me when she was with a client of
mine in Ingrid Bergman's show, "The Constant Wife." She's almost six feet tall.
I'm very tall myself and when I saw her, I thought, "God, honey, you're going to
have a tough time in this business because you're so huge."*

*And she floated in and she did something no one had ever done. She had this
big book with all her pictures from Bryn Mawr or Radcliffe of things she had done
and she opened this book and she comes around and drapes herself over my
shoulders from behind and points to herself in these pictures.*

She was hovering over me. And I thought no matter what happens with me, this

woman is going to make it. There was determination and strength and self-confidence and positiveness. Nobody's ever done that to me before.
Beverly Anderson

So, agents are looking for:

training	commerciality
experience	presence
talent	attitude
self-confidence	competitiveness
potential	looks

Well, I'd like to find all those things in an agent.

The Definitive Agent

If Beverly Anderson looks mainly for an actor who can get the job, I think the actor has to be primarily looking for an agent who can get him the audition. That sounds pretty simple, doesn't it?

Well, if the actor/agent relationship were based on getting auditions for everything, then the agent would have a right to say that you must get everything he sends you out on.

Getting an audition isn't necessarily the most important thing, either. Is he sending you on the right auditions? Does he see you accurately? Do you both have the same perception regarding the roles you are right for?

The agent has to know what the actor can do, what the range is, so he knows how to handle that particular artist.

Jeff Berg is the chairman of one of the industry's most important and powerful agencies, International Creative Management (ICM), which represents clients like Anthony Hopkins, Tommy Lee Jones, and Holly Hunter. He makes some good points about agents:

✦ *I'll tell you what I like about agents. I like the fact that agents look to make it happen. And a good agent can't take 'no' and expect to support himself. Agents have to develop a kind of resistance to rejection, and I think it makes you stronger and I think it makes you better.*
Bernard Weinraub, *The New York Times*[100]

I asked other agents what qualities they would look for if they were choosing agents. They mentioned integrity, client list, communication, background, and taste.

To know whether an agent possesses these traits, you'll have to do some research. *Reel Power*, written by Mark Litwak and published by William Morrow, is a good place to start:

✦ *One of the chief factors that determines the value of an agent is information. It is impossible for a small agent to possess the amount of information that a large agent can. We track hundreds of projects weekly at all of the studios and networks.*

If a client walks in and asks about a project, I can haul out 400 pages of notes and say, "Oh yeah, its at this studio and this is the producer and they're doing a rewrite right now and they're hoping to go with it on this date and talking to so-and-so about it." I have that information.

Gene Parseghian/Manager, Los Angeles

So, Gene thinks (and I certainly agree) that information is important. There are two other traits I want in an agent.

Access and Stature

The dictionary defines access as "ability to approach or admittance." Conglomerate agencies have so many stars on their lists, they have plenty of ability to approach. If the studios, networks and producers do not return their phone calls, they might find the agency retaliating by withholding their important stars.

Stature, on the other hand, is entirely different. Webster defines the word as "level of achievement." Other prestigious, mid-level agents like Mitchell K. Stubbs and Martin Gage surely have more stature than some lowly agent at William Morris, but possibly not as much access.

There's also the question of style. I know an actor who had a very effective agent who yelled at everyone (the client and the casting directors). That's not to say the agent didn't get the actor appointments; he did. The actor simply decided that wasn't the way he wanted to be represented, so he left.

In smaller marketplaces, the same qualifiers hold true. There may just be one agent in town for you to choose from who may not have stature and/or access. Then you will have to acquire these attributes yourself. It's not impossible. We (and they) build credibility by telling the truth, saying something, and carrying through. Don't promise something you can't deliver. If you can get someone to see you and you have something to sell, they will hire you. Perhaps not today, but it will happen.

Size

When you are shopping for an agent, make sure you get one that is your size. The most effective formula is the agency with the smallest number of credible clients and the largest number of well-respected agents. Many agents believe a good ratio is one agent to 20-25 actors.

For a successful partnership, you and your agent must have the same goals and visions. If you think you can be a star and your agent doesn't, or if he sees you as a star and you want a different kind of career, you're both going to be frustrated and the relationship won't work. Aggressiveness, enthusiasm, and integrity are all part of the mix.

In a fairytale business, it's comforting and necessary to know that at least one person is telling you the truth.

So in addition to actor/agent ratio, the chief assets to look for are:

stature	shared vision	enthusiasm	style
access	compatibility	aggressiveness	integrity

Let's say you have now landed the agent of your dreams (or the only agent in town). Now what?

The Relationship

All relationships take communication, thought, creative energy, and time in order to bond and be successful. This includes your partnership with your agent. As in other unions, it is important to know what you want from the alliance in order to get it. It is better to decide what you want before you sign a contract. What do you need from your agent in order to feel not only well-represented, but comfortable? There's a whole list of things I require.

It's important to me that my agent return my phone calls promptly. That might not be important to someone else, but it is high on my list of requirements.

I also want my agent to submit me for any job I am right for. I would like him to have the stature to get his phone calls returned from important casting directors and producers. I want him to have the imagination and aggressiveness to suggest me for roles that might be terrific for me, though unusual casting-wise.

I think we all want to be able to communicate honestly and easily with our agent, but trust doesn't happen in a day, from either one of you. There is going to be a period of getting acquainted and learning each other's signals. Don't be impatient. This person is your business partner. He needs to talk to you as much as you need to talk to him if he is going to represent you well.

Your agent doesn't have to be involved in your social circle, but he can be. Some people want their agents to console them when they're not working. If that is your need and your arrangement, fine, but it's really not part of the job description.

It's important to know what you want and to communicate that information to your prospective business partner, as well to find out what his needs are in order to negotiate the shape of your prospective partnership. It's going to be a marriage, after all, so you will need to have the same goals, tastes, value system, and vision regarding the possibilities of your union.

Getting Started

The best way to contact an agent is through a referral. If you know someone on the agent's list who can act as a go-between, that is fine. If you are friendly with a casting director, you might ask for advice about agents to contact. If the casting director volunteers to make a call for you, that would be terrific. But what if you don't have that entree?

If you are young and beautiful, drop your picture off looking as Y&B as possible.

If you are really Y&B and can speak at all, few will require you do much more. It's sad (for the rest of us), but true, so you may as well cash in on it. If you are smart, you will study while cashing in. Y&B doesn't linger long and you may want to work during those grey years of your thirties and beyond.

As I mentioned earlier, I think it's best to send a letter a couple of days before sending a picture and resume. Letters get read while pictures and resumes tend to sit in the as-soon-as-I-get-to-it stack.

Address your letter to a specific agent, preferably one of the associates. They get less mail than the owner so you might get attention sooner.

Remember, type your letter and use good paper. State that you are looking for representation and that you are impressed with the agency's client list (make sure you know who is on it) and that your credits compare favorably. Tell them your picture and resume will arrive in the next day's mail.

Make sure they do. Do not say you want this person for your agent (you don't know that yet). Mention a few key credits. If your credits don't look that impressive, but you did work with Martin Scorsese and Steven Spielberg, by all means note that. If your letter has piqued interest, your picture will be opened immediately.

Mail your letter so that it arrives on Wednesday or Thursday, away from the first-of-the-week rush. Every actor in town has been doing his homework over the weekend, so on Monday and Tuesday the agent's mail is full of 8x10 glossies. If your letter arrives later in the week, it will have less competition. Your follow-up call in the late afternoon should be brief and upbeat. Be a person the agent wants to talk to. If he doesn't want a meeting, get over the disappointment and go on to the next agent on your list.

When Carol Burnett went to New York, agents said to call when she was in something. Didn't they know if she was in something that she wouldn't need an agent? Finally, she enlisted her boyfriend (a writer) and the young women she lived with in a residence for young actresses. They produced their own show and invited all the agents in town. They all came.

When I interviewed New York agent Lionel Larner, he told me: "Tell actors to produce something in their living room and invite agents. I would come."

There really is an agent for everyone no matter where you live. Your focus, energy, and attitude can put you ahead of the pack. If you are committed, shoulder your responsibilities, do the work and pursue employment in a professional manner, you will prosper.

Reel

If you're not appearing at some venue where an agent can see you work, you really need an audition reel. Compile a DVD (no longer than eight minutes) as soon as you have any professional examples of your work. When you are just beginning, this might be several commercials (or moments from the commercials that feature you), a student film or even a non-union film. It can be two minutes or five, it doesn't have to be eight, but it should be something to show what you look like on film and give some idea of your range. This is a quick sales tool that can save you and the agent a lot of time.

A few years ago I received a frantic call from a woman who explained to me that she was enrolled in a seminar I was teaching that weekend for the American Film Institute, but that she needed to see me sooner. She had an appointment with an agent on Friday and she wanted to know if she could make an appointment for a consultation.

I told her to bring everything she had. Pictures, resumes, any examples of her work on film. She was about thirty-five, overweight, blowzy, very nice. I looked at her film and suggested that she not go to the agent without a reel. We selected the scenes we felt were best and she rushed to have a tape made.

A week later she called to tell me that when she got to the agent's office, the agent seemed unimpressed and passed her off to her assistant. The actress left her tape anyway. Over the weekend, she discovered another piece of film that she wanted to her tape. She called the agent's office to see if they had looked at the tape. They hadn't gotten to it yet and were annoyed that she had called. She explained that she had more film to add to it and that she would like to come by, pick it up, add the new material, and return the tape. There was a lot of sighing: "All right. Come and get it."

By the time the actress got there, the agent had looked at the tape. She was welcomed warmly: "Come in. Come in. We think you are wonderful. Can we sign you?"

Without the tape, she would probably have been passed over. It is pretty impossible to tell in an office meeting whether or not you are a good actor or to have any idea of someone's range.

Producing a tape of yourself is often a waste of money because most agents either will not look at a home-produced tape or will not give it much credibility. Therefore, one of your first goals should be to amass professional work on film. Call every theater and film school in your area and volunteer for student films. Do what you can with commercials and industrial film. This is an important entree into the business.

Another word about self-produced reels. I know a youngish actor who left another profession to pursue his dream. He has more money than a regular actor just starting out. You can tell by looking at his audition tape that it was expensive to put together. The problem is that it's all razzle dazzle. The actor doesn't really have that much to show and the reel totally points that up.

If you don't have anything to show, you're not far enough along to put anything together yet. Have patience. It will happen.

Also, there are many different places that will edit a tape for you. Some charge hourly and some by the job. It's been my experience that paying for hourly time is the way to go.

The Meeting

Okay, you've got an appointment. Now what will you do? How will you dress? How will you behave? What questions should you ask? Although you are there to present yourself to the agent, he is the salesman, afer all, so don't tell him he could make a lot of money on you. Agents have told me such self-serving remarks automatically conclude the meeting. He's not the agent for you if he can't figure that out by your presence and credits.

This is the time for clarity. Tell him you think you are due for a series, a film or whatever, but be realistic. Ask what he thinks is your realistic next step. Tell him what you think your strong points are.

Learn how the office works. If you're being interviewed by the owner, is he going to work for you or is he just the charmer? I know actors who signed with agencies because they were impressed with the owner, but after becoming his client, he rarely crossed the actor's path.

Can you drop by the office? Should you call first? Will the agents come to see your work? Will they consult with you before they turn down work? Are they good about returning phone calls? Explore your own feelings about these issues before you arrive.

If you need to be able to talk regularly to your agent, now's the time to mention it. He needs to know that's one of the things you require. You might want to ask if the office has a policy of regularly requesting audition material for clients at least a day in advance of the audition. Let him know your requirements to present yourself at your best. If that turns him off, this isn't the agent for you.

Isn't it nice to know there are specific things on your mind to ask about during the meeting so you won't just sit there quaking and hoping to be chosen?

Remembering how overeager people turn you off may help your perspective in these meetings. Remember, what you don't ask today can come back to haunt you tomorrow.

So, you were on time. You arrived with an attractive attitude. You met. You asked questions. You were respectful. You acted naturally. Now, be the one to end the meeting. Make it clear that you value the agent's time and view it as a precious commodity. He will appreciate that. Suggest you both think about the meeting for a day or two and then decide.

Be definite about when you will get back to him (it should be less than a week). You may have other agents to meet. Mention this. If he's last on the list, mention you have to go home and digest all the meetings.

Then go home and do just that. Let him know you were pleased with the meeting. Even if it wasn't your finest moment, or his, be gracious. After all, you both did your best.

Reality Check

I advise a 24-hour fantasy-shakedown period. I've interviewed so many agents in preparation for *The Los Angeles Agent* and *New York Agent* books and while I am in their offices talking to them, I'm having fantasies about almost every one of them. I think, "Oh, I wish he were my agent." They are salesmen, after all.

After a cooling-off period, I find my feelings to be more realistic. The hyperbole seems to drift out of my head and I am able to assess reality more clearly.

It is important to jot down your feelings and thoughts about each meeting as soon as you get home. Then, look at all the notes the next day and re-evaluate your feelings. Never forget you are choosing an agent. The qualities you look for in a friend are not necessarily the same qualities you desire in an agent.

Now you are ready to digest all your research and make a decision. You've done the hard part.

I heard a story about director Mike Nichols. He was giving a speech to the actors on opening night:

✦ *Just go out there and have a good time. Don't let it worry you that "The New*

York Times" is out there; that every important media person in the world is watching you; that we've worked for days and weeks and months on this production; that the investors are going to lose their houses if it doesn't go well; that the writer will commit suicide and that this could be the end of your careers if you make one misstep. Just go out there and have a good time.
Mike Nichols

I think this is the way many of us feel about choosing an agent. We act as if it is a momentous decision having irrevocable consequences on our careers. It's not. You can get a job without an agent. An agent can't book a job without an actor. Keep things in perspective. Do the research, weigh the evidence, then make the decision. The successful career is built on self-knowledge.

Trust your instincts. You already know what to do. Do it.

The Partnership

Once you have chosen the agent, visit him to sign contracts and meet (and fix in your mind) all the people in your new office. If there are several, note who is who and where they sit as soon as you leave the office. Until you become more familiar with everyone, you can consult your map before each subsequent visit and hope they don't play musical chairs in your absence.

Leave a good supply of pictures and resumes. If you have reels, leave those, too, as well as a list of casting directors, producers and directors with whom you have relationships. Alphabetize the list if you ever want the agent to use it. Keep abreast of current productions so that the next time Steven Spielberg has a project, you can remind your agent that you and Steven went to school together. After all, your agent has lots of clients.

Also leave a list of your quotes (how much you were paid for your last jobs in theater, film, and television), plus information on billing. The more background you give your agent, the better he can represent you. If it's a large office, leave each agent your quotes and contacts.

90%/10%

Now the real work begins. Remember the agent only gets 10% of the money. You can't really expect him to do 100% of the work. It's time for you to focus on your expectations. If you don't want him to be lazy, set a good example. Let him see how hard you are working to perfect and sell yourself. Let him see how enthusiastic you are. He will take his cue from you.

It's similar to one's relationship to one's children. If you have a positive view of life and act on it, the chances are that your children will also. If your children see you taking care of business, that's the norm. How you and your agent function together is a joint work-in-progress to which you will both contribute. I don't want to suggest that you can reform anyone's character. I'm assuming that with your diligence and investigation, you have already chosen a like-minded agent.

We hope agents are going to initiate work for us and introduce us to casting directors, producers, directors, etc., but their real contribution over a career span is negotiating, making appointments for us, being supportive in our dark moments, and helping us retain our perspective in the bright moments.

Give a good agent a real career to work with and he will build the momentum. Even then, successful actors don't just hand it all over. They continue to do 90% of the work.

What Does That Mean?

Your agent's job is to get the buyer enthusiastic about you. Your job once you get an agent is to keep your agent enthusiastic about you. When I finally signed with an agent in New York after successfully freelancing for a long time, I thought my part of the hustling was over. When I consider how much I might have contributed to my career if I had agented more, I'm annoyed with myself. My brain could have been teeming with all kinds of possibilities if I had even begun to think this way. It never even occurred to me that my agent might forget about me.

Consider this. If someone came into the room right now, gave you a script to read and then asked for your casting suggestions, who would you be able to think of?

My bet is the list would be heavy with the actors you have just seen in a movie, on television, stage, or in person. Is your agent any different?

Actor's Responsibilities

I know actors who are angry when they have to tell their agents how to negotiate for them. They feel the agent is not doing his job if he has to be reminded to go for a particular kind of billing or per diem or whatever. If the agent has it all together and does everything perfect, that's great, but it's your career. It's up to you to know what the union minimums are, how you go about getting more money and who else might be getting it. You are getting the 90%.

It is your responsibility to have your own plan for your career; it's a way for you to be in control of your destiny in a business where it is all too easy to feel tossed about by fate.

It's your vision and your focus that have gotten the agent's interest in the first place. Why would you want to hand over your business to someone else? The larger the support system and the more sources of energy focusing on a single goal, the larger the payoff. You can't afford to give up your role as your agent.

If you are looking for an agent in the Los Angeles or New York area, *The New York Agent Book* and *The Los Angeles Agent Book* detail agents, their background, clients, and agency information. These books also discuss how to go about having relationships with agents.

Managers

A manager is just an agent with (hopefully) a smaller client list and no restrictions. He can charge whatever percentage he chooses and sign you for as long as he likes. You could decide to be a manager tomorrow and just hang out a sign and work from your bedroom. Who would know?

There are, in fact, some licensed agents who also fit that description, but at least they have a license. Though the SAG/ATA agreement is no longer in effect, most of the agents still play by those rules. They have been screened, posted a bond, only charge you 10%, and can only legally sign you as a first time client for a year. They also observe the 91-day clause that gets both of you out of the relationship if things aren't working out.

While there are uncredentialed managers, there are many who are totally credible. Many were former agents who tired of all the regulations and wanted to produce, a restriction built into the old agreement. As the business continues to morph, I'm becoming more open to the wisdom of adding a manager to your team.

Attorneys

When I was starring in a series many years ago, it seemed to me to be a good idea to have a lawyer go over my contract. I contacted a successful visible friend of mine and asked for a referral. I spoke to the lawyer on the phone, sent him my contract, and waited to hear what he had to say about it. We started shooting and I still did not hear. After shooting seven episodes, we were cancelled and I still had not heard from my lawyer, much less laid eyes on him.

At that point, I got his bill for $5,000. As you can imagine, I was stunned and angry. When I called to say that I felt this fee was way out of line, he asked me what I thought I should pay. I replied that since as far as I could see, he had never done a thing. $200 would seem more reasonable.

"Done," he said.

I've never felt the need for a lawyer since then. Mostly, it's only big stars who add attorneys to their teams. I'm sure that the *Desperate Housewives* stars have powerful (and rich) attorneys working for them in addition to agents, managers, and publicists, but those people have such complicated careers that they probably need all the hands-on attention from each of those elements to keep their careers intact.

Until your career reaches that level, I wouldn't worry about it. If you don't have an agent and need a lawyer to negotiate for you, that would seem to me to be a legitimate reason to engage the services of an attorney.

When It Makes Sense to Have a Manager

Managers are a definite plus for child actors (see Chapter 10) who whose families have no show business background. A manager usually places the child with an agent, monitors auditions, and sometimes even accompanies the child to meetings.

If you are entering the business and need someone to help you with pictures, resumes, image, etc., managers can be helpful. There are, however, many agents who delight in starting new talent and consider this part of their service.

When you are at a big agency and it's too intimidating and time-consuming to bond with twenty agents, it might be advantageous to have a connected manager in your corner.

Changing agents is easier when you have a manager, because the manager does all the research, calling, and rejection of the former agent, so sometimes actors choose managers primarily for this reason. It's an expensive way to avoid discomfort. If the manager doesn't work out, you'll only have to go through the unpleasantness when you decide you can handle your own business after all.

If you have the credits to support getting a good agent, you can do that on your own. If you don't, the manager can't create them. I have a few friends who feel the presence of a manager enhanced their careers. One in particular said that when her agents were considering dropping her, that she and the manager read The Breakdown together, decided what she should be submitted for, and the actress delivered her picture and resume to the casting office. If the manager got a call for an appointment, the actress went in; if she got the job, they called the agent to make the deal.

The agent became more enthusiastic about the actress for a while, but ultimately dropped her. The agent's earlier disinterest signaled what he had already decided: that she was no longer appropriate for their list. In that case, the manager, though helpful, only delayed the inevitable.

Recently, I encountered a situation where I saw a manager work magic, so I have to recant any earlier statements I have made about managers being superfluous. This particular manager took a writer friend of mine from heavy debt to lots of money in two weeks. The combination of my friend's talent finally coming into focus at the same moment that the manager's career was catching fire was a lovely thing to watch.

Whether you have an agent, a manager or both, if you have the goods and they have the contacts, you're in business. If any part of that equation is missing, then it's not going to be your turn.

Changes in the Business

During the past several years as the business has compressed, the role of managers has changed. With increasing regularity, many agents are closing their doors as agents on Friday and opening on Monday as manager. They function largely the same, some charging more (15%) while being freed of all those pesky Screen Actors Guild rules and regulations that protect the talent.

Mike Ovitz, after playing a major role in creating what was for a time the most important talent agency in the world (CAA), and after unsatisfying stints at Disney and Livent, came back into the agent business as a manager when he formed Artists Management Group. Unfortunately, Ovitz spread himself so thinly and tried to do so many things at once that the business folded.

Though he wasn't in the management business very long overall, Ovitz's presence even for three years added to the growing clout of the managers. Though Screen Actors Guild has struggled for years to put some kind of regulations on contracts between managers and actors, at this point in time, managers are mainly agents with no rules.

Although there are many important, effective, and honest managers, there are many who are not. The Association of Talent Agents screens members before they confer membership, so that's worth something even if there continues to be no SAG/ATA regulations.

There are two different manager associations about which I've heard varying reports. The Los Angeles group seems to confer some sort of oversight on its members. If your manager is on the list and misbehaves, calling the association would get you results. They don't want scammers in the business any more than you do. The problem is that only a very tiny percentage of Los Angeles managers belong and most of the larger companies with track records are not members.

When Eddie Murphy became successful, an enterprising manager appeared from his past claiming part of the spoils. He had a valid contract. I don't know what Murphy ended up paying, but the aggravation and court costs were not inconsiderable. If you are entering into an agreement with a manager, be careful. You have no real protection if he turns out to be less than.

One of the main points of contention between SAG and the Association of Talent Agents concerns allowing agents to also be producers as well as have the right to sell off part of their companies to advertising and production agencies.

The guild's stand is that being both one's employee and employer is a conflict of interest and is nothing but bad news for actors. After a large referendum which went to the general SAG membership for a vote, the measure was defeated.

Although the agents vowed to become managers if they didn't get their way, most remain open as agents and are still abiding by the now defunct Franchise Agreement between themselves and the guild.

No one knows how this struggle will be resolved, but for the moment at least, it's pretty much business as usual with SAG warning members not to sign any new kind of agreement with their agents without having the guild legal department look it over for them.

Wrap Up

Agents

✓ self-agenting is always necessary
✓ strive to be the definitive client
✓ strive to get the definitive agent
✓ put together a good audition tape
✓ it's a relationship
✓ know your requirements
✓ be courageous about communicating
✓ get a meeting
✓ know what you are going to say
✓ remember that you're getting 90% of the money
✓ shoulder your responsibilities
✓ still forging an agreement with the Screen Actors Guild

Managers

✓ can provide access
✓ can provide guidance
✓ can be expensive
✓ are not governed by standard industry contracts
✓ be careful

⚔ 16 ⚔

Having a Life

Before you commit yourself to any career, you need to know as much as possible about yourself and what you want. If you haven't experienced any life yet, how can you know?

If you don't delineate who you are before you start chasing jobs, you not only won't have as much to sell, you may miss your opportunity to form yourself. You may end up as an empty vessel that only exists to be filled by someone else.

Who knows? You might find you are somebody entirely different than you thought, to whom unemployment or even employment might be less interesting than you thought.

Mira Sorvino says she missed her life.

✦ *"This summer was the first time I've taken off from work in five years, and I was able to reevaluate my life," she continued. "I thought about my grandfather, Poppy, who died in 1995 while I was making a movie. I missed his wake and his funeral because I couldn't get out off work. My LA life was so stacked up that way that I kept missing events that were happening in my real life."*
Mira Sorvino, interviewed by Dotson Rader, *Parade Magazine*[101]

David Duchovny was happier when *The X-Files* began filming in Los Angeles, allowing Duchovny to pursue a real life again. His candid remarks in an article in *Movieline* detail what it's really like to be the star of a successful television series. The reporter asked if he missed having a life:

✦ *"I thought I did. I miss it desperately at this point. But when I went back to LA recently, I was shocked to find that I didn't have a life there, either. I mean, I'm okay, I can take care of myself. But I feel isolated and lonely. I'm not happy."*
David Duchovny, interviewed by Martha Frankel, *Movieline*[102]

The reporter asked Duchovny if he would have taken the series if he had known what it was going to be like.

✦ *Can I also know what it would have been like if I didn't take the series? I hate those kinds of things, where people say, "Stop bitching, you could be working at Burger King now." As if those are the only two options for me either act or "Would you like a soda with your fries?"*

I love acting, and I love "The X-Files." But doing a television show is like riding an elephant: it goes where it wants, with or without your say. Does that make me an ungrateful bastard?

David Duchovny, interviewed by Martha Frankel, *Movieline*[103]

Angelina Jolie is another in a growing list who say it's not as they thought it would be,

✦ *I don't think I was ever more depressed in my life than the time I realized I was working in the business that I'd always wanted to be in. I was in love; I had money; and I wasn't struggling. I thought, "Well, I have everything I'd always thought would make me really happy, and I don't feel okay."*

Angelina Jolie, interviewed by Tim Roston, *Premiere*[104]

And that quote is from 1999, before Billy Bob. Now that she's with Brad and has all those babies, I'll bet she has a different slant. Kids tend to make one's life more meaningful. More chaotic perhaps, but definitely more meaningful.

Dan Hedaya is a well-respected actor who has survived for years in the business. He only became visible when he played the father of Alicia Silverstone in the hit movie *Clueless*. All of a sudden, he had job offers from every corner. Producers write parts into their movies for the express purpose of hiring Dan. An article in *The New York Times* (quoting Hedaya and others about his career) touched me greatly.

✦ *Mr. Hedaya is typical of any number of working actors, most of them with stage training, who are highly prized for their talents within the film and television business but not widely known outside it.*

"I wouldn't say I had years of struggle," said Mr. Hedaya, a disarmingly candid man who looks on his career with a blend of awe and amusement. "I was frustrated. I had lots of rejections. What actor doesn't? You get used to it."

....Scott Rudin, the producer who cast Hedaya in "Clueless," met Hedaya years ago and was impressed with his believability before the camera.

"Success has been really good for Dan. He went through a period of insecurity. He doubted he would ever have the kind of career he wanted. For a while he was angry. He had an edge. He wanted the kind of career that guys like Bob Duvall

or Harvey Keitel had, and never thought he would have one."

"I know brilliant actors who are struggling unbelievably hard," Hedaya
said.*"It breaks my heart. The rejection. The inability to get work. It can be so
corrosive to the spirit. I know actors who live with this struggle every day. It's
painful to watch. I've had good fortune. I'm working. That's what it's all about.
All I do is look around me to realize how lucky I am."*

Bernard Weinraub, *The New York Times*[105]

Sharon Stone isn't complaining, but the story of the life change
when she became instantly famous is a little chilling:

✦ *I got famous from a Friday to a Tuesday. On Friday, I worked. On Tuesday,
people were pounding on my car windows. Very shortly after that I went to Cannes
for "Basic Instinct." The roar never ceased, twenty-four hours a day for six days,
to the point where, by the fifth day, I was on the floor in the bathroom of my
friends' restaurant sweating and heaving.*

Sharon Stone, interviewed by Virginia Campbell, *Movieline*[106]

When Steven Jenkins left the business for a temporary job, he found
there were other ways to get the validation he had sought from acting:

✦ *I'd been offered a guest artist contract at the University of Florida and, of
course, just before I left, I'd given up my apartment, left my job, lost my girlfriend.
So when I came back to New York I had no money, I had no prospects and I'd
already been doing this acting for two years, which doesn't seem like a very long
time, but when you're twenty-two it seems like an eternity.*

*...so I got a job as a clerk. A year and a half later, I ended up at Dean &
DeLuca and that's where it all started.*

*I was so knocked out that I was getting a paycheck every week and finally
getting some responsibility. I wasn't freaking out every day about what I was going
to do for my next anything. So I applied myself. I scrubbed, I rubbed, I swept. I
showed up and I stayed late. I was doing everything I could do to keep from turning
tail and going back to my hometown.*

Steven Jenkins, interviewed by Laurie Ochoa, *Los Angeles Times*[107]

Steve is now an author and an internationally respected cheese
expert at Dean & DeLuca in New York City.

The late John Spencer's success on *The West Wing* came after many
years in the business. His perspective on the rewards of visibility bears
repeating:

✦ *Success is relative. People think, Oh my God, if I were just successful some people use the word 'famous' or if I just got to act all the time, everything would be better. Then, suddenly, you do, and you're still faced with an enormous amount of decisions and challenges and disappointments.*

They're just different. So, suddenly, Bob Duvall is doing the role you wanted. It doesn't feel much different from twenty years ago. Success doesn't make it all better. It just gives you a whole new set of challenges. And you don't know it until you have it.

John Spencer, interviewed by Danny Margolies, *Back Stage West*[108]

I've been in the business a long time and have watched the careers of many performers rise and fall and rise again. I have witnessed the downside of money, fame and power. It costs a lot. Not just that your relationships with those near and dear to you may falter, but what it does to your body. Elevated status is stressful. Your whole physical being has to adjust. Carroll O'Connor told me that when *All in the Family* hit, he was taking four Valium every day in an effort to calm himself down.

With elevated status comes power. You can misbehave without much repercussion. You can abuse people who have no recourse. If you have not learned early on to behave well because that is what is best for you in the long run, it's possible that you will lose control completely. Not only is it unconscionable to treat others badly, it will rot your soul and take its toll on you. You will have all those things you thought you wanted and still find yourself in constant pain.

Finding Out More About Yourself

If you are nineteen and play thirteen, you'd better cash in on that talent before you are too old. If you are exquisitely beautiful/handsome, perhaps you too need to get to Hollywood, Chicago, or New York right this minute. Otherwise, if you have already finished your education, I suggest you take some time to get your bearing. Whenever I travel abroad, I am impressed that young people in other countries routinely finish at university and spend a year traveling abroad. They call it 'gap' year.

Although there are many American colleges where junior year abroad is commonplace, not all colleges offer that option. Most of us don't get the life-enhancing experience of going to a strange place and improvising. Even if you have that opportunity, school is a protected environment that doesn't test your resources and spirit as does existing on your own. It's the old 'go out and spend a week in the wilderness' routine that used to mark the life passage from child to adult.

Writers are routinely told to "go live your life a little" in order to have something to actually write about. It's not just writers who need a store of experiences to nourish their art; actors need a vocabulary, too. No matter where you travel, if you are inventive, you can access the creative community.

Avril Thresh, a young British actress I met at The Court Theater in New Zealand, had been doing theater in Glasgow when she met a man who said, "If you are ever in New Zealand, call me."

Six months later, she was in Christchurch working at the theater as a stage manager, in the box office, and as an actress. Her two-month sojourn in N.Z. has not only turned into three years, but her parents came from Great Britain on holiday to visit her and immigrated to New Zealand permanently.

I'm not saying you're going to end up working as an actor or even in a theater-related job, but just having that traveling experience will change your whole vision of the world.

I've come to traveling late in life. I always thought I was going to get a job and go on location to exotic places like Julia Roberts does. A job did take me to Spain once, but New Jersey has been more my speed. Even now (and I'm much older than most of you reading this) I realize I can take what I have and use it to travel and bond with other people in the business.

When I was in New Zealand and Australia, I decided to do some research not only on the possibility of American actors getting work there, but also on how we could enter the system. It's not easy since (like us) those countries like to employ their own. However, since so many American films are shooting there, an appropriate American actor might have a much easier time being seen there than at home. After all, the producers would not have to pay airfare.

If you are going to spend energy trying to find work abroad, attending school there would give you a focus for your life and some help from Immigration in staying there for a period of time. Just as here at home, choosing the right school is an art in itself. Certain schools have cache with the buyers, just as they do here.

United Tech College of Performing Arts in Auckland, Toiwhakaari aka New Zealand Drama School in Wellington, and The National

Academy of Singing and Dramatic Art (NASDA) in Christchurch are the leaders in New Zealand. All but NASDA offer three-year programs, while NASDA's is two.

Production Centers

Peter Jackson's *Lord of the Rings* trilogy has made Wellington the film capital. Auckland leads in television production though. That's where they filmed *Hercules* and *Xena*.

The most famous and credentialed theater in New Zealand is The Court Theatre in Christchurch. It's the center for theater related jobs. Sheena Baines, the lighting designer at The Court, told me she feels privileged to be working at the only theater in N.Z. with its own staff across the board. The Court is committed to producing New Zealand playwrights plus new foreign classics. *ww.courttheatre.org.nz/*

If you have teaching credentials and are interested in working in New Zealand, I would research universities and theaters. Sheena told me that an American actor who teaches stage fighting queried the theater, was brought over to choreograph a particular show, and has now immigrated to New Zealand and works their regularly.

Casting Directors in New Zealand

As with all casting directors, do not fax picture and resume unless requested. It would be acceptable, however to fax a note indicating your interest in upcoming projects.

In order to work in any foreign country, you will need a work permit which will involve either a promise of work or a sponsor. If someone wants to hire you, they will usually help you find a sponsor.

Just like getting a union card, you can't work without a permit and you can't get a permit without work. And just like getting a union card, if you apply your creative powers, you'll figure out how to get over that obstacle.

As in any other market, the key to work is to involve yourself in activities that bring you in touch with people either already working in the business or close to it.

Casting director Liz Mullane (*King Kong, Lord of the Rings*) says it's probably not worth it for an actor to fly all the way to New Zealand just with the idea that he might get work. On the other hand, if you are in your year of experiencing life in N.Z., there's some great information at *www.zeroland.co.nz/new_zealand_film.htm*

Australian Work Opportunity

I interviewed Australian agent Mark Morrissey who told me that just as in America, foreign actors are 75% less likely to get work than native citizens. The Australian film community tells Australian stories and needs Australian actors. Although to my ear, our speech is not that different, Morrissey says:

✦ *The Australian accent is subtle and difficult to copy and the only real opportunity for an American actor would be in the rare instance when there is a part calling for an American or from American production companies who are filming in Oz.*

Work for female actors is limited even more in Australia than in the United States. There are more roles for women on television than in film as roles are more evenly divided between women and men in that media.

Even if you had decent American credits, you would still have to work yourself into the system, same as New York/Los Angeles.

Mark Morrissey/Agent, Sydney, Australia

In addition to getting chosen, you would have to procure a work visa. The Australian Embassy can tell you what is required. Although you need papers to work on an ongoing basis, papers are pretty easily come by that would allow enough work to keep you going on an extended holiday.

Travellers Contact Point

In Sydney, I happened across an amazing resource called Travellers Contact Point and Internet Café that provides mail-holding and forwarding, travel agent services, Internet and computers with word processing capability, as well as a job resource center.

When I checked the bulletin board, there were jobs for an au pair, a two-week stint in airline reservations, a business consultant opportunity, work for farm workers, and a job as a cook at a farmstay for three weeks. I was tempted to check that one out myself. It just sounded like a real adventure. Their brochure advertises placements for legal, secretarial, sales and marketing, accounting, hospitality, travel, health care, and trades.

You can get a Medicare card, insurance for your person as well as for loss of baggage, cameras, and other personal belongings, and cancellation fees. You can be covered from a week to a year. A personal e-mail address costs $10 a year and for $25 you can get a free address plus daily e-mail access.

There are TCP centers all over Australia and one each in New Zealand and London. *www.travellers.com.au/*

Many Internet Cafes around the world frequently provide either a job board or training. This link is international and will give you some good leads. *www.world66.com/europe/ireland/dublin/internetcafes*

Italy

The idea of working in some glamorous European city has always appealed to me, so when I was in Rome recently, I decided to check out work opportunities for non-star American actors. "Unless you can delve into your ancestry and come up with an Irish or British passport, your chances are pretty much nil" according to Gaby Ford, who runs the English Theatre of Rome. Oh darn!

Ex-patriate Ford has been working in Rome for many years and has struggled to keep her amazing English speaking theatre company viable in a city that, though excited to have the theatre, is not particularly supportive of her efforts.

Her troupe of international actors has produced everything from Chekhov to Durang. Any American actor with work papers and a one-person show could probably count on a stint at Gaby's theatre. To be a member of her troupe, you'd have to be able to support yourself on other than the small stipend the theatre is able to scrape together. *www.rometheatre.com*

Agents in Rome

Historically, casting calls in Italy go out from the Assistant Directors to their relatives' agencies for actors who are either friends or relatives, but when American agents Heidi Jarrett and Katharine Ronan opened Actors International, producers who were actually seeking credible actors finally had that option.

For an American actor to work legally in Rome, you need a British passport as Gaby Ford said, or some kind of proof on arrival in the country that you were hired as an actor before leaving the U.S. That pretty much rules out hoping to stumble into a job while you are on vacation. You could, however, make calls on agents and casting directors with your pictures, resumes and reels (PAL format), so that if a job comes up that you are right for, you might be considered.

If you do work without papers, you will be illegal, could be deported and not allowed to return to the country for 10 years.

If you plan to come to Rome and can get hold of some working papers, Katharine and Heidi would be happy to hear from you. They accept submissions online. *www.actorsinternational.it/*

Agents in London

Just as in Rome, more difficult than getting an agent to represent you is securing working papers, but if you have a British passport, searching the web for "agents in London" is rewarding. Gavin Baker Associates' webpage features pictures and bios of all its clients. They represent a host of top drawer actors that includes Vanessa Redgrave and Faith Prince. *www.gavinbarkerassociates.co.uk/index.htm*

Actor's Inc. bills itself as "the place for actors to see and be seen." You'll find a long list of agencies. A click on their website produces pictures of each of their clients. *www.actors-inc.co.uk/alist.asp?aid=k*

Typing in "casting directors London" gets reveals several different sites. *www.4rfv.co.uk/fulllisting.asp?scategory=68*

Cruise Companies

Cruise companies advertise in the trades and hire not only singers and dancers, but actors, magicians, costumers, and technicians as well. More and more ships are interested in straight theatre pieces so if you put together either a one-person show or your own acting troupe with some shows with minimal sets, this could be a great gig for you.

Basa Productions, who provide entertainment for the Orient lines, hires a British actor base and audition in London at least four times a year. You don't have to be British, you just need to be able to get there *www.vocalist.org.uk/cruise_ship_agencies.html*

There are many cruise lines and they all advertise in trade papers like *Back Stage West, Showbusiness,* and *Backstage,* so if you are interested, keep your eyes peeled for their ads.

If you're not in New York, Los Angeles, or Chicago and don't have access to those trades, go online to specific cruise line sights and search for an employment link or write for contact suggestions

The most famous alumnae of cruise ships has got to be Wayne Brady from *Whose Line Is It Anyway?* What a great way to perfect your talent and see the world at the same time.

Adventure at Home

There are opportunities for adventure within our own country. Imagine spending time in our Last Frontier: Alaska. University of Alaska at Fairbanks Coordinator, Maya Salgarek, told me that since their theatre department is composed of six staff members and thirty students, that faculty, staff and students function as a theatre company working on every aspect of every production.

The University of Alaska at Fairbanks' student ambassador program enables you to e-mail current students to ask questions about being a student at UAF. *www.uaf.edu/*

Hosteling

If you're going to embark on a year of adventure, you'll need some inexpensive places to stay. Hosteling is called backpacking in many parts of the world and it's perhaps best described as traveling cheaply with an adventurous spirit. The terms hosteler and backpacker are basically synonymous.

In many countries, especially Australia and New Zealand, it's customary for students and recent graduates to take trips of up to a year or more!

While hosteling, you see the world from a perspective that the average tourist will never see. You meet local people, learn customs, eat local food, and often have opportunities to do things you never imagined. Basically, backpackers stay longer, see more, and do more for less money.

The atmosphere at a hostel tends to be youthful, but people of all ages stay there. Hostelers are usually outgoing, friendly, and welcoming to newcomers. Hostels are an excellent place to stay for people traveling alone. Many solo travelers use hostels as a way of meeting others and sharing the travel experience.

At most hostels throughout the world there are no age restrictions. It is rumored that some hostels, such as some in Bavaria, will give priority to youths when the hostel is full. *www.hostel.com*

Hostelling International is a non-profit membership organization that promotes international understanding by bringing together travelers of all ages, backgrounds, and nationalities and represents more than seventy countries and 4.5 million members worldwide.

Hostelling International membership provides access to nearly 200 hostels in the U.S. and 6,000 hostels in worldwide. Cost varies from country to country so check the website *www.iyhf.org/*.

There are hostels in both New York and Los Angeles. Staying there seems to be quite inexpensive although I don't know how many of your belongings you might be able to stash safely, so more than a few days might be problematic.

For everything you ever want to know about hosteling in general, check out *www.hostels.com*.

In addition to hostels, international inexpensive places to stay include YWCAs and churches. Sit down at your computer and plan to make a day of it searching.

This May Be Your Only Chance

Once you embark on a career and gather any momentum at all, it's not only difficult to take yourself out of the marketplace, but you lose your forward motion. Consider pausing before you begin your career to focus on your life, find out who you are, and experience something other than the womb of your home and educational institutions.

I've always thought there should be two years between high school and college where one has to go out and work, do some kind of service job, join the Peace Corps or whatever. It's difficult right out of school to know what you really want to do. You've usually experienced so little.

Even if those two years didn't tell you what you want to do, they would certainly be instructive teaching what you don't want to do. Once you've existed on your own in unfamiliar, unprotected circumstances, slain your bear as it were, you would certainly bring more to your life and to the marketplace and be much less likely to lose focus with either success or rejection.

It's only a year. Think about it.

Wrap Up

✓ discover yourself before you embark
✓ explore all avenues
✓ delineate your value system first
✓ everything costs
✓ spend a week in the woods, test your resourcefulness
✓ traveling alone enlarges the actors vocabulary
✓ see what the opportunities are elsewhere
✓ test yourself

☙ 17 ☙

Unions

When I was in Texas dreaming of becoming an actress, my goal was to join Actors' Equity, the only actors' union I had heard of. Thrilled as I was to join SAG when it became my parent union, somehow I didn't feel like I was a real actor until I got into Equity. I wasn't any different from the day before, but I felt different and that is worth a lot; just like the Cowardly Lion getting courage with a medal in *The Wizard of Oz*.

One's goals and image of oneself aside, it is not always a good idea to join a union until you really have to. As I mentioned in Chapter 3, there is so much unemployment among all the actors who are already members of Screen Actors Guild that to presume that just showing up with a card is going to change things is merely wishful thinking.

If you are not a member of the union, at least all those more experienced actors with better credits are not your competition. There are many non-union jobs available that might net you some growth. Since the pay is low or non-existent, those out-of-work union actors (who have already done the groundwork you are now involved in) are not available for that work.

Non-union jobs include not only features with no union connection, but films for student filmmakers (they may be at regular colleges or in prestigious film schools like the American Film Institute, The University of Southern California, The New York Film School, etc.), plus documentaries, government, and educational films.

Investigate the project to see if it is worthwhile. Even a bad film will teach you a lot. You will see yourself on film, be on a set, watch set-ups, and learn to get along with people in unpleasant and stressful situations. Use discretion, Traci Lords is the only actress who ever made it out of porn movies to become a respectable actress and it still keeps her from some jobs.

All the performer unions are members of an alliance called the Association of Actors and Artists of America or the Four As.

Once you are a member of any actors' union, you are not allowed to work in a non-union venture involved in the jurisdiction of any of the Four As if that union is actively involved in bringing that production under union auspices.

So, if you are a member of SAG, but not Equity and Equity is trying to get a theater to become union affiliated, you cannot legally work in that project even though you are not a member of Equity. This circumstance doesn't happen very often. The concept is confusing, so check with your union before signing any contract; otherwise, you could be fined and brought up on charges.

Union Jurisdictions

Actors' Equity Association (AEA/Equity), founded in 1913, is the labor union representing actors and stage managers in the legitimate theater in the United States. Equity negotiates minimum wages and working conditions, administers contracts, and enforces the provisions of its various agreements with theatrical employers. There are currently about 45,000 active Equity members. *www.actorsequity.org*

The American Federation of Television and Radio Artists (AFTRA) represents 70,000 members in the recording business, news, broadcasting, industrial, entertainment programming, commercials, non-broadcast, and educational media. *www.aftra.org*

Screen Actors Guild (SAG) has jurisdiction over 120,000 members including the extras. In addition to filmed television shows and feature films, SAG has jurisdiction over Interactive multimedia, infomercials, low-budget films, student films, narration/voice-overs, dubbing promos and foreign films, music videos, experimental films, singer sessions, commercial demos, ADR (automated dialogue replacement), PSAs (public service announcements) trailers, industrials/corporate videos, and made-for-video productions. *www.sag.org*

Union Membership Requirements

AEA (Actors' Equity Association) — Currently, Equity's initiation fee is $1100. Basic Dues are $118 per year, payable semi-annually in May and in November plus a 2.25% Working Dues deduction from a member's gross weekly earnings when employed under Equity contract. (Gross weekly earnings don't include the minimum portion of out-of-town or per diem expense monies.) The maximum Equity earnings subject to WD is $300,000 a year.

Full membership privileges, including the right to vote, commence upon the signing of an application and the payment within six months of at least $400 of the initiation fee. Equity maintains a dues check-off system when performers are employed under an Equity contract that provides for the regular weekly deduction of any outstanding dues and initiation fees.

If a performer is not working under an Equity contract, any outstanding balance due on the initiation fee must be paid not later than the second anniversary date of the membership application signing.

Both membership status and any monies previously paid are forfeited should a performer fail to complete payment of the full $1100 initiation fee within this two-year maximum time period.

Rules for membership and all related membership information is available online at *www.actorsequity.org*.

AFTRA (American Federation of Television and Radio Artists) — New members must pay $1363.90 which includes the first six month's dues of $63.90. Dues are billed each May 1st and November 1st and are based on a member's AFTRA earnings in the previous year.

Requirements for membership are lenient in AFTRA.

As previously mentioned, it can be a hindrance to join unions before you are ready as that puts you out of the running to do non-union films, shows, etc., and begin to amass film of yourself, so be patient. For the most up-to-the-minute information about dues and benefits check out AFTRA's webpage at *www.aftra.org*.

SAG (Screen Actors Guild) — The most powerful actors' union is SAG. The initiation fee is $2277. plus the first semi-annual basic dues payment of $58 for a total of $2335. The fees may be lower in some branch areas.

SAG dues are based on SAG earnings and are billed twice a year. In addition members pay 1.85% of all individual earnings up to $200,000 and 0.5% of earnings from $200,001 through $500,000. Over $500,000 pay .24% to a maximum of $1,000,000. Details of eligibility may be found online at *www.sag.org*.

All unions have Honorary Withdrawal status for members who are not working. HW relieves you of the obligation to pay your dues, but you are still in the union and prohibited from accepting non-union work. As soon as you work again, you must reinstate yourself and pay the current dues and stay current for at least a year.

Union initiation fees are expensive, so wait until you have a reasonable expectation of actually working before joining.

Union Function

When you are ready to join the union, you are joining a group with a courageous legacy:

✦ *It took a lot of courage to join a union in the anti-labor climate of Hollywood in the thirties especially a union for motion picture performers. Actors' Equity made an unsuccessful attempt to organize the field in 1928-29, so when a ragtag group of theater-trained actors began a whispering campaign at a private men's club known as The Masquers in 1933, it was an uphill battle. They had to use passwords, backdoors, and secret alleyways to elude studio detectives. The group's goal: to correct the abuses heaped upon freelance players and to negotiate a square deal with fair wages and working conditions for all performers.*

With American Federation of Labor recognition in 1935, the organization became an affiliated union, but it wasn't until mid-1937, when the studios accepted SAG's jurisdiction, that suddenly every actor had to join.

Harry Medved, *Screen Actor*[109]

The unions fill an important need for actors. Powerless in many situations, actors are at least protected in the areas of basic working conditions. The unions provide hospitalization for members, keep track of residuals, and are helpful when an actor has any kind of problem, particularly financial. There are loans and grants available to members in time of need. In addition, SAG, Equity, and AFTRA all are participating in a work program to help non-working members educate themselves to change careers if they are interested.

As in any large collective of disparate parts, there is frequently a great deal of grousing from members regarding their unions. SAG members have considerable internal dissension and the union threatens to break apart from time to time. Equity was embroiled in disputes over casting in the Broadway hit *Miss Saigon*. Those disputes were not only with the employers, but were a source of strife between members of the union.

AFTRA and SAG faced a hard decision when they voted jointly to establish jurisdiction over extras. Now that the extras are in SAG and AFTRA, there is constant conflict between the extra and the principal performers because their needs are different.

Currently, SAG and AFTRA are in conflict over several issues:

+ *SAG had created an AFTRA relations committee in mid-July in the wake of a dispute over which union has the right to organize shows shot on digital. The actor unions also split in April over the hot-button issue of easing talent agency ownership rules and have not met formally to settle jurisdictional disputes since 1999.*
Dave McNary, *Variety*[110]

In every family there are disagreements, and the unions are no exception. It's also easy to take your unions for granted and bad mouth them when something doesn't go your way and you have not bothered to get the facts. This occurs particularly if you are not working and need a place to put all your anger and blame.

Scabbing

Some union members sabotage themselves and all the rest of us by working non-union jobs, hoping that the union will never find out. Sometimes union members work non-union unknowingly because they have not checked to see if the employer is a signatory to a basic contract with the union. Just because there is a major advertising agency or a visible star involved doesn't necessarily mean the job is union sanctioned.

Be diligent, for the union rules are very clear: a union member is not allowed financial gain from a non-union job. The union will bring you up on charges and fine you the amount of money you made on the job even if you thought the job was within the jurisdiction of the union. Therefore, it pays to make a simple phone call.

It is the actor's responsibility to call the union and find out if the producers have in fact signed an agreement with the union. Stationery stores sell blank Screen Actors Guild contracts, so just because you sign a form that has 'Screen Actors Guild' printed on it and the employer pays SAG rates doesn't mean the producer ever even had a conversation with the union.

When you work a non-union job, there is no protection of basic working conditions, no contributions to health and welfare on the actors behalf (and therefore no hospitalization), and no guarantee of payment. When a producer makes an agreement with the unions, he puts up a bond guaranteeing the actor's salary.

Hospitalization, decent pay, residuals, guaranteed meal times, and overtime compensation have all been won from employers over a long period of time through difficult negotiations. If you give these things away, you undermine your union and your own collective bargaining agreements.

Last but not least, *Variety* reviews almost every film made, listing the names of all the actors involved, so the union will most likely find out if you work non-union. You will be brought up on charges, possibly put on probation, fined, and/or excluded from the union. You may well work under an assumed name, but your face is still on the screen. You will be found out. I know you want to work, but it's really not worth it.

If you are not far along enough in your career to hold out for union jobs, don't join the union. If you are a professional, act like one. Live up to your responsibility by checking the status of projects you are considering.

Financial Core

While we are at it, let's discuss Financial Core, a situation whereby an actor resigns his SAG membership – essentially to play both ends against the middle – working both union and non-union jobs in order to cash in on reality television and non-union commercials.

I heard recently that a manager was recommending financial core to clients. That information caused me to review my history with the Screen Actors Guild and my own naivete when I first began my career years ago in Dallas, Texas – a non-union town at the time. I didn't know about any actor unions other than Actors Equity, and in my mind, I would become a *real* actor when I became a member of that union. But I was pretty sure I would have to go to New York to do that.

When I moved to New York years later, it was easier to establish a career in television commercials than onstage, so my parent union, and the one that made me a *real* actor, was Screen Actors Guild.

I was surprised to learn that as a SAG member, after earning a certain amount of money, I was entitled to medical coverage for my children and myself. That was just a nice plus, along with residuals, which were unheard of in non-union Dallas.

In addition, though totally unimportant to me at the time since the idea of my ever being older than thirty was not in my consciousness, I now had a pension fund. And if I were ever to actually age and become old enough to collect it (sixty-five for heaven's sake!), I would actually receive a monthly check.

Though union membership was pretty much a necessity in order to get good paying and respected work, the union was still an abstract thought to me. I appreciated the protection it offered when signing with an agent and the all important SAG minimum contracts with employers, but I never stopped to think what it cost to forge those contracts.

I'm amazed and respectful of those actors who put their careers on the line to form a union. Back in the thirties it was a different time and place; the prevailing thought was for the larger good instead of the individual. The union was originally formed to stand up to the powerful studios who controlled actors by signing them to long term contracts for very little money, and crushed the career of any actor who crossed them.

Can you imagine how hard the studios must have fought to keep the unions from forming? And how difficult it was to organize starving actors? You know how actors are: we'll work for free. I can't even imagine how difficult that journey must have been.

The union was formed to enhance actors' working conditions, compensation, and benefits, and to create a powerful unified voice on behalf of artists rights. That's still the job of the union. But never was the union more in need of a unified membership than today. New technologies enable buyers to use our images without appropriate compensation, and management wants to keep it that way.

It's odd to me that someone (an agent or a manager) who says he works for the actor, who supposedly has the actor's best interests in mind, would ever advise an actor to choose financial core.

Agents and managers who urge actors to go financial core are short-sighted. If the actor needs to pay his rent, it's better in the long run to get a day job rather than scab the union. Every time a union actor crosses over into fi-core territory, he undermines all the actors in the union. The union is only as strong as its weakest link. The union is only able to forge decent wages/working conditions contracts if all the professionals stand firm.

It used to be that when an actor worked in the business for a while, even if not a star, he was be able to establish a *quote* of more than scale.

These days having a *quote* means less and less, as producers routinely call and say, "we're paying SAG scale + 10%, take it or leave it?" What if there were no SAG scale? What would the actor be paid then? I wonder if those who advocate fi-core want to end up negotiating every single job that comes in for the working actor whose credits might not merit even SAG scale?

If you want a career, intend to live in a house and drive a car, and have a family, you'll find that pretty difficult to do without residuals, health coverage, and at least a minimum contract. You're not going to get that without union help.

For clarity, going financial core means you resign from the union so that you can work non-union work. The union will no longer let a member who has gone fi-core rejoin, but legally no one can keep you from working if someone wants to hire you. So the fi-core actor has his cake and eats it too. Moreover, he actually eats my cake too.

Anyone contemplating going fi-core should take a long hard look at why he chose to be an actor in the first place. I didn't know it at the time, but I became an actor to get a family. As time went by, I realized that the family created by my school plays was taking the place of the family I never had at home. Like many actors, I grew up feeling invisible and I appreciated finally being seen. I loved being in a play, being part of something, having people count on me.

If you are a member of Screen Actors Guild, remember – you do count, you are part of something, and people count on you.

Working as an Extra

While work as an extra gives you the opportunity to be on the set, unless you are looking for more extra work I would not list it on the resume. You want any agent, producer, or casting director thinking of you for principal parts, so don't cloud his vision.

✦ *Working as an extra could be valuable for someone who has never been on a set, to help you become familiar with cameras and absorb information. It's not something that should be on your resume or even brought up to the agent.*
Flo Rothacker

There are specific directors or producers that you might want to make an exception for:

An extra job on a Woody Allen film could turn out to be a good job because Woody sometimes notices extras, gives them lines and you can end up working for weeks. You could end up getting upgraded or if you got a chance to work on a Sydney Lumet film as an extra, think of what you could learn.
Marvin Josephson/Gilla Roos, Ltd.

If you plan to be a career extra, working as an extra makes sense. If your goal is to play principal parts, why amass a resume that advertises you in a different capacity? It's tempting to accept extra work to qualify for guild membership, pay rent, keep insurance active or get on a set. I understand that.

I asked an agent if he had "John Smith" work as an extra, wouldn't casting directors and producers now only consider John to be an extra?

We all do. I spoke to a casting director the other day about an actor and that's exactly what she said. The actor has to learn where to draw the line and say, "Okay, I can't do this anymore."
Anonymous Agent

A lot of people can't. They get used to the money and the insurance and their resumes reflect that they are full-time extras. A credible agent might encourage actors to work as extras (after all, he is making a commission), but he expects them to know when to draw the line and stop doing extra work.

To me it's like saying, "Here, these drugs will make you feel better. Just take them for a while, I know you will be able to stop in time." If you are not ready to get work as a principal on a regular basis, it may not be time for you to be in the union.

It would be more advantageous for you to work in some other capacity in order to pay your rent or to observe the business from the inside. Become an assistant or work in production. You will see what goes on, make some money, and you won't be fooling yourself into thinking you are really acting. You will be more driven to pursue work that will further your career.

SAG, Equity, and AFTRA all have financial assistance available to members in an emergency situation. If you are not a member of a union, ask your acting teacher for advice.

There are also many city agencies equipped to deal with people in need. There is low-cost counseling available through both the city of New York and through the schools of psychology of some universities.

Call the schools or look in the front of the white pages of the phone book for information.

Be Part of the Solution

Regardless of your union affiliation and jurisdiction, become an asset to your group. Too many of us become busy working and never take the time to go to meetings, become informed regarding the issues, join committees, and become part of the policy-making team. This frequently leaves the rule-making power to people not working the contracts that they are negotiating. They are looking for ways to fill their time and although they have good intentions, they are making rules they will not be bound by. You will. Unless you are willing to spend some time contributing, you have no right to complain.

When you join, become active. Read the literature and become aware of the issues. Know what minimum is. Know what isn't working in your current contract. Form an idea about what would make things better, then go to a meeting or write a letter and work to put those plans into action.

Besides joining your union, align yourself with any other local professional organization of actors. There are groups of actors in every city who are looking for other actors to work with. Join playwrighting groups and volunteer to read new material. In Los Angeles, there is a group of actors who have bound together to champion animal rights.

These groups not only provide another avenue of association with your fellow actors, but they supply a support group as well. Being involved in a theater group or playreading group also looks good on your resume. Take your place within the ranks of your own profession.

The unions are as weak or as strong as the members. My own opinion is that there should be more stringent rules for membership that would take into consideration such things as training, apprenticeship, and hours spent in the business. These types of rules govern craft unions such as hair and make-up.

Although it is difficult for a newcomer to join, there continue to be countless chronically non-working actors who are already union members. It is useless and expensive to join until you train yourself and have the tools (resume, craft, and experience) to realistically expect employment.

When you join the union, vow to be an active, informed member.

It's not always easy to obey rules others have made, so become involved and help make the rules. This is your profession. Take responsibility for your unions. It's important for working actors to become active members of their unions.

Wrap Up

✓ non-union jobs can be a source of film for your reel
✓ don't join until you are marketable
✓ scabbing hurts us all
✓ financial core hurts us all
✓ be an informed and active member
✓ be part of thc solution, not the problem

⚮ 18 ⚯

Finally

To make a living as an actor, you must inspire yourself to be active. If you are doing something for your career every day, I guarantee you will work. You may not get as much or as rewarding work as you want, but if you apply yourself, you will reap the profits. The things that make you successful or not are your habits. If you have bad habits, it's time to change them. If you already have good habits, hone them.

You need a firm schedule that you will honor every day and you need goals. You need goals for the day, the week, the month and the year. Without them, days turn into weeks, months and years and somehow you never get around to testing yourself, studying with a challenging teacher, getting your voice in shape, producing something, directing something, stretching yourself in every possible way.

People who succeed are working on their careers every single day.

I went to New York alone with three small children and didn't starve. I have been supporting myself in the business for forty years. I've had good years and bad. People ask me for my autograph and even though I've played fabulous roles at one time or another, I'm still going out on auditions for two scenes. Those times when I question whether or not it's a good career move to read for a few lines, I run into multiple Emmy winners as my competition.

I run into actresses who say, "At my age, it's insulting that I have to come in here and read". What are they thinking? This is the actor's life. We signed on to it. No one makes us do this. If you can't be happy and think it's fun to test yourself and get to visit with the friends you've made at auditions over the years, you should find something else to do.

Yes, when you are hot, it's great and when you are cold, it sucks. Whichever state you're in, I say to you: "This too shall pass."

Remind yourself, whether you are up or down, that it's just one blip on the landscape, but do enjoy the good blips!

I love my life with all its ups and downs and I continue to thank the universe that I am one of the 1% in the world who is actually living my dream. If you apply yourself and really want to, you can do the same thing. But I won't kid you, it's not for the faint-hearted!

⩗ 19 ⩘
Glossary

99-Seat Theater Plan — Actors basically work for free with Equity approval. Producers must also conform to Equity guidelines regarding rehearsal conditions, number of performances, complimentary tickets for industry, etc., minimal pay to cover parking, gas, etc. If you participate in this plan, be sure to stop by Equity and get a copy of your rights.

Academy Players Directory — See *Players Directory.*

Actors' Equity Membership Requirements — Rules for membership for the union covering actors for work in the theater state you must have a verifiable Equity Contract in order to join, or have been a member in good standing for at least one year in AFTRA or SAG.

Initiation fee is currently $1100 as of 4/01/07, payable prior to election to membership. Basic dues are $118 annually. Working dues of 2% of gross weekly earnings from employment is deducted from your check just like your income tax.

Actors' Equity Minimum — There are eighteen basic contracts ranging from the low end of the Small Production Contract to the higher Production Contract covering Broadway houses, Jones Beach, tours, etc. Highest is the Business Theater Agreement, for industrial shows produced by large corporations. All monies are discussed online at "contracts" at *www.actorsequity.org.*

Actor Unions — *Actors' Equity Association (Equity)* is the union that covers actors' employment in the theater. *The American Federation of Television and Radio Artists (AFTRA)* covers television and radio actors, broadcasters and recording artists. *Screen Actors Guild (SAG)* covers actors employed in theatrical motion pictures and filmed television product. The unions continue discussions about the potential of joining together under one overall labor organization.

AFTRA Membership Requirements — anyone expecting to work in the news and entertainment industries can join. AFTRA's current initiation fee is $1300. Minimum dues for the first six-month dues period are $63.90. Working dues are based on earnings in AFTRA's jurisdictions during the prior year and billed each May and November. Contract information at *www.aftra.org*.

AFTRA Minimum — Check AFTRA's web page for rates.

AFTRA Nighttime Rates — Check AFTRA's web page for rates.

Atmosphere — another term for Background Performers, a.k.a. Extras.

Audition Tape — A videotape usually no longer than six minutes, showcasing either one performance or a montage of scenes of an actor's work. Agents and casting directors prefer tapes of professional appearances (film or television), but some will look at a tape produced for audition purposes only. Increasingly, performers are making their work available on DVD or online.

Background Performers — a.k.a. Atmosphere and/or Extras

Billing — The size and placement of your name in the credits of motion picture, film or television are negotiated along with your salary and is called 'billing' which also delineates how many others are listed on the same line (theatre) or card (film or television).

Breakdown Service — Started in 1971 by Gary Marsh, the Service condenses scripts and lists parts available in films, television and theater. Expensive and available to agents and managers only.

Buyer — This term refers to anyone on the road to your future employment, whether it be a casting executive, a writer, producer, director, or an agent.

Clear — The unions require that the agent check with a freelance actor (clearing) before submitting him on a particular project.

Composite Cassette Tape — See Audition Tape.

Diversity Agreement — A contract providing financial incentives for producers who employ a significant number of under represented actors.

Equity-Waiver Productions — See Showcases.

Favored Nations — A clause entitling an actor to the same considerations given others.

Freelance — Term used to describe the relationship between an actor and agent or agents who submit the actor for work without an exclusive contract. New York agents frequently will work on this basis, Los Angeles agents rarely consent to this arrangement.

Going Out — Auditions or meetings with directors and/or casting directors. These are usually set up by your agent but have also been set up by very persistent and courageous actors.

Going to Network — Final process in landing a pilot/series. After the audition process has narrowed the list of choices, actors who have already signed option deals have another callback for network executives, usually at the network. Sometimes this process can include an extra callback for the heads of whatever studio is involved.

Guesting — Appearing in one or more episodes of a television show. This term is used to differentiate from those actors who are contracted to appear in all or a major portion of the shows.

Industrials — Industrial shows are splashy Broadway-type musicals produced by and for big business to sell their wares. They pay more than Broadway. The most famous is Monsanto in New York. These are also called industrial films.

Industry Referral — If you are looking for an agent, the best possible way to access one is if someone with some credibility in the business will call and make a phone call for you. This could be a casting director, writer, producer or the agent's mother, just so it's someone whose opinion the agent respects. If someone says, just use my name, forget it, they need to offer to make a phone call for you.

The Leagues — A now defunct formal collective of prestigious theater schools that offer conservatory training for the actor. The schools still exist, but there is no longer an association. As far as agents are concerned, this is the very best background an actor can have, other than having your father own a studio. Schools in this collective are American Conservatory Theater in San Francisco, CA; American Repertory Theater, Harvard University in Cambridge, MA; Boston University in Boston, MA; Carnegie Mellon in Pittsburgh, PA; Catholic University in Washington, DC; The Juilliard School in New York City, NY; New York University in New York City, NY; North Carolina School of the Arts in Winston-Salem, NC; Southern Methodist University in Dallas, TX; The University of California at San Diego in La Jolla, CA; and the Yale School of Drama in New Haven, CT.

Letter of Termination — A legal document dissolving the contract between actor and agent. Send a copy to your agent via registered mail, return receipt requested, plus a copy to the Screen Actors Guild and all other unions involved. Retain a copy for your files.

Major Role/Top of Show — See Top of Show

Mobisode — A short (up to three minutes) TV episode specially made for a mobile phone.

Open Call — refers to auditions or meetings held by casting directors that are not restricted by agents. No individual appointments are given. Usually the call is made in an advertisement in one of the trade newspapers, by flyers or in a news story in the popular press. As you can imagine, the number of people that show up is enormous. You will have to wait a long time. Although management's eyes tend to glaze over and see nothing after a certain number of hours, actors do sometimes get jobs this way.

Overexposed — Term used by nervous buyers (producers, casting directors, networks, etc.) indicating an actor has become too recognizable for their tastes. Frequently he just got off another show and everyone remembers him as a particular character and the buyer doesn't want the public thinking of that instead of his project. A thin line exists between not being recognizable and being overexposed.

Packaging — This practice involves a talent agency approaching a buyer with a writer, a star, usually a star director and possibly a producer already attached to it. May include any number of other writers, actors, producers, etc.

Paid Auditions — There's no formal name for the practice of rounding up twenty actors and charging them for the privilege of meeting a casting director, agent, producer, etc. There are agents, casting directors and actors who feel the practice is unethical. It does give some actors who would otherwise not be seen an opportunity to meet and be seen by casting directors. I feel meeting a casting director under these circumstances is questionable and that there are more productive ways to spend your money.

Per Diem — Negotiated amount of money for expenses on location or on the road per day.

Pictures — The actor's calling card. An 8x10 glossy or matte print color photograph.

Pilot — The first episode of a proposed television series. Produced so that the network can determine whether there will be additional episodes. There are many pilots made every year. Few get picked up. Fewer stay on the air for more than a single season.

Players Directory — Catalogue of actors published twice a year for the Los Angeles market. Must be a member of at least one actor union. Features one or two pictures per actor and lists representation. If you work freelance, you can list your name and service. Some list union affiliation. Casting directors, producers that track actors use the book as a reference guide. Every actor who is ready to book should be in this directory which also features online listing where you can add your audition reel.

Podcast — Downloadable file for use on portable devices.

Principal — Job designation indicating a part larger than an extra or an Under Five.

Process — People are continually talking about the process. This refers to the ongoing mechanisms involved in developing our personas, careers, and/or the rehearsal procedure in a play.

Ready to Book — Agent talk for an actor who has been trained and judged mature enough to handle himself well in the audition, not only with material, but also with the buyers. Frequently refers to an actor whose progress in acting class or theater has been monitored by the agent.

Resume — The actor's ID; lists credits, physical description, agent's name, phone contact and special skills.

Right — When someone describes an actor as being right for a part, he is speaking about the essence of an actor. We all associate a particular essence with Brad Pitt and a different essence with Jim Carrey. One would not expect Pitt and Carrey to be up for the same part. Being right also involves credits. The more important the part, the more credits are necessary to support being seen.

Rule One — The Screen Actors Guild requirement that all members are responsible for checking that a production is SAG signatory before rendering services.

Scale — See salary minimums of each union.

Scale Plus 10 — When a job only pays scale, in order for the actor to actually take home scale (which the union demands), the deal is made for scale plus 10% so that the agent's commission is not taken from the actor's pay. That means if an agent negotiates, he must negotiate his own 10%. If you had negotiated for yourself, you would only have gotten scale.

Screen Actors Guild Membership Requirements — The most prized union card is that of the Screen Actors Guild. Actors may join upon proof of employment or prospective employment within two weeks or less of start date of a SAG signatory film, television program or commercial.

Proof of employment may be in the form of a signed contract, a payroll check or check stub, or a letter from the company (on company letterhead stationery.) The document proving employment must state the applicant's name, Social Security number, the name of the production or commercial, the salary paid in dollar amount and the dates worked.

Another way of joining SAG is by being a paid up member of an affiliated performers union for a period of at least one year, having worked at least once as a principal performer in that union's jurisdiction.

The current SAG initiation fee is $2,211.00, payable in full by cashier's check or money order at the time of application. Fees may be lower in some branch areas. SAG dues are based on earnings and are billed twice a year.

If you are not working, you can go on Honorary Withdrawal which only relieves you of the obligation to pay your dues. You are still in the union and prohibited from accepting non-union work. For information on all things SAG related, *www.sag.org.* or call 323-549-6772.

Screen Actors Guild Minimum — As of 7-1-07, SAG scale is $757 daily. Overtime in SAG is considerably higher than in AFTRA. Check *www.sag.org* for more detailed info regarding rates. You don't have to be a member to check.

Seen — Term referring to an actor's having had an interview or audition and being considered for a part.

Showcases — Productions in which members of Actors' Equity are allowed by the union to work without compensation are called Showcases in New York and 99-Seat Theater Plan in Los Angeles. Equity members are allowed to perform, as long as the productions conform to certain Equity guidelines: rehearsal conditions, limiting the number of performances and seats, and providing a set number of complimentary tickets for industry people. The producers must provide tickets for franchised agents, casting directors and producers.

Sides — The pages of script containing your audition material. Usually not enough information to use as a source to do a good audition. If they won't give you a complete script, go early (or the day before), sit in the office and read it. SAG rules require producers to allow actors access to the script. Sometimes the script is still being written and is unavailable.

Stage Time — Term used to designate the amount of time a performer has had in front of an audience. Most agents and casting executives believe that an actor can only achieve a certain level of confidence by amassing stage time. They're right.

Station 12 — The Screen Actors Guild department that gives final clearance for talent to work.

Submissions — Sending an actor's name to a casting director in hopes of getting the actor an audition or meeting for a part.

Talent — Management's synonym for actors.

Test Option Agreement — Before going to network for a final back for a pilot/series, actors must routinely sign a contract that negotiates salary for the pilot and for series. The contract is for five years with an option for two more years. All options are at the discretion of management. They can drop you at the end of any season. You are bound by the terms of your contract to stay for the initial five years plus their two one-year options.

Top of Show/Major Role — A predetermined fee set by producers which is a non-negotiable maximum for guest appearances on television episodes. Also called Major Role Designation.

The Trades — *Daily Variety* and *Hollywood Reporter* are daily newspapers covering show business news. *Back Stage West* published weekly lists information about classes, auditions, casting, etc. and is particularly helpful to newcomers. *Ross Reports* published monthly lists names and addresses of casting directors, studios, advertising agencies, studios and networks in both New York and Los Angeles. All are available at good newsstands or by subscription.

Under Five — An AFTRA job in which the actor has five or fewer lines. Paid at a specific rate less than a principal and more than an extra. Sometimes referred to as Five and Under.

Visible/Visibility — Currently on view in film, theater or television. In this business, it's out of sight, out of mind, so visibility is very is very important.

Webisode — Short scripted entertainment made for the Internet.

⨁ 20 ⨁

Indexes

⚅ Index to Agents ⚆

⚅ Index to Managers ⚆

⚅ Index to Mentors ⚆

⚔ Index to Resources ⚑

⚞ Index to Web Addresses ⚟

ᴔ Index to Everything Else ᴂ

✄ Endnotes ✄

1. "FILM; Sticking to It, One Way or Another," September 24, 2000

2. "O to a higher power," December 11, 2005

3. "Rock 'n Roll," August 1997

4. "Acting on Impulse," September 28, 2003

5. "Great Isn't Good Enough," January 1991

6. Online, August 14, 1998

7. "Escape for a Scene Stealer," September 28, 2003

8. "Newest casting data shows highest ethnic minority representation on record," October 29, 2007

9. "Primetime Adds Some New Wrinkles," May 23, 2006

10. "For the Girls," July 16, 1995

11. "Power shifting," November 28, 2007

12. "SAG: More Roles for Minority Actors, experts say more must be done," November 21, 2007

13. "Actresses and Fear of the 'M' Role," April 30 1999

14. "Power shifting", November 28, 2007

15. "Robert De Niro," November 14, 1993

16. "Dialogue: Jodie Foster," December 2007

17. "Middle-Aged Lovers Jostle Onto the Screen," January 13, 2002

18. "SAG May Set Voting Limits," June 17, 2002

19. "Wage Wars Insiders' View of the Actors' Contract Dispute," July 17, 2001

20. "The Life of Hollywood: the Conversation," November 28, 2004

21. "After the Big Night, Is change Realistic?" March 29, 2002

22. Ibid.

23. "Will Smith: An uncommon man," December 13, 2007

24. "Who Says Hollywood Is Politically Correct?" May 9, 1995

25. "TV Study: Black Roles Are a Mixed Bag," June 5, 2002

26. "Morning Report: Small-Screen Diversity: A Long Way to Go," May 16, 2002

27. "Less Talk, More Action," May 15, 2002

28. "SAG: More Roles for Minority Actors, experts say more must be done", November 21, 2007

29. "Writing a New A List," November 12, 1995

30. Ibid.

31. "Will Smith: An uncommon man", December 13, 2007

32. "Iron Will," November 1998

33. Ibid.

34. Ibid.

35. "Muriel's Wedding Brings Bliss to Two Young Actresses," April 16, 1995

36. "A Showbiz Whiz", September 15, 2005

37. "Escape for a Scene Stealer", September 28, 2003

38. Bravo Television, February 12, 2006

39. "A Wild Desire to be Absolutely Fascinating," September 29, 1991

40. "These Actors Ply Their Craft for an Audience of Just One," July 23, 2002

41. "Servant of the Cause," June 2002

42. Princeton: Princeton University Press, 1971

43. "Singularly Susan," July 18, 1994

44. "She's Her Own Best Counsel," July 17, 1994

45. " When Race Isn't a Factor," August 27, 1995

46. "Making Movies," New York 1995

47. "From Pretty Woman to Pretty Busy," Sept. 19-25, 1991

48. "Carry'd Away," July 1994

49. "Confessions of a Reluctant Sex Godess," February 1993

50. "Comedy Club Salaries," March 3, 1998

51. "The Big Payoff," July 23, 1995

52. Ibid.

53. "Jim Carrey," July 26, 1994

54. "Next on the Stand-Up to TV Circuit," May 27, 1995

55. "Character Building," July 26, 1994

56. "Character Building," July 26, 1994

57. "Launching Pads," July 25, 1995

58. "Hittin' the Boards," July 25, 1995

59. "The Big Payoff," July 23, 1995

60. "It's Cho Time", September 2001

61. "Looking for Laughs in a Grim Race to Prime Time," August 27, 1995

62. "The Big Payoff," July 23, 1995

63. Ibid.

64. Ibid.

65. "Dialogue: Jodie Foster", December 2007

66. "Pearls of Wisdom from Liz," March 31, 1996

67. "The Hollywood Family," A&E, August 13, 1995

68. Ibid.

69. "Dialogue: Jodie Foster", December 2007

70. "Baby Talk," June 26, 1991

71. "I Wanted This So Bad, It Hurt," March 5, 2002

72. "Ibid

73. Ibid.

74. Ibid.

75. "Age of Innocence," November 1, 1994

76. "Casting a Spell," November 1, 1994

77. Ibid.

78. "2 Talent Agency Operators Given 30-Day Jail Terms," January 30, 1999

79. "Backstage at Yale Drama Admissions," October, 1996

80. "Acting Is One Thing, Getting Hired Another," May 25, 1997

80. "Acting Is One Thing, Getting Hired Another," May 25, 1997

82. "Acting Is One Thing, Getting Hired Another," May 25, 1997

83. "Perfect Casting: Okay, So There Are No Good Roles for Women. I Could Sit Around and Complain or I Could Do Something About it," Special Issue 1994

84. "Dish," May 16, 2002

85. "Close Ups," Spring 1988

86. "Gary After Gump," June 1995

87. "Dame Fame," June 1994

88. "Naked Ambition," August 10, 1998

89. "From Pretty Woman to Pretty Busy," Sept. 19-26, 1991

90. "Danger Is His Business," August 14, 1994

91. "Old Airport serving Local Film Industry," June 15, 2001

92. "City Spotlight," April 12, 2002

93. "Who Says You Have to Live in Hollywood or the Big Apple to Catch Your Rising Star?" November 1998

94. "The Woo Dynasty Comes to Hollywood," Nov-Dec 1995

95. M. Evans & Company, New York

96. "Bad News," Spring 1992, Volume 31 #1

97. "Funny Thing, Success," July 28, 2002

98. "Jessica Tandy, A Patrician Star of Theatre and Film, Dies at 85," September 12, 1994

99. "Muscle Man" December 1995

100. "Hollywood's No. 2 Agent View His Status and His World, Philosophically," March 2, 1994

101. "What I Love Most," October 11, 1998

102. "Hiding in Plain Sight." May 1997

103. Ibid.

104. "Wild Angel," January 1999

105. "Actor Fades Out of Anonymity," November 14, 1995

106. "Dame Fame," June 1994

107. "American's Cheesemonger," February 12, 1997

108. "Balancing Act," January 25, 2001

109. "The Founding Members," Sixteenth Anniversary Issue, 1995

110. "Unions Acting Nice," August 5, 2002

The Los Angeles Agent Book, 9th Edition
(How to Get the Agent You Need for the Career You Want)

If you're looking for an agent, this is the place to start. Callan's book profiles of Los Angeles agents includes their history, size of client list, client names and advice from the agents themselves on how actors can get their attention.

This guide to LA agents will help you make an effective and intelligent decision in your pursuit of the agent that is right for you. In the meantime, Callan gives advice on agenting yourself until the right agent is interested.

ISBN 1-878355-20-1
$20.00 + $5.00 Priority Mail US

The New York Agent Book, 8th edition
(How to Get the Agent You Need for the Career You Want)

This east coast companion to *The Los Angeles Agent Book* highlights the differences between looking for an agent in New York and in Los Angeles. Callan includes profiles of New York agents featuring their history, size of client list, client names, as well as quotes from the agents.

After studying this book you'll have a better understanding of how the business works in New York and be equipped to make an effective and intelligent decision in your pursuit of the agent that is right for you.

ISBN 1-878355-19-8
$20.00 + $5.00 Priority Mail US

The Script Is Finished, Now What Do I Do? 4th edition

(A resource book and agent guide for the scriptwriter)

The complete marketing and agent and manager guide for scriptwriters. This book gives you an overview of how the business really is, helps you understand the need to focus in order to succeed, and then teaches you how to do it. The book no scriptwriter should be without. This new edition profiles managers as well as agents.

ISBN 1-878355-18-8

$20.00 + $5.00 Priority Mail US

Directing Your Directing Career, 2nd edition

(A resource book and agent guide for directors)

Actress-author K Callan's best-selling directors' resource book and agent guide speaks candidly of the challenges facing directors, stresses the need to focus goals and energy, helps you evaluate whether you can be a working director in your own marketplace or whether it's time to move to New York or Los Angeles. The book features agent profiles, advice on how to agent yourself and attract an agent when you're ready.

ISBN 1-878355-11-2

$18.95 + $5.00 Priority Mail US.

order autographed copies online
20% web discount/www.swedenpress.com

or by mail
Sweden Press
Box 1612
Studio City, CA 91614

✁ ....

The New York Agent Book 8th edition	$20
How To Sell Yourself as an Actor 6th edition	$20
The Script Is Finished, Now What Do I Do? 4th edition	$20
Directing Your Directing Career, 2nd edition	$18.95
The Los Angeles Agent Book, 9th edition	$20
Priority Mail $5 for 1 or 2 books	

Name

Street

City, State, Zip

E-mail

Phone

How to Sell Yourself as an Actor 6th Edition

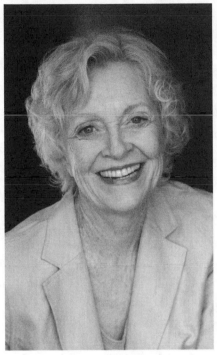

K Callan is tough. So is her book. In *How to Sell Yourself as an Actor*, the actress/author sets us straight right from the start, explaining that knowing how to act doesn't ipso facto make you an actor. If you're one of the actors who refuses to think of himself as a product which must be sold and prefers to believe that acting is art, Callan puts things in perspective — "show business is about making money; art is extra."

On any given day, 85% of the almost 120,000 members of Screen Actors Guild are out of work. Callan has always been a part of the working 15% and is living proof that it's possible to not only act and make a living but also raise a family and live a balanced life. This no-nonsense book provides both beginning and veteran actors with nuts and bolts information about how to be more appealing to casting directors, agents, producers, and directors. She encourages you to call upon your entrepreneurial skills, your courage, and your vision to take your career in your own hands and stop waiting to be asked to work.

As rough and honest as she is, Callan still offers a way of thinking about this business that will help you retain both your sense of humor and your sanity in good times and bad, as well as many concrete ideas, addresses, phone numbers, and web addresses for finding work.

Callan's theatre work includes The Public Theatre, Manhattan Theatre Club, South Coast Repertory in Costa Mesa and Alaska Rep in Anchorage, Alaska. Television and film work includes playing Superman's Mom on *Lois & Clark*, a repentant migrant on HBO's *Carnivale*, a demented Norman Desmond type on Tyler Perry's *Here Come the Browns*, Edie's evil mother on *Desperate Housewives*, Richard Gere's lover in *American Gigolo*, Peter Boyle's wife in *Joe* and Glenda Jackson's friend in *A Touch of Class*. She's a member of The Academy of Motion Picture Arts and Sciences, The Television Academy, and a past member of the Board of Directors of Screen Actors Guild.